To Steven

LET THERE BE BLOOD

Eva Carmichael

Happy Birthday

Eva Carmichael

Published in paperback, 2022, in association with:
JV Publishing
Tel: 07726366424
jvpublishing@yahoo.com

Dedication

To my dear friend, Lawrence.

R.I.P.

Acknowledgements

Grateful thanks to John & Vicky (JV Publishing) for enabling me to get this book to market. Your continued encouragement and patience are beyond thanks.

Again, I have to thank my beta readers, Mary, Maureen, Lindsey, Jane and Bill. Your contributions were invaluable.

A big thank you to Billy and Judith, who have gone out of their way to help me promote my books this year on Redcar Market.

Thank you also to my husband, Derek, who's still providing the tea, coffee and occasionally wine, and my family for their continued encouragement.

Last but by no means least, I would like to thank the people of Redcar and the surrounding area who have bought my books over the last eighteen months. The wonderful comments of support I have received make all the hard work worthwhile. Thank you.

Prologue

"Are you prepared to gamble?"

"What do you mean, gamble?"

Matthew smiled and walked towards the roulette table. "I suggest we sort this out with a spin of the wheel."

Karl scowled. "Are you fucking crazy?"

"No, I'm not crazy," Matthew said. "Joe and I are prepared to stake the casino and the whole of Alex's debt against all of your clubs. Winner takes all." He arched an eyebrow. "Well, Karl, what do you say? Are you in?"

Paul grabbed Karl's arm. "Don't do it, boss," he said. "We can sort this out another way."

Karl pushed Paul's arm away. "Let me get this straight," he said, "you'll put up this place and the money Alex owes against my businesses. Is that right?"

Matthew nodded. "That's exactly right."

Karl licked his lips. "Well, I'll say one thing for you, you've more balls than your old man had."

Matthew frowned. "Leave him out of this," he said. "This is between you and me."

Karl laughed. "And it's to be decided with one spin of the wheel?"

"That's right. Red or black? You choose."

"What do you think, Paul?" Karl said. "Do you think I should gamble?"

Paul shook his head. "No, boss. I think you should walk away and leave it to Beauchamp."

"But you were only telling me earlier to take a risk. Don't tell me you've changed your mind?"

"Karl, this is crazy. Don't do it."

Karl strolled over to the roulette wheel. He was silent for a moment. The pulse on his neck throbbed, and beads of sweat appeared on his forehead. "All right," he said. "Let's do it."

Matthew and Joe joined Karl at the roulette table.

"Well?" Matthew said. "What's it to be? Red or black?"

Karl stared at the wheel for a few seconds. "Black," he said. "I bet everything on black."

Matthew spun the wheel and carefully released the ball. It clattered noisily as it bounced from one compartment to another. The wheel rotated again and again before it slowed down and eventually came to a shuddering halt…

1

Karl Maddox sighed heavily as he gazed out the hotel window at the beach below. It had been almost two months since the operation on his heart. Now he felt recovered. He felt strong and robust, yearning to be back in England. Back to his nightclubs. Back to being kingpin once again.

Lisa sat at the dressing table, her tanned skin glistening beneath her floral sundress. "Hurry up, darling," she coaxed. "You're not dressed yet." She brushed her blonde hair, letting it fall onto her shoulders. "We're meeting Roger and Mary in ten minutes."

Karl grimaced. "There's something about that man I don't like," he said. "I don't know why you agreed to us having a drink with him."

"For goodness sake, don't be so miserable. Roger's all right, and Mary is fun. She makes me laugh."

"She has the face of a gargoyle," Karl said.

Lisa tutted and applied her lipstick. "Wear your blue shirt," she said. "It's in the wardrobe. Your navy-blue trousers are in there too. I got them back from the drycleaners this morning."

Karl walked over to his wife and, encircling her trim waist, began to nuzzle her neck. "I don't suppose there's time to—"

Lisa pulled away and tapped his arm playfully. "No, there is not. We're going to be late."

Karl huffed and picked up the telephone. "I have a couple of calls to make first," he said. "You go down to the bar, and I'll see you there."

"All right," she said, and gently kissed him on the cheek. "I'll order you Sangria, shall I?"

"If I never see Sangria again, it will be too soon," he said. "Now hurry up. You don't want to keep your new best friends waiting."

Lisa opened the door and blew a kiss. "See you downstairs," she said. "Don't be long."

Karl joined his wife and her two companions in the hotel

bar twenty minutes later. Roger Laverick leant against the bar, smoking a cigar.

"Good to see you again," he greeted, holding out his chubby yet well-manicured hand. "What'll it be? Sangria?" He winked mischievously.

Karl gave a slight scowl. "Whisky," he said, shaking Roger's hand.

Roger placed the order with the waiter, and they all made their way to a table. "I was just telling your lovely wife that we're going sailing tomorrow. We'd love it if you could join us."

"Oh, please say yes," Lisa said. "I love sailing."

Karl reached out and squeezed Lisa's hand. "Sorry to disappoint you, my love," he said, "but we're going home tomorrow."

Lisa pulled away. "What? No, we can't. You've not fully recovered. The doctor said—"

"The tickets are booked," Karl said. "The plane leaves at four o'clock, so you've plenty of time to pack."

"But—"

Karl glared at his wife. "There are no buts, Lisa," he said. "We're going home tomorrow, and that's an end to it."

Lisa huffed as she got up from the table and rushed towards the lift.

"I'll go and make sure she's all right," Mary said as she hurried after her. Finally, the lift doors opened, and both women stepped inside.

Roger rubbed his chin. "That's one unhappy wifey you've got there."

Karl shrugged as he took the whisky glass from the waiter. "She'll get over it."

"Lisa was saying you've been in the wars recently."

"I had a dodgy ticker," Karl said. "It's been fixed now, and I'm as good as new." He slowly sipped at his drink. "What line of business are you in, Roger?"

Tilting his head to one side, Roger waved his hand vaguely in the air. "Oh, a bit of this, a bit of that," he said. "Imports and exports mostly, but … Oh, the girls are back."

Lisa and Mary walked over to the table. Pouting, Lisa flounced into a chair, her arms folded in front of her. "I still think we should stay another week," she said. "If you go home now, you'll be working all hours again."

Karl leant forward and gently squeezed Lisa's hand. "I promise I'll take things easy," he said. "But I have a business to run. I can't do that sitting on a lounger drinking Sangria, can I?"

"I wish you'd get rid of those bloody clubs once and for all. They'll be the death of you."

"Nonsense," Karl said. "Peter and Paul do most of the work these days."

Lisa shrugged but remained silent.

Grinning, Karl clasped his hands together. "Good. That's settled. He drained his glass and indicated for the waiter to bring more drinks. "Now, where do you want to go for your last dinner in Spain?"

"Oh, please be our guests," Roger said. "Mary and I have found a little place that serves the most wonderful seafood, not fifteen minutes from here."

Lisa leant forward. "It sounds lovely, doesn't it, Karl?"

"If that's what you want," he said. "We'll finish our drinks and make a move."

Leaning over, Roger grabbed Karl's arm. "I was wondering if you and I might have a private word later," he said.

Karl furrowed his brow. "Oh? What about?"

Roger tapped the side of his nose with his forefinger. "Business. What else?"

2

It was raining heavily when the taxi arrived at Karl's house in Leeds the following evening. Thunder rumbled in the distance as Karl helped the driver remove the suitcases.

"Bloody English weather," Lisa said as she hurried towards the house. "I'm missing Malaga already."

Karl placed the last of the luggage inside the hall. "I'm going to the club," he said, "I won't be long."

Lisa scowled. "For goodness sake, can't that wait until tomorrow?"

"No, I'm afraid it can't," he said and kissed her lightly on the cheek. "You get unpacked, and I'll be back before you know it."

Before Lisa could object, Karl was back inside the taxi heading towards town.

Twenty minutes later, as the taxi drew up outside the club. Karl stared in disbelief around the car park, which was less than half full. He entered the foyer and stared at the usually bustling club, but it was almost empty tonight. He pushed open the door leading into the main club. Only two of the poles were in use, not the usual six. Scowling, he approached one of the hostesses, a thin, red-haired woman chewing vigorously on peppermint gum. "Where's Peter?" he said.

She shrugged her slim shoulders. "Don't know, mate," she said. "He's probably upstairs in the VIP lounge, but you can't go up unless you're a member." Karl huffed, pushed past her and hurried through the foyer and up the private staircase.

Peter Borowicz was sprawled across one of the couches, chatting to a hostess. As Karl strode into the room, Peter struggled to his feet. "We weren't expecting to see you, boss," he said. "You're… you're looking great."

Karl's eyes narrowed. "What the hell is going on?" he said. "There are no more than thirty punters downstairs and only half a dozen up here."

Peter shrugged. "Business has been slow, boss," he said.

"In fact, it's been bloody slow."

"Why the hell didn't you let me know?"

"You told us not to ring you while you were away. When things got bad, I rang Lisa. She said not to bother you."

The veins in Karl's neck pulsated. "Lisa doesn't pay your wages," he said, prodding Peter in the chest with his finger. "I do."

Peter exhaled deeply. "Let's go through to the office. There's stuff you should know."

Karl followed Peter through into his office and flung himself into a chair. "Well?" Karl said. "Why the fuck is my club empty on a Saturday night?"

Peter leant on the door jamb. "It's… it's like this, boss," he said. "A few days after your op, a new club opened in Leeds. The Fighting Tiger."

Karl frowned. "So what? The Emerald has always held its own with the competition."

"The club only charges the punters half what The Emerald does, and it pays the girls more money. As a result, most of the dancers left to work there."

Karl's frown deepened. "Who owns the club?"

"A bloke called Charlie Dexter."

"Never heard of him. Where exactly is this Fighting Tiger?"

"It's the old Harmony Club, boss, behind The Calls."

"That strip joint? I thought they'd closed that down last year?"

"Dexter bought it and did a refit. It's a lap-dancing club now."

"Have you been in to look around?"

"Me and Paul tried, but those gorillas on the door recognised us."

"I'm looking forward to meeting this Charlie Dexter," Karl said, reaching into his desk drawer and removing a cigar. "By the way, where is Paul tonight? He should be downstairs in the club."

"Paul's… Paul's working over in Sheffield at The

Sapphire."

"What's he doing there? Simon manages The Sapphire."

"He's quit. He left about two weeks ago."

Karl banged his fist on the desk. "Why am I only finding out about this now?"

Peter wiped the sweat from his forehead with the back of his hand. "I tried ringing you, boss. We both did, but as I said, Lisa told us you weren't to be bothered with work."

Karl strode over to the cabinet and poured himself a whisky. "Get Paul on the phone," he said. "We need to get this sorted."

3

"What time did you get home?" Lisa yawned as she entered the kitchen at eight o'clock the following morning. "I waited up until nearly midnight."

Karl did not reply as he continued sipping his coffee and staring out the window.

Lisa walked over to him. "Is everything all right?" she said. "You're looking a bit peaky this morning."

He put the mug down on the worktop with a bang and, springing forward, spanned Lisa's neck with his hands. "Why didn't you tell me Peter tried to get in touch?" he said, shaking her violently.

Lisa struggled to get free, but he held firm. "Please, let go," she whined. "You're hurting me."

Karl released his grip, pushing her into the wall. "Don't you ever interfere in my business again," he said, jabbing her in the chest with his finger. "You should have told me Peter rang."

Tears welled in Lisa's eyes as she rubbed her neck. "I… I'm sorry. I only—"

Karl growled as he pushed past her into the hall. "I'll be late home tonight," he said, opening the door and slamming it behind him.

Trembling, Lisa poured herself a coffee and entered the lounge. Tears trickled down her cheeks as she gazed out into the garden. The telephone ringing in the lounge startled her back into the moment.

"Hello?" she said.

"Mum? Mum, it's me. I heard you were back."

"Christina, how lovely to hear from you," she said, dabbing her eyes with a tissue. "I was going to ring you this morning."

"Is everything all right? You sound… you sound upset."

"I'm not upset, darling. I'm just a bit tired from the journey yesterday."

"How's Dad?"

"He's absolutely fine. The operation went well," Lisa said, gently stroking her neck. "The doctors say his heart is as good as new."

"What about his leg? Did he get that fixed?"

"Yes. He had metal pins put in. It seems to have done the trick."

"That's good. Actually, Mum, I was ringing to see if you could meet me for lunch today?"

"Darling, I'd love to. What time?"

"One o'clock. I thought we could try that new bistro on Lower Briggate, The Herb Basket."

"It sounds lovely. Will Matthew be joining us?"

Christina giggled. "No, not today," she said. "I'll tell you all my news over lunch."

"All right, darling, I'll see you at one."

Christina looked up as Lydia Glendenning entered the kitchen. "Was that your mother on the phone?" Lydia said. "I thought she was in Spain."

"She came back yesterday. We're having lunch later."

A look of amusement danced across Lydia's face as she poured herself a coffee from the cafetiere. "Do you think that's wise? I thought Karl had banned all contact between you and your mother."

Christina shrugged as she walked towards the door. "If I want to see my mother, I will. Karl can't tell me what to do. Not anymore."

"I'd love to be there when Karl learns you've married Matthew," she said. "The son of the man who shot him."

Christina flung back her head. "For goodness sake, let it drop. That's all in the past. We've all moved on since then."

Lydia banged her cup down on the table. "My husband's dead because of Karl. That's not in the past. It's something I have to live with every day."

Christina opened the kitchen door and walked into the hall. "Matthew and I are married now, and we're both happy.

I was hoping that you'd be happy for us too." She closed the door behind her and began to ascend the stairs.

Lydia's eyes narrowed as she picked up the cup and sipped her coffee. "Well, I'm not happy," she whispered. "I'm not happy at all."

4

When Karl arrived at The Emerald Club that morning, Peter and his brother, Paul, were already in the office.

Smiling, Peter stepped forward. "Good morning, Karl," he said. "Can I get you a coffee or something?"

"Thanks, that would be great," Karl said, "and a bacon sandwich to go with it. The café over the road is open."

"Sure thing," Peter said, bounding through the door.

Karl took out a cigar from the desk drawer and lit it. "Where are the others?" he said. "I told them to be here by nine o'clock."

"It's only half-eight," Paul said. "They'll be here."

Paul, the younger and more intelligent of the two brothers, was standing by the window looking down into the street, his hands thrust deep into his trouser pockets. "Good to have you back," he said as he slowly turned to face Karl. "You're looking well."

Karl scowled. "Never mind about that," he said. "What's this about Simon quitting The Sapphire?"

"He got a better offer. He's working in a club in Barnsley now."

"Didn't you try to stop him?"

"Of course I did, but you know what he's like when he decides to do something."

Karl drummed his fingers on the desk. "I can't believe Simon could be tempted away for more cash like some two-bit whore."

Paul took a deep breath. "I don't think he left because of the money."

"Then why? I've looked after him for years. If he had a problem, he should have spoken to me."

"It was you that was the problem," he said. "You're the reason Simon left."

Karl snorted, flinging back his head. "What the hell are you talking about?"

"That stunt you pulled at the casino. Gambling everything

you had built up on the spin of a wheel. It made him uneasy. It made us all uneasy."

"I won, didn't I? What's the problem?"

"What would have become of everyone if you had lost?" Paul paced the room, returning to the window. "You upset many people taking a risk like that. Some of the guys don't trust your judgement anymore."

Karl laced his fingers on the desk and leant forward. "What about you, Paul? Do you trust my judgement?"

"I was there that night, remember? I saw everything. You were reckless."

"I had no choice. You know that."

"That's not true. You could have got Beauchamp on the case. That's what you pay him for. Your gamble could have lost everything."

Karl shook his head and smiled. "That was never going to happen," he said. "Believe me."

"Of course it could. If the roulette wheel had stopped at red—"

Karl leant forward, banging his fist on the desk. "Do you think I'm a complete twat?" he said, his lip twisting menacingly. "Believe me, that wheel would only have stopped at black."

"You couldn't know that."

Karl grinned. "Couldn't I?"

"I… I don't understand."

"Roulette wheels can be fixed," Karl said, a look of triumph on his face. "You remember Alfie Novak and all that trouble he got into in Vegas a few years back?"

"Wasn't he charged with cheating in Caesar's Palace?"

"Yeah, that's him. He's very inventive, is Alfie."

"Karl, you're not making sense. What's Alfie Novak got to do with anything?"

"Alfie devised a small magnetic chip that, when placed underneath the roulette wheel, ensures that the ball lands in a particular spot."

Paul snorted. "And you just happened to have such a

device with you that night?"

"I certainly did," Karl said. "Alfie was very obliging."

"But… but how did you know what Joe and Matthew were planning? There's no way you could know unless… unless someone told you?"

"Ah, the penny has finally dropped," Karl said, clasping his hands together. "Of course, someone told me."

"Who?"

"Does it matter? The fact is I knew what those two bastards were up to, and I beat them at their own game."

"Who tipped you off? Was it Christina?"

Karl shook his head. "No, it wasn't my daughter. It should have been, but it wasn't."

"Then… then who?"

Karl drew heavily on his cigar. "My son is an arsehole," he said. "All the opportunities Alex had in life he threw into the gutter. The only good thing he did was marrying a woman with a conscience."

"Sarah? Are you saying it was Sarah who tipped you off?"

"Sarah isn't my greatest fan, but she was ashamed of how Alex behaved," he said. "She knew Matthew and Joe would be okay for money, so she told me everything they were planning."

Paul shook his head, giving a low whistle. "Bloody hell, Karl," he said, "you knew that, and you let me think—"

"Everything worked out perfectly," he said. "I cleared Alex's debt and got to keep my clubs and gain a casino in the process. In return, Sarah made me promise to leave her and Joe in peace from now on. To be honest, I don't think she was keen on him running a casino in the first place."

Paul flopped into an armchair, lowering his head into his hands. "I don't believe I'm hearing this," he said. "You deserve a bloody Oscar for your performance that night."

"I want you to keep this to yourself. The fewer people that know what really happened at the casino that night, the better. Okay?"

Paul shrugged. "Sure, if that's what you want."

The office door burst open, and Peter scurried into the room carrying several paper bags. "Sorry I've been so long," he said, placing them on the desk. "There was a queue."

Footsteps could be heard on the stairs leading up to the office.

"It sounds like the others are here," Paul said as he reached out and took a coffee cup from the bag.

"Good," Karl said, drawing on his cigar. "Perhaps now we can start to get this show on the road."

5

Karl narrowed his eyes, scrutinising the men sitting around the office. Peter and Paul Borowicz were his most trusted allies. His friendship with their father, Victor, went back many years. Freddie Smith managed The Topaz in Bradford, whilst Tommy Watson was the new manager of The Amethyst in Manchester. The other two men in Karl's office were cousins Terry and Wayne Richards. They were jointly managing the casino in Manchester.

Karl leant back in his chair and drew on his cigar. "Good morning, gentlemen," he said. "Thank you for coming over at such short notice."

"Good to have you back, boss," Wayne said. "You're looking well."

"Yeah, welcome back, Karl," Terry said.

"It's good to be back," he said. "Now, let's get down to business. Have any of you come across a bloke called Charlie Dexter?"

"Yeah, I know him," Tommy said. "We were on the doors in Birmingham a few years back."

"Tell me about him."

Tommy cleared his throat. "Well, from what I remember, he was a hard bastard. He didn't take prisoners. One time he broke a punter's jaw for giving him backchat. He liked the ladies too. He always had some flashy bird on his arm."

"When was the last time you saw him?"

Tommy frowned and rubbed his chin. "It must be five, no six years now. He got the push from the nightclub, and I heard he moved up north."

"And you haven't seen him since?"

Tommy shook his head. "No. Why? What's he done?"

"Dexter runs a lap dancing club in Leeds, The Fighting Tiger. Most of you will remember it as The Harmony Club."

Tommy frowned. "That dump behind The Calls?"

Karl nodded. "He's been enticing girls away from The Emerald to work there by offering more cash and charging the punters less entry fee."

"Naughty," Tommy said. "We can't let him get away with that."

Karl inhaled deeply, his hands curling into fists. "I have no intention of letting that little bastard get away with anything," he said.

6

Lydia Glendenning laid out the glasses and decanter on the occasional table alongside a box of cigars just as the doorbell rang. Glancing at the wall clock, she could see it was one-fifteen. *"A man who is punctual,"* she smiled to herself. *"I like that."*

Lydia walked through into the hall. The visitor's tall, broad silhouette visible behind the door's stained glass.

"Charles," she greeted. "On time as usual."

Charles Dexter smiled. "I never keep a lady waiting," he said as he leant forward to kiss her cheek. "It's good to see you again."

"Come through. I've got your favourite tipple waiting."

Charles followed Lydia into the lounge and went over to the couch after removing his overcoat and placing it on a chair.

Lydia smiled as she settled elegantly into an armchair. "Please, sit down," she invited. Charles burrowed into the couch and leant back, allowing himself to be enveloped in the soft velvet cushions.

Picking up the decanter, Lydia poured a large whisky into one of the crystal glasses. She handed it to Charles.

Reaching out, he took the glass and held it beneath his nose. "Is this what I think it is?" he said, sniffing the aroma.

Lydia poured herself a glass and nodded. "It's a Macallan," she said. "It was my dad's favourite."

Charles was silent for a moment as he swirled the golden liquid around the glass before putting it to his lips. "Perfect," he said. "If god made anything better, he kept it for himself."

Lydia gave a satisfied sigh. "I'm glad you like it."

They both sipped their drinks for a couple of minutes in silence. It was Charles who spoke first. "This is all very pleasant, Lydia," he said, "but what exactly am I doing here?"

Lydia lifted the decanter and began to pour more whisky into his glass. "I hoped you and I could escalate our little… our little arrangement," she said.

Frowning, Charles leant forward. "What did you have in mind? Undercutting another of Maddox's clubs?"

Lydia hunched her shoulders. "Perhaps later," she said. "I was thinking about targeting the escort agency he runs."

Charles's frown deepened. "Are you suggesting I set up an agency to compete with Cupid's Angels?"

Lydia smiled and shook her head. "No, no, of course not. That would take far too long. I had something quite different in mind."

"Like what?"

"Booking his tarts out on false calls, for a start," she said. "I want them running all over town on fake bookings."

"I suppose I could manage that," he said.

"You could also arrange for violent and abusive clients. His girls will soon get fed up with the hassle."

Charles rubbed his chin. "Mm," he said. "I suppose it could work, but it won't be cheap. You do know that?"

Lydia sipped her whisky. "Don't worry about the money, Charles. Money is one thing I have plenty of."

"That's just as well. The Fighting Tiger is running at a loss every week."

Lydia flung back her head. "It can run at a loss for a whole year. I want Maddox out of business once and for all, and I don't care how much it costs."

Charles drank the remnants of his whisky. "You must really hate his guts. What's he done to piss you off so much?"

Lydia stood up and walked towards the fireplace, resting her hand on the mantelpiece. "Never mind about that," she said. "Let's just say we have a score to settle."

"Okay, Lydia. It's your money. When do you want me to start?"

"Tonight. Do you think you can arrange that?"

Charles walked over to the chair and began to put on his coat. "I'll see what I can do," he said.

Lydia reached for a brown envelope on the mantelpiece and handed it to him. "This will cover the club's running costs for a few more weeks," she said. "In addition, there's money for our new venture."

Charles reached out and took the envelope from Lydia. "Thanks," he said, placing it in his coat pocket. "It's a pleasure doing business with you."

He turned and walked into the hall, followed by Lydia.

"Oh, by the way, Charles," she said. "Karl Maddox is back in Leeds. He arrived last night. I thought you should know."

7

Lisa sat across from her daughter in the restaurant. "I am happy for you, darling," she said, squeezing her hand. "But I think it's best if we don't tell your father that you and Matthew are married, at least not for the time being."

Christina huffed. "If you think that's best," she said, "but he's bound to find out sometime. You know that."

Lisa reached into her bag and produced a small, red-leather box. "I bought you this," she said, handing the box to her daughter.

Christina took the box and opened the lid. "Oh, Mum," she said, taking out the gold bracelet. "It's beautiful. Thank you." She got up and flung her arms around her mother's neck, kissing her gently on the cheek. It was then she saw the bruising. "Mum, what happened?" she said, lifting Lisa's hair up to reveal more bruising.

Lisa turned away from her daughter, pushing her hair back down. "It's nothing," she said. "I…"

Christina gritted her teeth. "He did this, didn't he?"

"Karl lost his temper, that's all," Lisa said. "He didn't mean it. Your father hasn't been well and—"

Christina went back to her chair. "That's no excuse, Mum. You know it isn't. You don't have to stay with him if he's violent. You know that."

Lisa dabbed her eyes with a tissue. "Karl isn't violent with me, not really. He was angry this morning, that's all. I think there's some sort of trouble at The Emerald."

Christina shook her head. "That damned club. I hate it. I wish Joe and Matthew had—"

"How is Matthew?" Lisa said, desperately trying to change the subject. "What is he doing now?"

"He's gone into partnership with a property developer," Christina said. "He buys and renovates rundown buildings, then rents them out." She sipped at her wine. "They're refurbishing an old warehouse by the river at the moment. There'll be ten apartments when it's completed."

"That sounds wonderful, darling. I hope it goes well."

"To be honest, I wouldn't mind moving into one of them myself when they're finished."

Lisa frowned. "I don't understand. I thought you were living at Matthew's family home?"

"We are. The house is beautiful, but … it's Lydia. She hates me being there and takes every opportunity to ensure I know it."

"I thought she was in a nursing home since her breakdown?"

"Lydia's supposed to be fully recovered. She moved back into the house about the same time you and Dad went to Spain."

"Have you spoken to Matthew about it?"

"And say what? That his mother is rude and makes me feel uncomfortable?"

Lisa sighed. "If you'll take my advice, darling, you'll get out of that house as soon as possible."

Christina tilted her head. "I could say the same to you," she said.

The waiter came to the table. "Will there be anything else, ladies?" he asked, smiling. "We have a large selection of desserts."

"Why not?" Christina grinned mischievously. "I think I'll have lemon meringue. What about you?"

Lisa smiled. "I'll have the same," she said. "Sod the diet for today. Oh, and can we have another bottle of Chardonnay, please?"

The meal was drawing to a close when Lisa leant forward and took Christina's hand, a serious look on her face. "I… I don't suppose you've heard anything from Alex since… since he went away?" she said. "I'm so worried about him."

Christina tensed. "No, I haven't heard a thing. He'll keep out of Dad's way if he knows what's good for him."

"Alex is still my son. Despite the wicked things he has done."

"Mum, stop worrying about Alex. He can take care of

himself. He always has."

Lisa tilted her head, and Christina could see her eyes were moist. "You will let me know if he does contact you, won't you?" she said.

Christina squeezed her mother's hand. "Of course I will, but I think I'll be the last person Alex will want to speak to."

"What about Sarah? Have you spoken to her since she ran off with Joe?"

"I spoke with her a month ago. They're living near Joe's sister and her family. She seemed really happy."

Lisa huffed. "Poor Alex has lost everything," she said. "It was a wicked thing Sarah did, leaving him like that."

"Alex only has himself to blame for the mess he made of his life."

Lisa indicated to the waiter to fetch the bill. She turned to face her daughter. "Sometimes you can be very hard, Christina," she said. "A little compassion towards your brother might be nice."

Before Christina could respond, Lisa handed her credit card to the waiter and followed him to the counter.

"That was lovely," Lisa said once they were outside. "We must meet up again soon."

"Yes, Mum, I'll look forward to it, and thanks again for the bracelet."

Christina was behind the wheel of her car before she dialled a number on her phone. "Alex, it's me," she said. "Can we meet?"

8

It was eight o'clock that evening when Cherry arrived at Balmoral Close on the outskirts of Leeds. Cherry had worked for Cupid's Angels for over a year and was confident going into a stranger's house for paid sex.

She parked her Mini Metro under a streetlamp and hurried along the road to number forty-two. On reaching the house, she stopped and gazed in disbelief. The door and windows had been boarded up, and a *For Sale* sign was nailed to the wall. She took out her mobile and rang the office.

"Cupid's Angels," said a husky female voice over the phone. "How can we help you this evening?"

"Mavis, it's me, Cherry," she said. "That address you gave me in Balmoral Close. Are you sure it was forty-two?"

"Of course I'm sure," Mavis said. "Why? What's the matter?"

"The house is empty. It's boarded up."

Mavis sighed. "Oh, I'm sorry, love. It happens sometimes," she said. "Some twat's playing silly beggars. I'll blacklist the phone number he gave me. He won't be able to pull that trick again."

"I hope not. That's the second time tonight."

"Cheer up, love. A booking has just come in from Jepson Court. Flat 66."

Cherry sighed. "Text me his number, and I'll ring him," she said. "I don't want another wasted journey tonight."

"Okay. Ring me when you get there and let me know everything's all right."

Sharon hurried along the dimly lit corridor of Bernie's Motel. The client was Michael Wills. It was nine o'clock when she knocked on the door of room 149.

"It's open," said a man from inside the room.

Sharon ran her tongue over her red-painted lips. She brought her long auburn hair over her shoulder before gliding into the room.

It was difficult to focus at first. One small lamp was the only source of lighting in the room. She could make out a bed on the far wall and the silhouette of a man standing in front of the window.

"Hello," she said, striding confidently into the room. "I'm Sharon." She slipped off her jacket and walked slowly towards the man. Suddenly, she felt someone grab her from behind and push her to the floor. Terrified, she attempted to scream, but the man bent down and dragged her to her feet, striking her across the face. Sharon was thrown against the wall, and both men began punching her about her face and body, causing her to collapse onto the floor.

"That's enough," said one of the men. "I think the bitch has got the message. Let's go."

Sobbing, Sharon struggled to her feet and slowly made her way out of the rear of the hotel and into the night.

Kathy was new to escorting. It was only her third assignment. She took a deep breath as she knocked on the door of number seventeen at the Lyndon Hotel. She could hear movement inside the room, and after a few minutes, the door was opened by an elderly woman wearing a bright-blue dressing gown.

"Yes, dear?" she said, squinting over the top of her spectacles. "Is everything all right?"

Kathy gripped her bag tightly. "I… I was looking for Mr Jones," she said.

The woman shook her head. "I'm sorry," she said. "I think you've got the wrong room."

Kathy smiled weakly. "Sorry to have bothered you. I'll check with reception." She turned and hurried down the corridor. Then, taking out her phone, she rang the number she had been given for Thomas Jones. It rang unobtainable.

She hurried out of the building and rang Cupid's Angels.

Karl was in the office at The Emerald when his phone rang. He could see the call was coming from Cupid's Angels.

"Yeah?" he said. "What is it?"

"Karl, it's Mavis at the agency. We've had some trouble. Big trouble."

He exhaled, banging his whisky glass down on the desk. "What the fuck's happened now?" he said.

"One of the girls is in hospital," she said. "She has a broken jaw. Her client beat her up pretty bad, and… and we've had seven false callouts tonight. Cherry went to three of them. She's so pissed off she's threatening to go to another agency."

Karl ran his fingers through his hair and sighed. "You are taking the punter's credit card details before you send the girls, aren't you?"

"That's… that's not always possible," Mavis said. "Most men don't want to leave a paper trail for their wives to find. They insist on paying cash."

Karl banged his fist down hard on the desk. "To hell with that," he said. "No more bookings are to be made without a credit card. Do you hear me?"

"Sure, Karl, if that's what you want, but—"

Karl slammed down the phone and buzzed Peter on the internal line. "Come up to the office," he said. "I have a job for you."

Peter drove Karl to The Fighting Tiger and parked on the street opposite. It was almost two o'clock.

"What do you want to do, boss?" Peter said nervously. "Should we get some help?"

Karl scowled. "No. I can handle this on my own."

"Let me come with you."

Karl leant over and put his hand on Peter's shoulder. "No, you stay here. If I'm not back in fifteen minutes… well, you know what to do."

Karl got out of the car and strode towards the club's entrance. As he approached, a stocky, balding man standing in the club's doorway moved forward. "Sorry, mate, we're closed," he said. "We're open from seven tomorrow, so—"

Karl grabbed the man's arm, twisting it behind his back.

"Is Dexter in?" he said.

The man struggled, but Karl held fast. "I asked you a question," he said.

"Inside," the man spluttered. "Charlie's inside."

Karl released his grip before flinging him to the ground. "Now, piss off," he said as he walked through the revolving door and into the foyer.

Charlie Dexter stood by the table in reception. On sight of Karl, the man standing beside him lunged forward, fists raised. Karl dodged the blow and landed a punch on the man's jaw, causing him to fall to the floor in a crumpled heap.

Dexter raised his hands and took a step backwards. "Stop," he spluttered, "there's no need for this. Let's talk."

Karl rushed towards Dexter, grabbing his shirt with one hand and raising his fist to his face with the other. "Come near my business again," he said through clenched teeth, "and I'll kill you."

Dexter's breathing became erratic. "I… I don't know what you're talking about. I—"

Karl sprang forward, head butting him in the face. "You know exactly what I'm talking about," he said. "It stops now, understand?" He pushed Dexter against the wall, spanning his neck with his hand. "I can make your life hell," Karl said, his eyes narrowing into slits. "One word from me, and you're a dead man."

Karl released his grip, and Dexter attempted to regain his composure. "I… I run a legitimate business," he said. "I've never—"

"Bollocks," Karl said, poking him in the chest with his finger. "I know what you've been up to. It stops now."

Dexter glared at Karl but remained silent.

"Who put you up to this? Who's footing the bill?"

"I don't know what you're talking about."

"My girls will all be back at The Emerald tomorrow. I can promise you that."

"You can't tell them where they can work," Dexter said.

"If they want to work here, they can."

Karl's eyes narrowed as he pressed his face close to Dexter's. "They'll do as I say," he said, "and so will you."

The man on the floor began to stir. Karl laughed coarsely as he strode over him and walked out into the street.

He climbed into the waiting car, and Peter drove him back to The Emerald.

9

"Here's what I want you to do," Karl said, addressing his club managers the following morning. He handed out cards containing the addresses of the girls who had left to work at The Fighting Tiger. "Split these between you and visit each one personally. Explain how it's in their best interest to come back to The Emerald."

"What if they refuse?" Freddie asked. "We can't make them."

"Saying no is not an option. I want to see their arses in this club tonight. If they don't work at The Emerald, they don't work at all."

Freddie's cheeks flushed. "Sure, boss," he said. "Don't worry. They'll be back."

Paul was standing by the window. "What about Si? Do you want me to have a word?"

Karl shook his head. "Leave Si to me. I'll call round this morning."

"I heard Sharon has been released from hospital," Peter said. "She won't be working for some time, though."

Karl scowled. "Who the hell's Sharon?"

"She got beaten up last night at Bernie's Motel."

Karl turned to Paul. "Get over there and speak to the manager," he said. "I want to know who these heroes were."

"Sure thing," he said.

Karl took a cigar from his desk drawer, and a wry smile danced across his lips. "I want you all back here by four," he said. "Tonight, I want the world to know The Emerald is back in business."

Simon Crosby lived in a smart apartment in the centre of the city. He stepped out of the shower to the ringing of the door buzzer. Wrapping his bathrobe around himself, he looked through the door's spyhole. Upon sight of Karl, he took a step back. Karl rang the buzzer again. This time, Simon opened the door.

"I was beginning to think you were ignoring me," Karl said, pushing his way past Simon and into the apartment. "How are you, Si? Enjoying your new job?"

Simon closed the door and followed Karl into his comfortable lounge. "When did you get back?" he said. "I thought you'd retired to Spain."

"Why would you think that?"

Simon walked through into the kitchen. "I'm making coffee. Do you want one?"

Karl flung himself into an armchair. "Sure, why not?"

Simon returned to the lounge a couple of minutes later, carrying two mugs of coffee. "So, how are you these days?" he said, placing the mugs down on the coasters on the occasional table. "You're looking well."

Karl leant forward with his eyes fixed on Simon. "What the fuck are you playing at?" he said. "Why did you leave The Sapphire to work at that shithole in Barnsley without talking to me first?"

Simon perched on the edge of the couch. "Why do you think?" he said. "After that stunt you pulled at the casino I—"

"Why is everybody so fixated with that bloody roulette wheel? I walked out of that place clearing my son's debts and owning the place, didn't I? That should be a cause for celebration."

Simon stood up and walked over to the window. "You take too many chances, Karl. You always have. One of these days…"

Karl laughed coarsely. "What? You think I'll get beaten?" He picked up the coffee cup and took a sip. "You're probably right. Maybe one day I will, but it hasn't happened yet, and it's not going to any time soon."

"You know Charlie Dexter's got most of your girls working at his place?"

"Don't worry. They'll be back at The Emerald. The guys are working on that right now."

"You need to be careful. Charlie Dexter can be a vicious

little bastard."

"So can I," Karl said, placing the mug back on the table. "So, what are your plans? Do you intend to stay in Barnsley?"

Simon shrugged. "It's a job. The pay's better too."

Karl arched an eyebrow. "You're not trying to hustle over money, are you?"

"If I come back to The Sapphire, I want your assurance that you'll never pull a stunt like that at the casino again."

Karl held up his hands in mock surrender. "Okay, if that's what it takes," he said. "You have my word. Does this mean I can put you back on the payroll?"

"When do I start?"

Freddie parked outside the address he had been given for Lola and Ruby Jones. It was a run-down four-storey apartment block on the outskirts of Leeds. He knocked on the door of the ground floor flat. It was opened immediately by Ruby.

"Freddie, what are you doing here?" she said, attempting to block his entry. "What do you want?"

Freddie pushed the girl into the room and closed the door behind him. Lola emerged from the bedroom and joined her sister. "Karl's back," Freddie said. "He wants you both back at The Emerald."

Lola shook her head. "We work for Charlie now," she said. "He pays more and—"

Freddie sprang forward and, grabbing her upper arms, shook her violently. "If you don't do as I say, I'll make sure you never work again." He released his grip and pushed her into a chair.

Ruby ran to her sister. "Are you all right?" she said, putting her arm around Lola's shoulders. She turned to Freddie. "Get out of here," she screamed. "If you're not gone in five seconds, I'll—"

"You'll what? Call the police? I don't think so."

"I'll call Charlie," she said. "You can't come here and—"

Freddie crouched down in front of the two girls. "Karl

wants you both working back at The Emerald tonight. If not… well, you'll just have to wait and see, but I warn you, it won't be pleasant."

He stood up and walked towards the door. "Seven o'clock," he said, "and ladies, don't be late."

10

Bernie's Motel was a shabby, single-storey building on the far side of Chapeltown. Paul parked his car at the front and entered the foyer. A chubby, middle-aged man with ginger hair was leaning against the desk. A silver badge on his lapel bore the inscription *Larry – Here To Help*. Larry was engrossed in reading the local newspaper. Giving Paul a cursory glance, he went back to his paper. "Yeah?" he grunted. "What'll it be?"

Paul walked over to the desk, leant over and grabbed the newspaper from Larry's grasp.

"What the fuck—" Larry yelled. He reached out to retrieve it, but Paul held it out of reach.

"I need your full attention," he said. "I have some questions for you."

"Fuck you," Larry said, rushing from behind the desk towards Paul. "Give me that back."

Paul held the newspaper behind his back. "You can have your paper when you tell me what I need to know."

Larry glared at Paul. "What's that?" he said.

"Who booked room 149 last night?"

Larry sniffed, wiping his nose on the back of his hand. "That's privileged," he said, returning to the desk. "I can't discuss guest's details. It's covered by data protection."

Paul leant over the desk and grabbed Larry's lapels. "Fuck data protection," he said. "I won't ask you again. Who booked that room?"

Beads of sweat ran down Larry's face. "All right," Larry said, opening the ledger. "It was a bloke called Michael Wills."

"What address do you have for him?"

"I don't. He only booked the room for a couple of hours, him and his mates."

"What mates?"

"There were two of them. They paid in cash."

"Did you see a girl arrive last night?"

Larry smiled and licked his lips. "Yeah," he said. "She got

37

here about nine o'clock. Pretty little thing she was too. I wouldn't have minded a piece of her myself."

"Did you see the men leave?"

Larry scratched his head. "Yeah, they left about ten. They didn't have the girl with them, though. She must have left already by the back door."

"How do you know?"

He chuckled. "I went to the room to see if there were any leftovers, if you know what I mean, but the room was empty."

"Do you know what car the men drove?"

Larry shook his head. "No idea, mate. They must have been parked around the side."

"Is there anything else you can tell me about them?"

He frowned. "Why should I? Who are you anyway, coming here asking your questions? I've a good mind to ring the police."

"I'll ring them for you," Paul said, taking out his phone. "They'll be interested to know you rent out rooms by the hour."

Larry stepped back. "Look, mate, let's not be too hasty," he said. "We've all got to make a living. I'm not doing anything that every other fleapit at this end of town isn't doing."

"Tell me what these men looked like," Paul said. "I want to know everything you can remember."

Larry scowled. "I didn't pay much attention," he said. "I was watching the boxing on the telly. I remember one of them had a spider's web tattoo on his neck and up the side of his face. Is that freaky or what?" He reached inside his trouser pocket and removed a card. "He gave me this," he said, handing the card to Paul. "He said I can get in free if I show this at the door."

Paul looked at the card. It advertised The Fighting Tiger. "If you take my advice, you'll stay as far away from that place as you can get."

"What about my paper?"

Paul threw the paper down and made his way towards the door. "Fetch," he said as he walked towards out his car.

38

11

Matthew leant over and gently kissed his wife on the cheek. "Wake up, sleepyhead," he teased. "It's nearly ten o'clock."

Christina opened her eyes and smiled. "Why don't we spend the day in bed?" she said.

Matthew pushed a strand of her hair back from her eyes. "Sounds tempting, but we have things to do, my love."

Christina propped herself on her elbows. "Oh? I thought you were working over at the flats today?"

Matthew pulled back the duvet. "I have a surprise for you, darling," he said. "Hurry up and get ready. I have something to show you." He walked towards the bedroom door. "I've run your bath, so hurry up. You don't want it to get cold."

Matthew left the bedroom and went downstairs, leaving Christina to get ready.

Scowling, Lydia peered over her newspaper. "Isn't that girl up yet?" she said. "I've never known anyone sleep so much."

Matthew kissed her lightly on the forehead. "She's getting up now, Mother," he said. "There's nothing spoiling." He walked over to the kitchen cupboard and took out a box of cereal. "I'll make her breakfast, and then we're going out for the day."

"Going out? Aren't you supposed to be working?"

Matthew grinned. "That's the joy of being the boss," he said. "If I don't feel like going to work, I don't have to."

"But Matthew, you can't just—"

"Good morning," Christina said, entering the kitchen. "I'd love a coffee, darling, if it's not too much trouble."

"No trouble at all. I've put out some cereal. It's your favourite."

Christina blew Matthew a kiss as she poured milk into the dish. "Are you going to tell me where you're taking me?" she said. "Or do you want me to guess?

Matthew winked mischievously as he passed his wife a mug of coffee. "You're going to have to wait and see. It's a surprise."

Lydia tutted as she returned to her newspaper. "Will you be home for dinner? It would help if Molly knew how many to prepare for."

"Tell her not to bother about us," Matthew said. "We'll eat out."

Lydia snorted. "That really isn't good enough, Matthew," she said, flinging down her newspaper. "You're treating this place like a hotel. I won't have it."

"I'm doing no such thing. This is my home too and—"

"I think you'll find it's my home," she said. "At least, that's what the deeds said the last time I looked."

Matthew shrugged and turned to Christina. "Hurry up with your breakfast," he said. "We have an appointment."

Lydia watched as her son and Christina drove down the drive. "That bloody bitch," she said through gritted teeth. She raised her arm and threw the cup she held against the wall. "I hate her."

The sound of breaking crockery brought Molly rushing into the kitchen. "Is everything all right, Mrs Glendenning?" she said. "Have you hurt yourself?"

"I dropped a cup," she said. "Clean it up, will you?"

"Yes, of course," Molly said as she scurried to the cleaning cupboard and took out a brush and pan. She busily set to work sweeping up the broken crockery, then got a cloth to mop up the spilt liquid. "Will Matthew and Christina want dinner tonight?" she asked. "I've got some fillet steaks and—"

"No," Lydia said sharply. "My son and that woman will make their own arrangements."

"Very well, Mrs Glendenning," Molly said as she turned to leave the kitchen.

"Oh, by the way, Molly, I will have a guest this evening, so if you could prepare dinner for two?"

"Of course, madam. Will there be anything else?"

Lydia shook her head. "No. I think that will be all for now."

It was two o'clock. Lydia was in the rear garden deadheading flowers when Molly came dashing down the path towards her.

"Mrs Glendenning," she said, "there's a gentleman at the door. He says it's urgent he speaks with you."

Lydia raised an eyebrow. "Does this gentleman have a name?"

"Dexter," Molly said. "Mr Charles Dexter."

Lydia removed her gardening gloves and threw them into the basket, along with the flower heads. "Show him through to the patio," she said. "And arrange some tea and biscuits."

"Yes, madam," Molly said. She turned and ran back to the house.

Lydia walked up to the patio where a white wrought iron table and four chairs were arranged under a large yellow sunshade. She sat just as Charlie Dexter came through the French doors.

"Charles, this is a surprise," she said. "I wasn't expecting to see you again so soon."

He spun a chair round and straddled it. "I had a visit from Maddox last night," he said, snarling, pointing to his bruised and swollen left eye. "He did this."

"Oh, it looks painful," Lydia mocked concern. "What happened?"

"He warned me to back off or else."

"And are you going to back off?"

"Going toe-to-toe with that mad bastard wasn't in the arrangement," he said, rubbing his chin. "You told me Maddox was a sick man, about to retire."

"Christina told me he was abroad convalescing," she said. "I had no idea he would be coming back to Leeds."

"It will cost you a lot more cash if you want me to go up against him. You do know that? I'll need more muscle for a start."

"Then get it, as much as you need. I want to see the end of the Maddox family. All of them."

"Does that include your daughter-in-law?"

Lydia's eyes narrowed. "Yes. It includes that bitch and… oh, here's Molly with the tea." She watched as Molly put the tray on the table. "Thank you, dear," she said. "I'll take it from here."

"Yes, madam," Molly said, scurrying back into the house.

Lydia smiled sweetly. "Now, Charles, shall I be mother?"

12

"Well, what do you think?" Matthew said, smiling. "Can you see yourself living in the penthouse?"

Christina gasped as she took in her surroundings. Floor-to-ceiling windows gave panoramic views of the city and the river below. The deep-mahogany floor and log-burner oozed luxury, along with the large, sparkling white kitchen/diner. Two double bedrooms with ensuite completed the apartment.

Christina flung her arms around his neck, kissing him passionately on the lips. "Darling, it's perfect," she whispered. "When can we move in?"

Matthew took a bunch of keys from his trouser pocket and handed them to Christina. "Whenever you want," he said. "I thought we could go looking for furniture this afternoon."

Christina clasped her hands in excitement. "I've seen a fantastic leather couch in Harvey Nick's. It would look perfect in here," she said, rushing over to the far wall. "We could put the television here. I've seen just the one in town, and—"

Matthew laughed. "You seem to have got it all planned."

Christina rushed over to the door. "Come on, darling," she said. "Let's go into town now. The sooner we fit out the apartment, the sooner we can move in."

"All right," he said as he locked the door behind him. He turned to Christina and put his hand on her arm. "I was thinking, maybe your mother could stay with us for a while if she's having trouble with Karl."

Christina shook her head vehemently. "No, I don't think that's a good idea," she said. "We don't want any more trouble from Dad, do we?"

Matthew hunched his shoulders. "Well, the offer's there," he said. "Now, where do you fancy going for lunch? You can't shop on an empty stomach."

It was four o'clock, and all the club managers were assembled in Karl's office at The Emerald.

Karl sat behind his desk, a glass of whisky in his hand.

"Before we begin," Karl said, "the good news is Simon will be coming back to manage The Sapphire. He'll be starting tonight."

Paul blew out. "Thank god for that," he said.

Karl gave him a cursory glance but ignored his remark. "Right, now to business," he said. "How did you all get on?"

Freddie nodded, the colour rising in his cheeks as he folded his arms across his chest. "Ruby and her sister will be here at seven," he said. "I think Elsa will be coming back too, but you can never tell with her."

"I persuaded the three that share the flat in Cheapside," Tommy said. "By the way, do you know they're using their place as a brothel? There were two punters in the flat when I got there."

Karl frowned. "I'll deal with them later. Did you contact anyone else?"

"I saw Jenny," Tommy said. "She was reluctant at first, but she'll be here tonight."

Karl sipped his whisky. "I take it she needed persuading?"

Tommy shrugged. "Like I said, she'll be here."

"Me and Terry called on the rest," Wayne said. "They'd all been told by Dexter that you'd left the business for good. That's why they went to The Fighting Tiger."

Karl turned to Paul. "What did you find out at the motel?"

Paul relayed his conversation with the receptionist and the link to The Fighting Tiger.

Karl's hands curled into fists. "Just as I suspected," he said. "It was down to Charlie Dexter and his lot."

"What are we going to do about it?" Peter asked. "We can't let them get away with knocking the girls around."

"Did you get a description of the men?"

"Not really. One of them had tattoos over his face and neck. So, he shouldn't be hard to find."

Karl inhaled deeply. "Well, I think that's all for now," he said. He turned to Freddie. "Have the minders on standby to come over to Leeds if there's trouble from Dexter."

"No problem," Freddie said as everyone made to leave the

room.

Wayne remained seated. "Boss, could me and Terry have a private word?"

Karl nodded. Everyone else left, and Karl walked to the cabinet and refreshed his drink. "Want one?" he asked. They both declined. He returned to his seat behind the desk. "So, what's the problem?"

Wayne cleared his throat. "When we took on the casino three months ago, it was on the understanding that it was just a temporary thing," he said. "The thing is, Karl, we've been offered a casino down in Brighton to manage."

"When do you want to leave?"

"As soon as you can get a replacement," Terry said.

Karl took out a cigar from the desk drawer and lit it. "How does next week sound?"

Wayne looked startled. "We can hang on a bit longer, Karl. We don't want to leave you in the lurch."

"You aren't. I've got somebody lined up already. He'll be here tomorrow, as a matter of fact."

13

It was eleven o'clock that evening when Matthew and Christina approached the house just as a dark-red Audi was being driven out through the gates.

Matthew smirked. "It looks like Mother has had a visitor," he said.

Christina began to chuckle. "You don't think she's got a bloke, do you? A secret lover?"

"Let's hope so. She might keep her nose out of our business."

They both got out of the car, walking arm-in-arm into the house. Lydia was lounging on the couch, a half-empty glass of brandy in her hand. Matthew bent down and kissed her on the cheek. "Good evening, Mother," he said. "I see you've had a visitor."

Lydia sipped at the brandy. "A family friend," she said, getting up from the couch and walking unsteadily towards the hall. "I'm going up. I'll see you in the morning."

Matthew turned to his wife. "Do you want a nightcap? I'm having one."

Christina nodded and kicked off her shoes, snuggling back into an armchair. "Did you recognise the car?"

Frowning, Matthew passed her a gin and tonic. "I've never seen it before," he said. "No doubt Mother will tell us all about her visitor tomorrow." He perched on the arm of the chair, placing his arm protectively around Christina's shoulders. "Do you think we should tell her about the apartment?"

"No, darling," she said. "Let's wait until the furniture is ready. Then we can surprise her."

Matthew reached out and kissed the top of her head, gently running his fingers through her hair. "It will be wonderful having our own place. I can't wait."

Christina smiled contentedly, stretching her arms above her head. "Neither can I. It will be perfect."

Matthew cosied up to his wife, drawing her close. "Maybe, when we're settled, we could think about starting a family," he said and nuzzled her neck. "What do you think?"

Christina tensed and pulled away from Matthew's embrace. "Are you serious?"

"Of course, I'm serious. I thought two kids, maybe three. We'd be a proper family then."

Christina banged her glass down hard on the table. "I'm tired," she said. "I'm going up." She hurried out of the room, leaving Matthew staring after her, open-mouthed.

Geoffrey Lawrence parked his red Audi in the garage and entered his spacious bungalow on the outskirts of Harrogate. He hurried towards his study. Nurse Walters was hovering in the hallway and followed him into the room.

"How is she?" he said. "Has she—?"

"Mrs Lawrence has waited up to speak with you," she said, a look of disapproval spreading across her face. "She refused her injection until you got home."

Geoffrey sighed heavily as he walked towards his wife's bedroom. "All right," he said. "I'll sort it."

Amanda Lawrence sat propped up with pillows waiting for him to enter the room. Her pale face looked gaunt, with dark shadows beneath her eyes. On sight of her husband, she smiled weakly and leant forward, lifting her arms towards him. Rushing to her side, Geoffrey gently guided her back into the pillows, kissing her lightly on the cheek. "Darling, you should be asleep," he said. "It's almost midnight."

Amanda grasped his arm. "I couldn't sleep until you got back," she said.

"Darling, I'll tell you all about it tomorrow. You need your rest."

Amanda's breathing became erratic. "Don't fuss," she said. "I have to know why Lydia invited you over to dinner. We've barely seen her in years, not since her father died."

Geoffrey perched on the edge of the bed, gently stroking his wife's hand. "She'd heard about the book I'm writing," he said. "She asked me if I would include a chapter about the shooting. She's convinced Maddox caused David to do what he did."

"David killed himself. Everybody knows that."

"Yes, but why? That's what Lydia wants to know. Why did David Glendenning shoot Karl Maddox? What had gone on between them to make him do that?"

"I thought the investigation concluded David had had some kind of breakdown?"

Geoffrey gently eased his wife back into the pillows. "That was the official verdict," he said. "There was no evidence to prove otherwise, but there are those at the nick who think differently."

"So, what are you going to do? Are you going to investigate?"

"Perhaps," he said, leaning over and pushing back a stray lock of hair from his wife's face. "Anyway, that's enough excitement for now. You need to sleep. Nurse Walters is waiting outside with your medication."

Amanda grabbed Geoffrey's arm. "Oh, do I have to have that? The pain isn't so bad today."

Geoffrey lifted Amanda's hands to his lips and kissed them gently. "It's for the best," he said. "You need a comfortable night's sleep. We can talk more about this tomorrow."

Lydia closed her eyes. "I suppose you're right," she said. "You'd better tell her to come in."

Writing his memoirs now that he had retired had been Amanda's idea. Geoffrey Lawrence prided himself that most of the cases he had been involved in throughout his long career as a police officer had been solved. It had never been established to anyone's satisfaction why David Glendenning, a senior police officer, had shot and wounded Karl Maddox before turning the gun on himself. There had been rumours, of course. David was known to frequent the various lap-dancing clubs owned by Maddox, and it was also suspected, although nothing had been proven, that he frequently used the services of prostitutes.

He opened the copy file notes on the case that he had squirrelled out of the station years earlier and began to read. Everyone involved in the investigation had concluded that it was an argument over money or women. No one had looked at the possibility of anything more sinister behind the shootings. Not until now.

Leaning back into his chair, Geoffrey gave a contented sigh of satisfaction as he slowly sipped his drink. If he played this right, he thought, and with a little help from Lydia, there was a possibility he could make a real name for himself. Maybe even write a best seller.

14

It was eleven-thirty the following morning. Karl was in his office when Peter knocked and leant into the room. "There's someone to see you, Karl," he said, a broad grin on his chubby face. He stood to one side to let the newcomer enter.

"Danny, you old bastard," Karl said, rushing towards his guest, hand outstretched. "I'm glad you decided to come."

Danny shook Karl's hand and put his arms around him in a man-hug. "How could I refuse?" Danny said. "It's great to see you again, mate."

"Fancy a drink?"

Danny shook his head. "It's a bit too early for me."

"I meant tea," Karl said, "or coffee if you prefer."

"I'll pass, thanks. I want to see what you've done to this place while I've been away."

Karl rubbed his hands together. "You won't recognise it," he said. "Let's start with the VIP Lounge. This used to be your living room back in the day."

Danny followed Karl through into the lounge. He stopped abruptly in the doorway, his mouth gaping wide. "Bloody hell, Karl," he said. "I can't believe this. It looks like a tart's boudoir."

"When were you ever in a tart's boudoir?"

He grimaced as he followed Karl into the room. "What's with the mirrored walls and fancy couches?"

Karl waved his arm around the room. "It gives the place class," he said. "It's not cheap being entertained up here. It has to look seductive."

Danny wrinkled his nose. "They don't actually… they don't shag in here, do they?"

Karl laughed and shook his head. "No, of course they don't. They just fantasise about shagging."

Danny plonked himself on one of the velvet couches. "Well, it's certainly changed since my day," he said. "How's business?"

"I can't complain," he said. "While I was away, the wolves

began circling. There was a bit of trouble with some arsehole trying to muscle in, but it's sorted now. They won't be back in a hurry."

Danny chuckled. "So, you're still keeping your hand in, eh? Aren't you getting a bit long in the tooth for that sort of thing?"

Karl grinned. "Piss off," he said. "I'm not old. I'm in my prime."

"If you say so, mate."

"I take it things didn't work out too well in Spain?" Karl said. "I thought you were planning to end your days out there."

"I was, but… well, I guess you can have too much of the high life. I didn't have anything to occupy me. That was the problem. Sitting on a beach all day and clubbing all night is great, but… the truth is, I missed my old life too much. When I bumped into you in Malaga last month, I realised I was homesick."

"So, you wouldn't recommend a life in the sun?"

"Too bloody right, I would. But just make sure you have things to occupy yourself. That's where I went wrong." He got up from the couch and walked over to the window. "Seriously though, isn't it time you thought of taking it easy? Start enjoying your money."

"It has crossed my mind these last few months," Karl said, "but what would I do if I did?"

"Relax. Start to enjoy life a bit more. You're a long time dead, you know."

Karl frowned. "You're a miserable sod these days," he said.

There was a knock on the door, and Peter stepped into the room. "Do you still want me to take that booze over The Amethyst, boss, only my car's in for service today?"

Karl huffed. "Take mine," he said, throwing the car keys towards him. "But make sure you're back before six. I'll need the car tonight."

"Sure, boss," Peter said, giving a nod of acknowledgement to Danny before hurrying out of the room.

"I see you've got Victor's lad working for you. Do you see much of Victor?"

"Not much. He's set up with his brothers in Sheffield. They're running a security business."

"Good for him," Danny said. "Now, are you going to show me the rest of the club?"

Both men descended the staircase into the foyer.

"Through here," Karl said, opening the door at the side and walking into the main club. Danny followed

"So, this is where the bitches wiggle their arses, is it?" he said. "I still can't believe men pay good money to watch that."

"Well, they do," Karl said, making his way towards the six gleaming poles erected on podiums. "They pay lots of money. There are no wolves around my door, mate." He reached out and, wrapping his arms around one of the poles, attempted to spin.

Danny chuckled. "Bloody hell, Karl, don't give up your day job."

Karl struggled to his feet. "Do you know something? That's the second time someone's said that to me."

"Oh? Who was the first?"

"Joe, when I first bought this place. That was a long time ago."

"I heard he took off with your missus. Good riddance to both of them if you ask me."

Karl shrugged but remained silent.

Danny walked over to the far wall of the club with its fleur-de-lis fretwork set in oak panelling. "I'm glad to see some things haven't changed," he said. "I take it nobody knows about the hidden passage?"

Karl shook his head. "No. Just me and Victor's two lads."

"Take my advice and keep it that way. You never know when a hideout might come in useful." He glanced at his watch. "It's nearly twelve," he said. "What about that drink you mentioned?"

Karl walked to the bar and poured two whiskies, handing one to Danny. "By the way, did you manage to take care of that other business we talked about?" Karl said.

Danny rested his hand on Karl's arm, a broad grin on his face. "The villa was burnt to the ground," he said. "The woman managed to get out, but I heard she had severe burns."

"And Clutterbuck? What about him?"

"He wasn't so lucky. Burnt to a crisp, so I heard."

Karl pursed his lips and slowly shook his head. "I wish people would learn it doesn't pay to rip me off."

"Oh, I think they've got the message," Danny said and slowly sipped his whisky. "Now, tell me about this casino of yours. I heard you won it on the spin of a wheel."

"Something like that," he said. "I've renamed it *The Four Aces.*"

"You're full of surprises. I'd never have taken you for a gambler." He took another sip of his drink. "When do you want me to start?"

"Next weekend," Karl said. "Terry and Wayne are leaving at the end of the week."

"Sounds good. I'm looking forward to it. It's been a while since I worked in a casino."

"There are staff there that can show you the ropes," Karl said. "Oh, by the way, what happened to that ginger nut you went off to Spain with? Billy, wasn't it?"

Danny chuckled. "There've been a few Billies since him," he said. "Right now, I'm free and single."

"But probably not for long, eh?"

Danny winked mischievously. "We'll see," he said and drained his glass. "One more for the road?"

15

It was midday. Christina parked her car on the top level of the multi-storey and looked through her rear-view mirror for the person she had come to meet. It was fifteen minutes before a familiar figure came hurrying towards her.

"Sorry I'm late, Sis," Alex said as he climbed into the front passenger seat. He leant over to kiss Christina on the cheek, but she pulled away.

"I want you to ring Mum," she said. "She's out of her mind with worry about you."

Alex huffed. "I can't do that, Chris. If Dad finds out—"

"Don't worry about that. She won't tell him."

"You think she's forgiven me for what I did?"

Christina scowled. "No, of course she hasn't, but you're still her son. She's worried about you." She turned to face her brother. "What are you up to these days? Where are you living?"

Alex shrugged. "Around."

"You're looking very thin, Alex. Are you eating?"

"Yes, I'm eating,"

"What about work? Do you have a job?"

"Don't worry about me. I'll be all right."

"You'll have to come out of hiding sooner or later."

"I think it's best if I make it later, don't you?"

"Did you hear what happened at the casino?"

Alex chuckled. "Yes, I can't believe Karl actually risked everything like that. I thought I was the gambler in the family."

Christina placed her hand on Alex's arm. "I'm sorry to hear about you and Sarah splitting up," she said. "Have you heard from her?"

"No, and I don't want to. Plenty more fish in the sea."

Christina sighed. "I liked Sarah," she said. "She seemed a decent person. By the way, did you know Matthew and I got married?"

Alex's posture stiffened. "You've got to be kidding. You can't be married to him. Not Matthew."

Christina removed her hand from Alex's arm. "What do you mean by that? Matthew is a wonderful man. He's kind and generous."

"His father tried to kill Karl, or have you forgotten?"

"You can't hold Matthew responsible for what his father did. That's not fair."

"Isn't it? Believe me, you're making a big mistake being with him. Walk away now while you still can."

"You're talking nonsense. That business between David and Karl happened years ago. It's all over with now."

"Really? What about what happened with the casino? Karl could have lost everything because of Matthew's scheming."

"Well, he didn't. Anyway, you're to blame for that too, don't forget. You almost bankrupted Dad."

Alex hunched his shoulders. "I was a gambler," he said. "I suppose I'll always be a gambler. It's a sickness, an addiction. But Matthew and Joe took advantage of that. They encouraged me."

"You can't keep blaming other people," she said. "You have to take responsibility for what you did."

"I don't know why you're defending Dad," he said. "He took the salon back off you as soon as you went to live with Matthew."

"There was a clause in the lease that if I didn't work in the salon for five consecutive years, it reverted back into Karl's ownership."

"I bet you didn't know about that when he gave you the salon, did you?"

"I couldn't care less about the damned salon," she said. "I'm married to Matthew, so I don't have to work again if I don't want to."

"Lucky you," Alex mocked. "You've really landed on your feet."

"What about you? What are you going to do for money?"

Alex smirked. "I'm not entirely without funds," he said. "Even gamblers get to win occasionally."

16

It was just before four o'clock that afternoon when Police Inspector Wilson arrived at The Emerald Club. One of the cleaning staff showed him to Karl's office.

Karl looked up from his desk as the officer approached. "Yes?" he said. "What do you want?"

"Mr Maddox, there's been an accident involving a Mercedes motor vehicle registered in your name."

"What the hell happened? Was anyone hurt?"

"I'm afraid the driver has serious injuries. He's in St James's Hospital."

Karl grabbed his desk for support.

"Do you know the identity of the driver?" Wilson said.

"Peter," he said. "Peter Borowicz. He works for me. He was on his way to Manchester on business." Karl stumbled over to the drinks cabinet and poured himself a whisky. "What… what happened? How badly hurt is he?"

"All I can tell you is that the Mercedes appears to have collided with the central reservation and landed on its roof. It's a miracle that the driver wasn't killed."

Karl swayed as he returned to his chair and flopped down heavily. He picked up the telephone on his desk and dialled a number. "Paul? Paul, I need you to get back to the club straight away."

He replaced the receiver, gulped the whisky, and lowered his head into his hands.

Left alone, Karl leant back into his chair and closed his eyes. He gulped more whisky before reaching over for the phone. It was answered on the third ring. "Victor? Victor, it's Karl," he said. "I'm afraid I have some bad news, old friend."

17

As instructed, Karl attended the police station a week after the accident. He arrived at three o'clock, accompanied by Paul. Both men were shown to an interview room to await the arrival of Inspector Wilson.

"Sorry to keep you gentlemen waiting," the inspector said as he bustled into the room, a young constable by his side. Wilson sat down at the metal table across from Karl and Paul and removed papers from a blue file he had been carrying.

Karl scowled and flung back his head. "What's this about?" he said. "Why am I here?"

Wilson looked up from his papers. "You're here, Mr Maddox, because we have found that the incident involving your vehicle was not an accident."

Karl's hands clenched into fists. "What are you talking about? Not an accident?"

"The brakes had been tampered with."

Karl inhaled deeply and shook his head. "No, that can't be right," he said. "I don't believe it. You've got it wrong."

"I'm afraid there's no mistake," Wilson said. "Our traffic lads are the best in the business. The brake cables had definitely been cut."

Paul banged his fist on the table. "Are you saying someone tried to kill my brother?"

Wilson turned to face Karl. "Did Peter often drive your car?"

"Sometimes," he said, "when he had an errand to do for me, but I drove it most of the time."

"Tell me about the day of the crash. You say he was on his way to Manchester?"

Karl nodded. "That's right. Peter's car was in for a service, so I said he could drive mine."

Wilson stroked his chin. "I see. So, you would normally have been behind the wheel?"

"Yes, but… what the hell are you implying?" Karl jumped to his feet. "You can't think someone was out to get me?"

"Sit down, Mr Maddox," Wilson said. "Can you think of anyone who might wish you harm?"

Karl plonked himself back into his chair, scowling, but remained silent.

"Well?"

Karl shook his head. "No one."

"But surely in your line of business—"

"I've told you there's no one. Now, if we're finished, I have things to do."

"We'll need you to make a statement," Wilson said. "The constable will write it for you." He turned to face Paul. "What about your brother? Do you know if he has any enemies?"

"Everyone likes Peter," he said. "He doesn't have an enemy in the world."

Karl huffed. "Can we get on with this? I'm a busy man. We've told you all we know."

Wilson stood and turned to the young policeman. "Take a statement from these gentlemen," he said.

"Yes, sir," the officer said, taking out his notebook.

18

Paul drove Karl to The Emerald Club in silence. Karl was pensive as he made his way up to his office. "It's got to be Dexter," he said. "I thought that bastard had got the message."

"The police will never prove it was him. I think we both know that."

"Police? I wouldn't rely on them to find a cat." He flounced into his chair and leant forward, steepling his fingers on the desk. "Call the lads together," he said. "I think it's time we paid Charlie Dexter a visit he won't forget."

"Do you want me to ring Dad?"

Karl nodded. "Yes. Victor will want to be in on this."

Lydia was startled by the banging on her front door. As she hurried along the hall, she could see Charlie Dexter's familiar silhouette behind the glass. "What on earth's the matter?" she said, opening the door. "I thought we'd agreed to meet next week?"

Charlie pushed past her and made his way through to the lounge. "Word's out somebody's tried to kill Maddox," he said. "They'd messed with his car's brakes or something."

"Is he dead?"

Charlie shook his head. "No. One of his lackeys was driving. I've heard he's in a bad way."

"I don't see what this has to do with me, Charles," Lydia said, perching on the edge of the couch.

"He'll blame me." Charlie gulped. "Karl and those mad dogs of his will be looking for me."

"In that case, you'd better lie low for a while, hadn't you?"

"Lie low? I need to get away. Far away. I'll need money for that."

Lydia pursed her lips. "Not from me," she said. "This has nothing to do with me. I only told you to disrupt his business, not kill him."

"It wasn't me," Charlie wailed. "I didn't do anything, but

Karl will think I did." He grabbed Lydia by her upper arms and shook her. "You've got to help me," he said, his voice trembling. "You've no idea what Maddox is capable of."

Lydia pulled away from him. "I think you'd better leave," she said. "Our… our arrangement has come to an end."

Charlie raised his hand as if to slap her, then lowered it again. "You bitch," he said, pointing his finger. "If he gets to me, I'll make damned sure he finds out about you too."

Lydia took a step back. "Get out," she screamed. "Get the hell out of my house."

Charlie Dexter closed the front door with a loud bang. Christina, who had been standing on the stairs, turned quickly and went back to her room. Ten minutes later, she was in her car and heading in the direction of The Emerald Club.

19

Karl paced the office, beads of sweat running down his brow. A turf war with Charlie Dexter was the last thing he wanted. He was about to pour himself a whisky when Freddie burst into the room. "Boss, he's gone," he said. "Dexter's gone."

Karl lunged forward. "What do you mean, gone? Gone where?"

Freddie recoiled. "The Fighting Tiger is shut down. It's been boarded up, and there's no sign of him," he said. "I've spoken to a couple of the blokes that worked there. They don't know where he is. They're pissed off because he owes them money."

Karl's nostrils flared. "So, the cowardly little bastard has run for the hills, has he?"

"I'll get the lads out looking," Freddie offered. "He can't have gone far."

The opened, and Christina bounded into the room.

"Doesn't anybody ever knock?" Karl said, striding menacingly towards her. "What the hell do you want? You're not welcome here, you know that."

"Dad, I—"

Karl raised his hand. "I don't want to hear it. You've made your bed. Now lie in it."

"But, Dad… it's about Peter's accident."

"What do you know about that?"

"I know Charlie Dexter had nothing to do with it."

"Bollocks," Karl said. "Dexter's been trying to take over my business for months."

"Dexter was out to cause trouble for your business, but that was down to Lydia. I just found out today that she's been paying him to disrupt the club, but Dexter had nothing to do with the accident." She reached out and put her hand on his arm. "He's been around the house trying to borrow money to help him get away. Lydia refused. Dexter's scared shitless, but he insists he had nothing to do with the accident."

"You say you've only found out what Lydia's been up to

today?"

She nodded. "We're not close. She's not happy about Matthew and me being together."

"I heard you'd married Glendenning."

"I love him," she said. "He's a wonderful man."

"That bastard tried to take everything from me," Karl said, "and you, my own daughter, were part of it."

"Dad, that's not true. You've got to believe me. I didn't know what Matthew and Joe were planning. It was nothing to do with me."

"You don't belong in that family, Christina. You'll realise that one day. He's no good, just like his father."

"You're wrong about Matthew. He's nothing like his father."

"I don't suppose you know where your brother is?"

She shook her head. "I haven't seen Alex in months."

"Well, if you should happen to bump into him in some gutter, make sure he knows I'm looking for him. We have a score to settle."

"You can't mean that. Alex is a fool, but he's still your son."

Karl pointed towards the door. "I'm sure you can find your way out," he said, "and, Christina, don't come back."

"Well, that's a relief," Freddie said when Christina left. "If what she said is right, it wasn't Charlie Dexter after all."

"What do you mean relief?"

"It means we won't have to fight Charlie's lot."

Karl shook his head slowly and sighed. "It's not a relief," he said. "If Charlie Dexter isn't responsible for tampering with the brakes on my car, who the fuck is?"

Freddie shrugged. "I don't know, boss," he said. "It could be anybody, I suppose."

"Christina could have it wrong," Karl said. "He deserves a good kicking for the trouble he's caused."

"You mean we're going ahead with fighting him, boss?"

"Yes, Freddie. That's exactly what I mean."

20

Geoffrey Lawrence steered his Audi alongside the address in Liverpool his ex-colleague had given him for Joe Stevens.

A young woman answered the door. Lawrence deducted this must be Karl's ex-daughter-in-law, Sarah. "I was looking for Mr Stevens," he said, conjuring up a broad smile. "Mr Joe Stevens?"

Sarah frowned, crossing her arms across her chest. "Who are you?"

"My name is Geoffrey Lawrence," he said, handing her his card.

She gave the card a cursory glance. "Joe's not here. I'm not expecting him until this evening."

Lawrence painted on his warmest smile. "It really is quite urgent. Perhaps I could call round later this evening?"

She turned to close the door. "I'm sorry, Mr... Mr Lawrence," she said, glancing at his card again. "That won't be convenient. We're going out this evening. What is it you want to speak to my husband about?"

"I'm a retired police officer," Lawrence said, "and I'm writing my memoirs. I want to include the incident between your father-in-law, Karl Maddox, and Superintendent David Glendenning. I was hoping Joe might be able to shed light on what happened."

"How could he? He wasn't there."

"No, but he may be able to fill in the background. It would be helpful if I could speak to him for a few minutes. I—"

Sarah slammed the door shut.

"Was that the front door?" Joe asked as he took off his gardening boots and walked into the kitchen.

Sarah handed him the card she had been given and relayed her conversation with the visitor.

"Geoffrey Lawrence? I know that name from somewhere," he said, scrutinising the card. "What did he look like?"

She shrugged. "Late fifties, early sixties, maybe. Smartly dressed and well-spoken."

Joe stroked his chin. "You say this bloke's writing a book about Karl and David? I think… wait a minute," Joe said and struck his forehead with the heel of his hand. "Geoffrey Lawrence, of course. He was David's boss at the nick. David said he was a real bastard. He made his life hell."

"So why would he want to speak to you? David's dead, and Karl's… well, he's just Karl."

"Whatever he's up to, I want no part in it. If he calls again, slam the door in his face."

21

After his encounter with Sarah, Lawrence returned to his car. His mood was pensive as he studied the other names in his notebook. Glancing at his watch, he saw it was almost midday. He headed towards The Red Lion pub, which he had passed on his way to Joe's house. According to the board outside, the pub offered home-cooked food and a fine selection of specialist beers.

Lawrence had just about finished his quiche and salad when Sarah and Joe walked into the pub and stood by the bar. He got up from his table and walked over to them. "Joe Stevens?" he said. "I'm Geoffrey Lawrence. I wonder if—?"

"I have nothing to say to you," Joe said, turning away. "Leave me alone."

"I just want to ask you some questions about Karl Maddox. I understand you used to work for him."

"I said I have nothing to say to you," Joe said. "If you want to know anything about Karl's business, go and ask him yourself if you dare." Joe gripped Sarah's upper arm and steered her towards an empty table. Geoffrey followed.

"Joe, all I want to know is why David Glendenning shot Karl. What had Karl done to piss him off?"

"The police investigated at the time," Joe said. "Check the files."

"I have. They're not helpful. There's no explanation for why they fell out. What could have been so serious for David to shoot Karl and then kill himself?"

Joe shrugged. "I don't know. I wasn't there."

"Not when the shooting took place, but you were there immediately before. You must have some idea what went wrong."

Joe's eyes narrowed. "I've told you, I have nothing to say." He picked up the menu from the table. "Now, if you don't mind, I'd like to have my lunch in peace."

Lawrence turned to leave. "If you change your mind, Sarah has details on how to reach me."

"I won't," he said as he scrutinised the menu.

Sarah placed her hand on Joe's. "What did happen between them?" she said. "You never did tell me."

Joe leant over and gently cupped Sarah's chin in his hand. "There's nothing to tell," he said. "It all happened a long time ago. It has nothing to do with us."

"But Joe, I—"

Joe removed his hand. "I've told you, forget about Karl and all that shit. It's in the past. Now, what do you fancy for lunch? I think I'll have the cod."

22

It was early evening when Lawrence got back to Harrogate. When he arrived, Amanda was propped up in bed, the latest Eva Carmichael novel in her hand. Upon seeing her husband, she put the book down and reached out to him.

"Darling, there you are," she said. "I didn't hear you leave this morning."

Geoffrey bent over and kissed his wife gently on the cheek. "I made an early start," he said. "I've been to Liverpool."

"Oh?"

"I went to see Joe Stevens. He's the guy who was working for Karl just before David shot himself."

"What happened? Did he tell you anything useful?"

Geoffrey shook his head. "He was cagey. He refused to tell me anything."

"That's that then, I suppose," Amanda said.

"I'm not sure. I think Joe has a pretty good idea of what went on between them. It's just a question of giving him the right incentive to tell me what he knows."

"What sort of man is he?"

Geoffrey tilted his head. "A decent bloke, from what I can make out. He did a spot inside for causing death by dangerous driving when he was young, but apart from that, he's kept his nose clean."

"Didn't he run off with Karl's wife?"

"Erica? Actually, she was his common-law wife. They were never married."

"Maddox must have been raging at Joe, taking her away like that from under his nose."

"Erica had a pretty miserable existence with Karl by all accounts. She died a couple of years later."

"You don't think …?"

"No. Cancer," he said. "The funny thing is, Joe's now with Karl's daughter-in-law, Sarah."

Amanda frowned. "He certainly seems to have a liking for the Maddox women, doesn't he? Will you try to speak to Joe again?"

"Later," he said. "I'll let him brood about what I've said for a few days."

"Who are you going to speak to next?"

"I think I'll pay Victor Borowicz a visit," he said. "I've had dealings with Victor in the past. He's not the sharpest knife in the box, I seem to remember."

"Who's Victor Borowicz?"

"He used to work for Danny Davies back in the days when The Emerald Club was a snooker hall. Danny sold it to Karl, and Victor stayed on at the club for a while. His two boys both work there now, as a matter of fact."

"Why do you want to speak with him? I would have thought you would be better speaking to his two lads."

"I'll speak to them in due course," Geoffrey said, "but Victor can give me some background about what was going on at the club before the shooting."

"I suppose so, but… but I…" Amanda closed her eyes, and her head slowly lolled forward.

Geoffrey reached out and gently manoeuvred her back into the pillows. "Keep still, my love," he said. "I'll get the nurse." He hurried out of the room and rapped on Nurse Walters' door. It was opened immediately. "Hurry," he said. "Amanda's having another one of her turns."

They both rushed along the corridor to Amanda's bedroom. "Stay out here, Mr Lawrence," Nurse Walters ordered. "I'll see to your wife." She closed the door firmly, leaving a dejected Geoffrey Lawrence standing alone. Head bowed, he ambled back to his study. It was ten minutes before he was joined by the nurse.

"You really shouldn't exert your wife," she said. "She needs rest. As much rest as she can get."

Geoffrey hunched his shoulders. "We were just talking," he said. "Amanda likes me to discuss my work."

"Mrs Lawrence is a sick woman," she said. "Excitement of any kind affects her blood pressure. We've discussed this before. I really must insist."

Geoffrey put up his hands in mock surrender. "All right, I hear you," he said. "Can I see her?"

The nurse shook her head. "Not right now. I've given her something to help her sleep."

23

Paul was in Karl's office the following morning. "Are you sure Christina got it right?" he said. "She's not trying to protect the little scumbag?"

Karl shrugged. "Why would she? As far as I know, Dexter's pissed off. He wouldn't do that if he wasn't scared."

"What about the bitch who put him up to it?"

"Lydia Glendenning is a sick woman. She's only just been released from the looney bin. I don't think she'll give us any more trouble now she hasn't got Dexter to do her bidding."

"You're not going soft, are you? That heart thing you had, it's not affected the way you do business?"

Karl banged his fists on the desk. "How dare you say that? I'm not going guns blazing until I know who to aim at. I don't think that person is Charlie Dexter."

"Then who the fuck is it that's trying to kill you? I can't think of anyone who'd have the balls."

Karl leant back into his chair. "Do you think Alex could be involved?"

"Alex? No. He's reckless and a gambler, but he's not a killer."

"Still, he must be pretty pissed off with me," Karl said, "being cut off from the family business."

"Alex got what he deserved. Besides, he's resilient. He'll bounce back. No, my money's on Patrick Flynn and his sidekick. They've a million reasons to hate your guts."

"I don't think so. They're lying low abroad somewhere. If they were back in the country, I'd have heard about it."

"I still think it could be them. They ran a pretty big operation before you destroyed it."

Karl huffed. "They were lowlife sex traffickers," he said. "The sooner they get put away, the better."

"Let's hope you're right," Paul said, walking towards the door. "I'm going to the hospital to visit Peter. I'll be back about seven."

"How's he doing?"

"A concussion and a few broken bones, but he's tough. He'll be out of there in no time. Dad hasn't left his side since the accident."

"I'll try and call in to see him, but things have been manic here since the girls came back. The club's never been so busy."

"Good. It's great getting things back to normal."

The desk phone rang. Karl picked up the receiver. "Oh, Roger," he said, "it's good to hear from you, mate. Hold on a minute." He turned to Paul. "Give Peter my best," he said, putting his hand over the receiver. Taking the hint, Paul nodded and left the room.

Peter Borowicz was propped up in his hospital bed, a large bunch of black grapes by his side. "Thanks for these, Dad," he said, placing three grapes into his mouth.

"I'm glad you're enjoying them," Victor said. "Is there anything else I can get? A glass of water, perhaps?"

"I wouldn't mind a pint," Peter said, winking playfully. "A nice cold beer would go down a treat."

Victor placed his hand on Peter's arm. "I'll see what I can do, son," he said, smiling. "You'll have to be careful, though, that staff nurse over there looks pretty fierce."

Peter grinned. "Bethany's all right. I wouldn't be surprised if she'd drink one too." They both chuckled, and neither one noticed as she came over to the bed.

"You seem a lot better today," she said. "It's good to hear you laughing."

"My son is on the mend," Victor said. "He'll be ready to come home with me in a day or two."

The nurse leant over to straighten the covers on the bed. "We'll have to see what the doctors say about that. Peter has undergone quite a trauma." She turned to face Victor. "There's a gentleman to see you, Mr Borowicz," she said. "He's waiting in the day room."

Victor arched an eyebrow. "Someone to see me?"

"That's right. He said it's important."

"I'll be right back, son," Victor said as he walked down the corridor in the direction of the day room.

"Hello, Victor," Lawrence said. "Remember me?"

Victor scowled at the visitor. "What the hell do you want?"

"I was sorry to hear what happened to your boy. How's he doing?"

"He's on the mend," Victor said. "Why are you here?"

"I need a little chat," Lawrence said, indicating for Victor to sit on the chair across from him.

Victor perched on the edge, his arms folded across his chest in defiance. "Well?" he demanded. "I don't have long. I need to get back to my boy."

"I want to ask you some questions about Karl Maddox," Lawrence said, "more specifically, Karl's relationship with David Glendenning."

Victor's posture stiffened. "Glendenning's dead," he said. "He shot himself."

"Yes, I know that, but why did he shoot himself? What happened between him and Karl to make him do something like that?"

"How the hell should I know? I wasn't working for Karl when it all kicked off."

"Did David and Karl get on well?"

Victor shrugged. "I suppose so," he said. "David liked the women, but there's nothing wrong with that, is there? Karl provides adult entertainment, and David liked to be entertained."

"Then what caused them to fall out? Was it over money?"

Victor frowned. "No, I don't think so. David always seemed to have plenty of cash."

"Then it must have been over some girl? Is that what happened?"

"You're best speaking to my son, Paul, about that."

"Did I hear my name mentioned?"

Both men turned to see Paul Borowicz standing at the door.

Victor got to his feet and walked towards his son. "Paul, I was just telling the policeman about—"

"Policeman? Geoffrey Lawrence isn't a policeman anymore. He's retired. Isn't that right?"

Lawrence clasped his hands together. "Yes, that's right, I am, but—"

Paul lunged forward. "Then what the fuck are you doing here asking questions of my dad? You've no right."

"Keep your hair on," Lawrence said. "I was just asking Victor a few questions."

"About what?"

"I'm researching the incident between David Glendenning and Karl. I'm writing a book, my memoirs, and I want to dedicate a chapter to what happened."

"What is there to research? David shot Karl and then turned the gun on himself."

"But why would he do that? It just doesn't make any sense. I was hoping Victor might have some theory about what caused it to happen."

"Well, he hasn't. Now piss off and don't bother my family again."

"Paul, this isn't going to go away. I intend to find out exactly what happened."

"Good luck," Paul said, as taking Victor's arm, he steered him towards the door. "Come on, Dad. Let's get back to Peter."

24

After Paul left the office, Karl busied himself checking the previous night's takings. Things were certainly picking up since he got back in the driving seat. He gave a satisfied grunt as he noted how well the casino was doing. It had been a good move bringing Danny into the team. He was about to pour himself a drink when there was a knock on the door, and the cleaner came into the office. "Sorry to bother you, Mr Maddox," she said, twisting the belt of her tabard, "but there's a man downstairs who wants to speak to you urgently."

Karl scowled, lowering the whisky bottle. "I'm busy," he said. "Tell him—"

The door pushed open, and a well-groomed young man dressed in a smart dark-grey suit stepped into the room. "Karl," he said, walking towards him with an outstretched hand. "It's so good to meet you at last."

Karl's scowl deepened. "Who the fuck are you?"

"I'm Ryan," the newcomer said. "Ryan Maddox. I'm your nephew."

Karl's eyes narrowed. "I don't have a nephew.'

"I'm Jason's son."

"I didn't know Jason had a son."

"My dad died when I was five," Ryan said. "He talked about you all the time. He used to call you *Big K*." He began to chuckle. "Sometimes he called you *Special K*."

Karl blinked rapidly, remembering how Jason thought it hilarious and would often tease him with the name. "You'd better sit down," Karl said. "Do you want a drink?"

Ryan shook his head as he perched on the couch. "Never touch the stuff," he said, "but don't let me stop you."

Karl raised an eyebrow as he poured a whisky and sat behind his desk, studying the young man before him. He could definitely see a family resemblance, the same thick black hair and the same dark eyes. He slowly sipped his whisky. "Jason and I more or less lost touch when I… when I moved away."

"Dad said you'd been inside. It was while you were in prison that he met my mother. Her name's Roxanne."

"Jason never mentioned her the last time I saw him," Karl said. "In fact, he never mentioned you either."

Ryan shrugged. "Mam and Dad lead a pretty chaotic life," he said. "They were apart as much as they were together."

"By chaotic, I take it you mean drugs?"

"Drugs and alcohol. That's why I was adopted after Dad died. Mum couldn't take care of me. She could barely take care of herself."

Karl leant back into his chair. "Nobody told me about you," he said. "Maybe… maybe I could have helped?"

Ryan smiled. "Oh, don't feel bad. I did all right. I was adopted and spent my childhood in Devon. It's beautiful there. Have you ever been?"

Karl grinned and shook his head. "Too much fresh air down there for my taste. I'm a city boy." He sipped his drink. "So, what brings you to Leeds after all these years?"

"I got transferred here with work."

"What sort of work?"

"I'm a social worker," he said.

Karl smirked. "A do-gooder, eh?"

"I like helping people," he said. "Many people have problems and need that extra bit of help."

"There are a lot of wankers," Karl said. "They don't want work. They're afraid of work. I don't have time for them, and if I'm honest, I'm surprised my brother's kid has time for them either."

Ryan frowned. "That's a bit harsh, isn't it?"

Karl's mobile rang. He saw it was Paul ringing and cancelled the call.

"Aren't you going to answer it? It could be important."

"He'll call back," Karl said as he placed the mobile back in his pocket.

"I couldn't do that. I can't bear to hear a phone ringing. I have to answer."

Karl placed his glass firmly on the desk. "What is it you

want, Ryan? Why have you come here after all this time?"

"I came to meet you," Ryan said. "Apart from my mother, you're the only family I have."

"It's a bit late to play happy families, isn't it?"

"I was hoping we could get to know each other, but if you don't want to…"

"I didn't say that," Karl said, leaning forward. "Leave me your details, and I'll get in touch."

Ryan grinned as he handed Karl his business card. "This has my office number," he said, "and I've written my private number on the back."

Karl took the card. "Thanks," he said. His mobile rang again.

"I can see you're busy," Ryan said, walking towards the door. "I look forward to getting to know you, Karl, or should I say, Uncle Karl?"

"Karl's fine," he said, taking the mobile from his pocket. It was only when Ryan left the room that Karl answered the phone. "Yes, Paul? What's so urgent?"

25

Karl was pacing the office when Paul arrived. He turned sharply to face him. "Geoffrey Lawrence, you say?"

Paul nodded. "He used to be Glendenning's boss back in the day. He was the one who got David suspended."

"What does he want to dredge that business up for? David's dead. He's been dead for years."

"He says he's writing his memoirs. A lot of ex-cops write books when they retire."

"A book about David?"

"About you and David," Paul said. "He's trying to find out what led to the shootings."

Karl plonked onto his chair behind his desk. "David was off his fucking rocker. That's what led to the shootings. What did Victor tell him?"

"Nothing much. He just said David had a weakness for women. Lots of women."

"He didn't mention… he didn't say anything else?"

"Such as?"

Karl began to drum his fingers impatiently on the desk. "Lawrence must know something to make him take an interest in the shooting."

"It's history," Paul said. "As you said, David was off his rocker. He was about to be kicked out of the police, and he… well, he just flipped."

"If Lawrence tries to speak with you, tell him—"

"I'll tell him to piss off, just like I told him at the hospital." Paul walked over to the cabinet. "I need a drink," he said. "Want one?"

Karl nodded and leant back into his chair, stretching out his legs and placing his hands behind his head. "I had a visitor while you were at the hospital. You'll never guess who."

Paul poured two whiskies. "Give me a clue," he said, handing a glass to Karl.

"A bloke claiming to be Jason's son."

Paul's eyes widened. "What, your Jason?"

Karl nodded. "That's right. It seems Jason got himself a wife and kid while I was inside."

"Bloody hell, Karl, your family doesn't do things by halves, do they? What's he like, this long-lost nephew?"

"His name is Ryan. I have to admit he does have a look of our kid."

Paul frowned. "What did he want?"

"What makes you think he wanted something?"

"Why else would he get in touch after all this time? Jason's been dead for close on twenty years."

"He works in Leeds. A social worker, would you believe?"

"You're having a laugh. Jason's son, a social worker? I don't believe it."

Karl handed Paul the card Ryan had given him. "That's what he says."

"What are you going to do?"

"I'm not sure. I'll invite him to the club and have a proper chat."

"Okay, but… be careful."

"What do you mean, be careful?"

"I don't know. It doesn't quite sit right, does it, coming out of the woodwork after all this time."

"You've a very suspicious nature," Karl said, wagging his finger playfully. "You see a con behind every bush."

Paul shrugged. "Maybe," he said, "but I'm usually right. Oh, by the way, I've traced Dexter and his mob."

"Where are they?"

"According to my source, they're holding up in Newcastle."

"Is your source reliable?"

Paul shrugged. "As reliable as an alcoholic whore can be."

"You'd better get up there and see who he's got with him."

"Sure," Paul said. "I'll drive up tonight."

26

Paul stood in the shadows, his eyes transfixed on the two-storey red-brick house in front of him. Lights blazed in every window. Occasionally, someone would come out of the house and smoke a cigarette on the doorstep. He counted three different men in the two hours he had been watching. In the distance, a church clock struck twelve. Still, there was no sign of his prey. Then, ten minutes later, a green Ford screeched to a halt outside the house, and Charlie Dexter stepped out.

Paul watched as Charlie strode up to the front door. Before he could knock, it was flung open by a tall, stocky man with a shaved head. The light from the hallway revealed a spider's web tattoo on his neck extending onto his left cheek. From their body language, Paul deduced aggression between the two men. He watched as Charlie entered the house, slamming the door shut behind him. Eventually, the lights were turned off one by one, and the place was in darkness.

"Gotcha," Paul whispered as he took out his mobile from his pocket and dialled Karl's number.

It was mid-afternoon when Paul joined Karl in the office at The Emerald. "You did well last night," Karl said. "I heard you sent Dexter running for the hills."

Paul smirked. "To be fair, by the time our lads got there, Dexter and his crew were tucked up in their beds asleep. They were all pretty drunk too."

"I hope you didn't go easy on them," Karl said. "That bastard has cost me money, lots of money."

"Don't worry, they got the message."

"What about the bloke with the tattoo?"

"Steve, one of the minders at The Sapphire, took care of him. Steve was really fond of Sharon."

"Let's hope that's the last we hear from Charlie Dexter and his mob," Karl said, walking over to the stand and putting on his coat.

"Going somewhere?"

"I thought I'd pop over to the hospital whilst things are quiet and see how Peter's doing."

"Do you want me to come with you?"

"No. You stay here. I've got a delivery of knock-off booze coming shortly. Make sure you put it in the storeroom."

Paul grinned. "You mean the secret storeroom behind the panelling?"

"Just do it," Karl said, "and make sure nobody sees you doing it."

It was three o'clock when Karl arrived at the hospital. He walked briskly across the car park carrying the bottle of whisky inside the carrier bag. Suddenly, a white van came screeching around the corner, heading directly in his direction. Karl dodged between two parked cars, hurtling to the floor as the van raced past him.

"Are you all right, mate?" Karl looked up to see an elderly man leaning heavily on two walking sticks standing over him. "That stupid bastard could have killed you."

Shaken, Karl got to his feet. "I… I think so," he said. "I don't suppose you got the number?"

The old man shook his head. "No, sorry. It all happened so fast, but the hospital should have CCTV. If you speak to reception, they could probably help."

"Yeah," he said, "I'll do that."

As Karl made his way to the hospital's entrance, two porters came hurrying towards him. "We saw what happened," one of them said. "We've called the police. It looked like someone was deliberately trying to run you over."

"I'm all right," Karl said. "Can I have a look at the CCTV?"

The porter shook his head. "No, sorry mate, the public aren't allowed. The police will be here in a minute. They can check it for you."

Karl muttered under his breath as he made his way into the hospital. "I'm going to Ward fourteen," he said. "I'll speak to the police later."

Karl took the lift to the first floor. Peter was propped up, chatting to the patient in the next bed when he arrived.

"Thanks for coming, boss," Peter said, his face beaming with excitement. "The doctor said I can come home tomorrow. I'll be back at work in no time. Isn't that great news?"

Karl plonked heavily onto the chair next to Peter's bed. "Are you sure you're feeling up to it?"

Peter nodded. "Sure, I am," he said. "I… Karl, are you all right? You're as pale as a sheet. Has something happened?"

"What do you mean?"

"Your trousers are ripped, and they're covered in mud."

Karl leant forward in the chair. "Oh, that?" he said, gently rubbing at the mud splatter. "I tripped in the car park and fell down, that's all."

"Do you want me to get the nurse to have a look at you?"

"I said I'm fine," Karl said, handing Peter the carrier bag containing the whisky. "I brought you this."

Peter peered into the bag at its contents. "Thanks, boss," he said. "I'd better not let the nurses see this."

"Why? Will they confiscate it?"

"No, they'll probably want to help me drink it." Both men laughed. "What the fuck are the police doing here?" Peter said.

Karl turned to see two uniformed officers heading towards them. "I think they need to speak to me," Karl said, getting to his feet.

"But what do they want?" Peter said. "They've no right barging into a hospital like this."

Karl leant over and patted Peter's arm. "It's nothing to worry about," he said. "You get some rest, and I'll see you back at the club."

27

"So, it's official then," Paul said when Karl returned to The Emerald. "Somebody is definitely out to get you?"

Karl huffed. "It certainly looks that way. The CCTV clearly shows the van drove directly at me."

"You say the van had been stolen?"

"According to the police, it was stolen from Wakefield yesterday."

"Who the fuck can it be? After that trouble with Alex, I thought things had settled down."

"We need to make a list of possibilities."

"It's going to be a bloody long list, Karl."

"What do you mean by that?"

"Well, let's face it, you've pissed off a lot of people over the years."

"Not enough for anyone to want me dead, though," he said.

"I've drawn up a list," Paul said, reaching over the desk and passing Karl a hand-written sheet of names.

Karl took the list. "Alex? You think Alex could be behind this?"

"He has a strong motive," Paul said. "That casino business proved he has absolutely no loyalty towards you."

"I thought we'd agreed he was a hapless gambler. A drifter from one disastrous encounter to another."

Paul shrugged. "As far as I'm concerned, Alex is still up there as the main contender. With you gone, he gets his hands on everything you own."

"No, I can't see it. He's a useless wanker, but he's not a killer."

"Maybe not, but perhaps he knows people who are."

Karl waved his hand dismissively. "I see you've put Christina and Matthew down."

"Are you saying the thought hadn't occurred to you? Your daughter has been totally disloyal since she got mixed up with David's son. You can't deny it's not beyond the realms of possibility that they're involved in this somehow?"

"That's bollocks. Christina is my daughter. She would never harm me."

"Are you sure about that? You know she is meeting up with Lisa and—"

"Lisa is her mother. Of course, she wants to see her. That doesn't mean they want me dead."

"Doesn't it?"

"It's not family, Paul. I know it isn't. It has to be someone else."

"Someone who works for you, you mean? Like me or Simon? You think we could be responsible?"

Karl shook his head. "No, that's not what I'm saying."

"Then what are you saying?"

Karl lowered his head into his hands. "I don't know," he said. "I haven't got a fucking clue."

"We've eliminated Charlie Dexter," Paul said. "If you believe Christina, he was only interested in getting money from Lydia Glendenning."

Karl nodded.

"Then we must look at Patrick Flynn and his sidekick, Luke," Paul said

"I've told you, they're hiding out abroad. I'd have heard something if they were back in England."

"You can't be sure of that," Paul said. "I don't think you can dismiss them out of hand."

"Okay, they're a possibility, I suppose."

"I've put Joe Stevens on the list," Paul said. "We both know he hates your guts."

"Joe is off the scene," Karl said. "It's not him."

"How can you be sure? He could still be bearing a grudge."

"Joe has settled down with Sarah. He has no quarrel with me anymore."

"You don't think Lisa—?"

Karl banged his fist down on the desk. "Are you out of your mind? You seriously think my wife is behind this?"

"I don't know, Karl, but somebody is. You have to look at

everyone in your circle."

"It's most likely a business rival," Karl said, "some toe-rag trying to muscle in the easy way."

"Like Charlie Dexter?"

Karl huffed. "This is crazy. We're just going round in circles."

"What did the police say?"

"Not much. They're concerned it's the beginning of some kind of gang war. The trouble is, they don't know who the other party is."

"We're just going to have to be vigilant."

Karl grinned. "Are you offering to be my bodyguard?"

"Sorry, too busy, but I can arrange one if you think it's necessary."

"No. We can take care of it in-house. Just make sure the guys know what's going on so they can keep an eye open."

Paul walked towards the door. "I'll go downstairs and make sure they're ready to open up."

Karl picked up the list. "Okay. I'll have another think about these names."

28

The following morning Geoffrey Lawrence finished his breakfast before making his way to his wife's room. "How are you this morning, love?" he said and gently kissed her on the cheek.

Amanda smiled weakly and stretched out her arms for her husband's caress. "I didn't sleep too well," she said. "I kept thinking about this Maddox business. Poor Lydia must be distraught."

"I don't want you worrying about things," he said, patting his wife's hand. "I'm meeting Lydia later this morning, as a matter of fact."

"But you haven't made any progress, have you? You still don't know what made David do what he did."

"Patience, my dear," he said. "I haven't begun my investigation yet. I've just rattled a few cages, that's all."

Amanda sighed. "You will be careful, won't you, Geoffrey? These are vicious criminals you're mixing with."

"Darling, stop fretting. I've been doing this for thirty years, don't forget."

"I know, but you're not a young man anymore. From what I've heard about Karl Maddox, he'll—"

"Don't worry about Karl Maddox," he said and gently kissed her hand. "That animal might not be around for too long. I've heard from a reliable source at the nick that somebody is out to get him. They nearly succeeded too."

"Do you know who?"

Geoffrey shrugged. "I have no idea. I just hope I get this business sorted before they succeed." He made his way to the door. "Now, darling, I want you to stop worrying about Lydia Glendenning and get plenty of rest. I'll be home tonight with news."

Amanda nodded as her husband headed towards the hall. She heard his key in the lock as he opened the front door and, a few seconds later, heard the Audi burst into life. Within minutes she had succumbed to the medication the nurse had given her earlier, and she drifted into a troubled sleep.

Lawrence decided to call into the local nick before visiting Lydia. Earlier, he had telephoned John Bennett, a detective inspector, to arrange a meeting. Bennett had worked under Lawrence for years. He considered Bennett one of the more intelligent and observant police officers and a personal friend.

"Great to see you, sir," Bennett said, walking towards Lawrence, hand outstretched.

"No need for the sir," he said, shaking his hand. "I'm just plain mister these days, don't forget."

Bennett smiled. "I thought we could go to the canteen. It's empty at this time of day."

Lawrence followed his companion up the familiar staircase to the police canteen. With two exceptions, all of the blue plastic-topped tables were empty. Bennett asked the waitress to bring over two coffees before making his way to a table by the window. "So, how's the book coming along? It must keep you busy."

Lawrence shrugged. "You think you've remembered every last detail about a case, and then, after a bit more research, you realise your mind plays tricks."

Bennett chuckled. "I think it's a sign of getting old," he said. "What is it you're working on at the moment? You know I'll do all I can to help."

Lawrence leant back in his chair and rubbed his chin. "I'm looking into Karl Maddox," he said. "I'm trying to find out why Glendenning took a pot shot at him."

"David was having a breakdown, wasn't he? He was about to be booted out of the service."

"Yes, I know that. I was the investigating officer," Lawrence said. "I confiscated his warrant card and suspended him from duty."

"Well, there you are," Bennett said. "The shame of being sacked was too much for him."

Lawrence shook his head. "No, I don't think so. David Glendenning was never a dedicated officer. He always had things too easy. Having a father-in-law as chief constable helped."

The chubby waitress sauntered over to the table, carrying two mugs of coffee. "The canteen's supposed to be self-service," she muttered, banging the cups down, causing the liquid to splash onto the table. "I'm not supposed to wait on tables."

"Not even for your favourite policeman," Bennett said, a broad grin on his freckled face. "You remember Chief Superintendent Lawrence, don't you, Maggie?"

The woman peered at Lawrence for a few seconds. "Oh, sorry, sir," she said. "I... I didn't recognise you. I'll get a cloth and—"

Bennett picked up one of the paper serviettes and began to wipe the spillage. "Don't worry, Maggie. I'll do it."

Crimson-faced, Maggie returned to the counter.

"Sorry about that," Bennett said. "Maggie's not the most refined of people, but she means well."

Lawrence sipped at his drink and grimaced. "I see the coffee has lost none of its flavour," he said.

"Wet and warm," Bennett said. "What more could you ask for?"

Lawrence pushed his cup to one side. "Going back to Glendenning, did he ever mention anything to the lads about his relationship with Maddox?"

"I think most of the crew had heard rumours he was a frequent visitor to Maddox's club. No one would admit they had actually seen him there, of course. It would have had consequences." Bennett sipped his tea. "David was a good-looking bloke," he said. "Women liked him, and from what I heard, he liked them."

"He never indicated any animosity towards Maddox?"

Bennett shook his head. "No. He kept his cards close to his chest. David wasn't one for mixing with the crew socially. That's probably because he was married into a wealthy family and had his own social circle."

"According to Lydia, David didn't mix much with her

friends, just the occasional family dinner party."

Bennett shrugged. "I wouldn't know about that."

"You're sure he never said anything about his private life that might shed some light on what happened?"

"I only wish there was, but… well, it's probably nothing. After all, it happened years ago, so …"

"Go on," Lawrence encouraged. "At this stage, anything you know might be helpful."

"Well, like I said, it happened years ago. We were on night patrol together, and he got talking about some girl he'd been seeing for over a year. I got the impression she was on the game. He seemed crazy about her. He was even talking about leaving his wife to be with her."

"Do you think he was serious?"

Bennett shrugged. "I don't know. He was certainly smitten. I told him it would probably end his career, but he didn't seem to care."

"What happened?"

Bennett hunched his shoulders. "I was on shift with him a couple of weeks later, and he was really down. I've never seen anyone so low."

"Did he say why?"

"He said the girl had disappeared."

"Disappeared?"

"They'd had an argument. He didn't say what about, and before he'd had the chance to make up, she left. He never heard from her again. He was heartbroken for a long time."

"I don't suppose you remember the girl's name?"

"As a matter of fact, I do," Bennett said. "She had the same name as my sister. Paula."

29

Lydia was in the garden when Lawrence arrived. "Geoffrey, it's so good to see you," she said as he sat opposite her at the patio table.

"You're looking well," he said.

"Would you like some coffee? I can get Molly to—"

Lawrence raised a hand. "No, thank you. I've had more than enough coffee this morning. I'll be getting high on caffeine if I have any more."

"How are your investigations going? Have you come up with any explanation for what happened yet?"

Lawrence shook his head. "Nobody involved seems to want to talk about it."

"That's probably because they're hiding something. I knew I was right."

"It's more likely these people don't like talking to the police, even if they are retired."

"Have you managed to speak to Maddox yet?" Lydia said.

"No, but I will. I'm just piecing together the background."

"Well, what have you found out? Somebody must know something."

"Lydia, I… I need to ask you some rather delicate questions."

She stared at him. "Ask whatever you want. I have nothing to hide."

"I've heard a rumour that David was involved with some woman a few years ago, a prostitute by all accounts. Did you know anything about that?"

"David was always hanging about with prostitutes."

"Maybe, but this one was special. He was planning to go away with her."

Lydia sniffed. "I wondered how long it would take you to find out about her."

"You knew?"

"Of course, I knew. I'd hired a private detective to follow David for weeks."

"What did you do?"

"I warned her to keep away from my husband. The cow just laughed in my face. She said she could take David away from me whenever she wanted."

"Did you speak to him about it?"

She shook her head. "No. I was afraid of losing him, I suppose. Then a few days later, he seemed upset... no, it was more than that... he was distraught. I'd never seen him like that before. He wouldn't tell me what was wrong, but I knew it must have been something to do with her."

"That must have been terrible for you," he said. "But at least their affair was over."

Lydia took out a tissue and dried her eyes. "You'd have thought so, wouldn't you? There were other women after her, of course, but I don't think he ever felt the same about any of them."

Lawrence patted her hand. "I don't know what to say. I knew David could be a selfish bastard but to treat you like that."

She threw back her head. "Oh, that's not the worst of it," she said, delving into her bag and removing a cigarette. "Years later, I discovered that David and his whore had had a child together."

"Are you sure?"

"Of course, I'm sure. Her name was Charlotte. I heard she was brought up in Ireland by Karl's wife's family."

Lawrence scribbled notes in his book. "Do you know where this girl is now?"

Lydia hunched her shoulders. "I've no idea," she said, "and I have no intention of meeting David's bastard."

30

It was mid-afternoon when Ryan entered The Emerald. Karl was waiting in the foyer to meet him. "Glad you could make it," he said. "Come in. I'll show you around."

Ryan smiled. "I've never been inside anything like this before," he said. "Dad… I mean, my stepdad would have a fit if he knew."

"Is he a social worker too?"

"No. He was a vicar. He died a few months ago. My stepmum too."

"Oh, I'm sorry to hear that. What happened?"

"There was a fire at the vicarage. Neither of them managed to get out."

"Bloody hell, that's terrible. What about you? Were you there at the time?"

"Fortunately for me, I was staying with friends that weekend."

"You were lucky then."

Ryan shrugged. "If you don't mind, I'd rather not talk about it. It's still too painful."

"Sure, I understand," Karl said as he led the way into the main club. Paul stood by the bar supervising auditions for new dancers. "Paul, I'd like you to meet Ryan," he said. "He's Jason's boy I was telling you about."

Paul nodded an acknowledgement. "Nice to meet you," he said.

Karl walked towards the bar. "Fancy a drink?" he said, addressing Ryan. "Oh, sorry, I forgot. You don't drink alcohol, do you? What about a coke?"

"A coke would be great," Ryan said, his gaze firmly fixed on a young woman as she coiled her body seductively around the silver pole to the beat of the music.

Paul smiled mischievously. "You'll have to come to the club tonight and see the show."

"Yeah," Ryan said. "I might do that."

Karl returned with the two drinks. "I'll show you upstairs," he said. "There's a lounge up there for special guests."

Ryan followed Karl through the foyer and up the stairs to the empty VIP Lounge.

"Take a seat," Karl said. "Make yourself comfortable."

Ryan perched on the edge of one of the velvet couches. "Wow, this is great," he said.

"Yeah, not bad, is it? I have three more clubs like this and a casino."

"Impressive," Ryan said. "You've certainly done well for yourself."

"I can always find you a job here if you want. There are lots of opportunities for a bright lad like you."

Ryan grinned. "I'll think about it. What I really want is for you to tell me more about my dad."

"What do you want to know?"

Ryan shrugged. "Anything really. I was only five when he died, so I don't remember much. But I remember him teaching me to ride a bike, and he was always playing music and singing along."

Karl laughed. "Yeah, Jason always did like his music. He once talked about joining a band."

"I didn't know that. What happened?"

"It never came to anything. He was hooked on the drugs, and… well, things never really worked out for him."

"Do you have any photographs of when you were kids? Mum didn't have any."

Karl shook his head. "Sorry, mate," he said. "We never had a camera, and there weren't mobile phones back then."

"Dad was a good person though, wasn't he, when he wasn't on the drugs, I mean?"

Karl sipped his drink and looked away. "Jason and I were best mates once," he said, "before the drugs took over. We didn't have the best upbringing in the world. I left home when I was sixteen."

"Mum told me. She thought that's when Dad started with the drugs."

"Probably," Karl said. "I feel bad about that, but I had to

get out of there. I was only a kid myself."

"I'm not blaming you," Ryan said. "From what Mum says, Jason was headstrong, always getting into trouble."

Karl shrugged. "He was certainly a handful, but he had a good heart." He took another sip of his drink. "Is your mother still around?"

"She's in a hostel at the moment. I do what I can to help her, but it's hard. She's been in the lifestyle a lot of years."

"You kept in touch with her after you were adopted?"

"I got a letter from her every so often. I eventually got to meet her last year just before the fire."

Karl leant back into his chair. "Tell me about you," he said. "What are your ambitions?"

Ryan smiled. "I'm not really an ambitious person. If being brought up in the church teaches you anything, it teaches humility."

"So, you're happy being a do-gooder then? Helping other people?"

Ryan gave a wry smile. "It has its own rewards. The majority of offenders I supervise go on to lead perfectly law-abiding and productive lives."

Karl sat upright. "What do you mean offenders?"

"I work in prisons, Karl. Didn't I mention that?"

31

Matthew put down the telephone, a broad smile on his handsome face. "Darling," he said, "guess who that was?"

Christina yawned and stretched her arms above her head. "What time is it?"

Matthew leant over and kissed her lightly on the lips. "Wake up, sleepy head," he said. "Charlotte's back in England. She wants to meet up."

Christina's eyes opened wide. "Charlotte?"

"Her train gets into Leeds at ten. She wants us to meet her."

Christina propped herself on her elbows. "I thought she was in the Caribbean with her grandmother."

"She was, but now she's back. Won't it be wonderful to see her again?" He made his way to the ensuite. "I'll run your bath," he said. "Do be quick, darling. We don't have much time."

As the train rattled through the English countryside, Charlotte Flynn finished her breakfast of poached eggs and toast.

"Would you like more juice?" the attendant said, holding a glass jug of fresh orange juice.

Charlotte smiled. "No, thank you. How long before we get into Leeds?"

"Thirty minutes, madam," he said as he removed the breakfast setting. "Can I get you anything else? A newspaper or magazine, perhaps?"

She shook her head. "No, I'm fine, thank you."

Left alone, Charlotte reached into her handbag and removed the letter she had received from Joe a few days earlier.

"Dearest Charlotte," it began, *"I hope you and Marion are both well and are continuing to enjoy your extended holiday. I'm not sure when you intend to return to England if indeed you do, but I thought I should*

warn you of a worrying incident which has occurred recently. I was approached by an ex-policeman called Geoffrey Lawrence. Apparently, Lawrence is writing his memoirs concerning his time with the police, including the incident between David Glendenning and Karl Maddox. It would seem he is interviewing everyone whom he believes could shine a light on what happened, however tenuous their involvement. It is possible that he will be aware of your existence, so I thought it best to warn you... just in case. Please get in touch if and when you decide to return to England. Give my love to Marion. — Joe"

Charlotte read and re-read the letter before placing it back in her handbag. Her mobile rang. It was Marion. "Hello, Grandma," she said. "I'm fine. Stop worrying... Yes, Matthew is going to meet me at the station... Of course, I'll be careful.... Joe? I haven't spoken to him yet, but I'll give him a ring when I get settled... Yes, of course, I'll give him your love... Goodbye, darling, speak soon."

The shrill sound of the train's intercom with its familiar message filled the carriage. "*We will shortly be arriving at Leeds Station. Please make sure you take all your personal belongings with you when you leave the train. Thank you for travelling with us this morning.*"

Charlotte collected her luggage and stepped from the train onto the platform. Two familiar figures came hurrying towards her. "Matthew," she said, "and Christina. How wonderful to see you both."

32

Paul and Victor arrived at the hospital at ten o'clock. Peter was already dressed, his small overnight bag propped on the chair next to the bed.

"Dad," he shouted, "hurry up and get me out of here before they change their mind."

Victor flung his arms affectionately around his son. "Don't worry. The car is outside."

The nurse came over to the bed. "We need you to sign these discharge papers," she said, "then you are free to leave us, Mr Borowicz." She handed Peter a pen and several papers, which he signed immediately.

"So, I can go now?" he said.

"Of course, but you must rest. You're far from fully recovered." She turned to Victor, handing him a prescription form. "Please remember to call at the pharmacy for your son's medication," she said. "Your GP will be in touch shortly to check on his progress."

Victor nodded. "Don't worry, nurse, the family will look after Peter, and thank you, all of you, for taking such good care of him."

Paul picked up the overnight bag, and the three of them left the hospital and drove off in Paul's car.

"Are you sure somebody's trying to kill Karl?" Peter said once Paul had told him what had been happening. "Why would they do that? He's no real beef with anybody, has he?"

Paul shrugged. "Not that we know."

"You're sure it isn't Charlie Dexter?"

"To be honest, Peter, we're not sure of anything anymore. We gave his lot a good kicking the other night, and they've scattered, but you never know."

"Whoever it is, they must have some balls to fuck with Karl's car. You say they deliberately cut through the brake cables?"

"That's what the police said. If Karl had been behind the

wheel, he'd be dead, the speed he drives."

"I suppose I've been lucky then, getting away with a broken leg and three cracked ribs?"

Paul grinned. "Very lucky," he said. "It's a good job you drive like an old lady."

Victor came into the bedroom carrying a mug of tea. "Drink this," he said, "then you need to rest. Remember what the nurse said?"

Peter huffed. "Dad, I'm feeling better already. I'll be up and about tomorrow."

"We'll see about that," he said, handing him two white tablets. "Take these. They'll ease the pain."

Peter swallowed the pills with one gulp of his drink.

"Come on," Victor said to Paul. "Let's go downstairs and let your brother rest."

33

Charlotte checked into the Park Plaza Hotel. Matthew and Christina accompanied her to her suite.

"This is a fantastic room," Christina said, bouncing on the corner of the king-sized bed. "Have you stayed here before?"

Charlotte nodded. "Once, with Patrick," she said. "It's convenient for the shops and the trains."

Matthew walked to the window. "Our new apartment is just over there," he said, pointing in the direction of the river. "We'll be moving in about four weeks."

"You must come and stay with us," Christina said as she joined her husband. "I'm sorry we can't put you up now. We're staying with Lydia at the moment."

"I understand perfectly. Don't worry. I'm sure I'll be comfortable here."

"How long are you staying? Will you have time to do some shopping? There are so many new shops opening. It's fabulous."

"I'm not sure. I'm meeting Joe tomorrow for a catch-up. He's coming up to Leeds."

Christina scowled. "You know Joe's living with my sister-in-law?"

"Yes, I had heard, but that's their business, isn't it?"

Christina huffed. "Alex is devastated. I can't forgive Joe for being disloyal to Dad. He was supposed to be his friend." She turned to face Matthew. "I understand you wanting to hurt Dad, but Joe had no reason to."

Matthew put his hand on Christina's arm. "Chris, we've talked about this before. I don't want you getting mixed up in anything to do with Joe or your dad. They can sort out their differences without you."

Christina folded her arms, sauntered to the corner of the bed and sat down.

"Is anybody hungry?" Charlotte said in an attempt to break the uneasy silence. "I'm going down to the dining room if you both care to join me."

"Sure," Matthew said. "You can tell us all about your cruise."

Geoffrey Lawrence spent the morning perusing police files relating to Karl Maddox's businesses. He had been searching for the names of the women who had been working the streets around about the time when Paula had gone missing. He inhaled sharply. One name stood out, a name he recognised from his own dalliance some years previously. It had only been the once, and he hadn't realised when he bought her a drink in the hotel bar that she was a working girl.

A wry smile crept across his lips. Magda West would have been around twenty at the time. Tall and slim with shoulder-length auburn hair and eyes the colour of dark chocolate. He felt a jolt, even after all these years. Sex with her had been on another level, a level he had never experienced before or since.

Lawrence had to call in several favours before he was able to locate Magda. She was still living in the area, but she had reverted back to her proper name of Marie West. Lawrence felt a pang of excitement as he knocked on the green-painted door of 32 Florence Mews. It was several minutes before the door was opened.

"Yes?" said a plump, middle-aged woman. "What do you want?"

"Good afternoon," Lawrence said. "I'm looking for Marie West. I believe she lives at this address?"

The woman squinted suspiciously at him. "Who are you?"

"Is Marie West at this address?" he said. "It's important I speak with her."

"Marie's out," she said. "She won't be back until tonight."

"Where can I find her?"

The woman folded her arms over her ample breasts. "What do you want to speak to my sister about? You're not from the social, are you?"

Lawrence shook his head. "No, madam," he said. "I'm not from the social."

She sniffed loudly. "Marie's working behind the bar at the

Mariners. Do you know where that is?"

"Yes, I know the place," he said as he turned to leave. "Thank you."

34

Lawrence parked his Audi outside The Mariner's Rest, one of the oldest pubs in Leeds. It was an ugly red brick building with decades of the city's industrial grime clinging to its fabric. Back in the day, The Mariner's had been a favourite haunt for working girls where they met their clients, and as far as he knew, it still was.

The pub was almost empty. Two men stood by the pool table while a small group played the slot machines on the far wall. Lawrence walked up to the bar, which was being tendered by a middle-aged man with a goatee beard.

"Yes, mate," he said. "What'll it be?"

"A pint of bitter, please," Lawrence said.

"You'll have to wait a minute, I'm afraid. The barrel's being changed." He went to the cellar door behind him and shouted. "Will you hurry up with that bloody barrel? A customer is waiting."

"Keep your hair on," a female voice bellowed from the cellar. "I'm going as fast as I can."

"Sorry about that, mate," the man said. "Women are bloody crap at changing barrels. Can I get you something else instead?"

Lawrence shook his head. "No thanks. I can wait. I'm in no hurry."

"I don't think I've seen you in here before. Just passing through, are you?"

"Yes, that's right. I fancied a pint and saw this place."

"What line of business are you in, then? We don't get many suits in here." Before he could respond, the cellar door flung open, and Marie West entered the bar. Geoffrey recognised her at once. A little older, a little plumper, but still a beautiful woman with the same auburn hair and dark-brown eyes.

The landlord huffed. "About bloody time," he said. "This bloke's dying of thirst waiting for you."

Muttering under her breath, she took down a beer glass from the shelf and, sauntering over to the pumps, began to pull a pint. "Anything else?" she said, not making eye contact with Lawrence.

"No, just the beer," he said, "and one for yourself. You too, landlord."

"Thanks," she said, giving a faint smile. "I'll have a vodka and coke."

"I have to make a phone call. Could you be so kind as to bring my drink over?" He removed a twenty-pound note from his wallet and placed it on the bar. "Keep the change," he said, making his way over to a table by the window.

"Sure," she said, glancing at Lawrence's bulky wallet. "I'll be right over."

Lawrence telephoned home and briefly spoke to Nurse Walters. On being assured that Amanda was sleeping, he put the phone back into his pocket just as the barmaid brought over his drink.

"Thanks," he said. "Why don't you bring your drink over and join me for a minute?"

"Why not? I'm due a break anyway." She picked up her drink from the bar and joined Lawrence at the table.

"My name's Geoffrey," he said. "What's yours?"

"Marie."

"Well, it's nice to meet you, Marie. I must say, you do look familiar. Have you always lived in Leeds?"

She sniffed. "Most of my life."

"I'm sure I've seen you before, but for the life of me, I can't remember where."

"I worked in The Black Bull for ten years. Perhaps you saw me in there?"

He shook his head. "No, I don't think so… I've got it. Didn't you use to call yourself Magda? Yes, that's it. You worked for Karl Maddox as an escort in Chapeltown. I'm right, aren't I?"

Marie scraped back the wooden chair and attempted to get to her feet. Lawrence grabbed her wrist, pulling her back into the chair. "Sit down," he said through clenched teeth. "You and I need to talk."

"What do you want with me? I haven't done that sort of thing in years."

"I want to know about one of the girls you used to work with. Her name was Paula."

"Who are you?" she said. "A fucking copper?"

"Never mind who I am. Just answer my question."

Marie shuffled uncomfortably in her seat. "I haven't kept in touch with any of the girls since I quit."

"Did you know Paula?"

"What do you want with her anyway? I'd have thought she'd be past it by now."

"So, you did know her?"

"I knew who she was, but we weren't close."

"What do you know about her?"

Marie rolled her eyes. "Not much, only that she was big mates with Erica. Erica was Karl's missus."

"Karl Maddox?"

"Yeah. This was back in the day when he pimped most of the girls in Leeds. Before he moved up in the world with his fancy clubs, that is. If you want to know anything about Paula, ask Erica. She'll know."

"Erica's dead."

"Oh, I didn't know that."

"Who else was close to Paula?"

Marie leant back in her chair, slowly rubbing her wrists. "If I tell you that, it'll cost you a lot more than the price of a vodka and coke."

35

Karl and Paul were in The Emerald just before it was about to open for the evening. "Well, what do you think of Ryan?" Karl said. "Isn't he the image of our kid?"

Paul grinned. "He certainly is. Let's hope he doesn't have his father's temper."

"He seems fine to me. He told me he's been brought up by a vicar."

"You're joking?"

"That's what he said."

"Where's this vicar now?"

"Dead. He died a few months ago in a house fire, his mam too."

"Bloody hell, that's tough luck."

"You haven't heard the best bit. Ryan's not just a social worker, he's involved with the rehabilitation of prisoners. He actually works inside prisons. Can you believe it?"

Paul scowled. "He's a proper little do-gooder, isn't he?"

"What do you mean by that?"

"Karl, Jason was a wrong 'un. I can't believe that any sprog of his isn't a wrong 'un too. You know as well as I do that the apple doesn't fall far from the tree."

Karl shrugged. "I think you're wrong, mate. Ryan's had a decent upbringing."

Paul hunched his shoulders. "Okay, if you say so, but you won't mind if I have a little dig around, will you? Just to make sure."

"Dig as much as you want, but you're wasting your time." Karl picked up his coat from the stand and walked towards the door. "I'm going over to Manchester to see how Danny's getting on in the casino."

"Are you taking a couple of the lads with you?"

"Yeah, they're bringing the car around. See you tomorrow."

It was ten o'clock when Ryan entered The Emerald. He

went straight to the bar and ordered a coke. On seeing him, Paul walked over and stood beside him. "So, you decided to come back?" he said. "Karl's not here tonight, I'm afraid."

Ryan looked around the club. "Isn't that the girl who was auditioning earlier? The blonde one on the far podium?"

"Yeah, that's Phoenix. She's stunning, isn't she?"

"She's very beautiful. Do you think she would have a drink with me?"

"I'm sure she would," Paul said, smiling. "But I don't think she'll be drinking coke."

Ten minutes later, Phoenix was sitting with Ryan at the far side of the club, in front of the oak panelled wall inset with fleur-de-lis fretwork. Phoenix sipped the house champagne. "Well, darling," she purred. "Here we are."

Ryan reached over and attempted to run his fingers through her hair.

"Sorry," Phoenix said, pulling back. "You're not allowed to touch. It's against the rules."

"Fuck the rules," Ryan said.

"Be sensible. You don't want me to get fired before I've even started, do you?"

Ryan sighed heavily, leaning back into the couch. "Sorry," he said. "You're right. I have to act like one of these sad punters."

"Darling, it won't be for long."

"I know, but it's not easy seeing you parading in front of this lot with next to nothing on."

"If our plan is to work, you have no choice. Now stop acting like a twat and buy me another drink, and for goodness sake, smile. You're supposed to be enjoying yourself, remember?"

Paul frowned. Unsure what to make of the conversation he had overheard between Ryan and Phoenix. Something was definitely not right. Slowly he ascended the concealed staircase behind the panelling which led up to Karl's office.

36

Karl arrived at the casino half an hour before it was due to open. Danny was standing at the Black Jack table chatting to the croupier. From Danny's body language, Karl could see he was angry. Frowning, Karl walked over to him, placing his hand on his shoulder. "How's it going?" he said. "Everything all right, mate?"

Danny huffed. "It will be if this idiot did his job right."

"What's the problem?"

"This table's been losing every night this week."

"How much?"

"A lot. I'm beginning to think—"

The croupier, a handsome young man with dark hair pulled back in a ponytail, looked anxious. "Boss, sometimes people get lucky. What can I say?"

Karl scowled. "It's your job to ensure they don't get too lucky, understand?"

The croupier nodded. "I… I'll see what I can do," he said.

"You do that," Danny said, striding towards the bar, followed closely by Karl.

"You don't think he's on the take?" Karl asked, glaring over at the croupier. "It wouldn't be the first time some joker has tried it on."

Danny shook his head. "No, I don't think so. He hasn't got the balls."

"Well, keep a close eye on him anyway. I don't want him getting ideas."

The bartender poured two large whiskies, and taking their drinks, Danny and Karl made their way to one of the booths.

"Have you figured out who's trying to bump you off yet?" Danny said, leaning back on the leather couch. "I heard they had a second pop at you at the hospital."

Karl sipped his drink. "Yeah, some bastard tried to run me over. He nearly succeeded too."

"You've no idea who?"

"I've drawn up a list, but… well, to be honest, I don't fancy any of them."

"What about Charlie Dexter? I thought that mad bastard would be top of your list."

"My lads have dealt with Charlie and his boys," Karl said. "They've all fucked off to Scotland."

"And you think they'll stay there?"

"They will if they've any sense." Karl drained his glass, and Danny signalled for the bartender to bring more drinks.

Danny scowled. "I can't believe you took Lisa back after what she did," he said. "I'd have shown her the door. In fact, I'd have kicked her arse through the fucking door."

"I was tempted, but there were the kids. I'd no idea they existed."

"Didn't Alex gamble away most of your assets? You could have gone under because of that little shit."

"I could, but I didn't," Karl said, taking the glass of whisky from the waiter.

"And that girl of yours, Christina, isn't it? She goes and shacks up with the guy who was trying to bring you down."

"According to her, she didn't know anything about what was going on."

"And you believe her?"

Karl hesitated, took a sip of whisky and placed it on the table. "I don't believe a word that comes out of her mouth," he said. "But sometimes it's wise to keep your enemy close."

"You consider her the enemy?"

"She's got hitched to my enemy," Karl said. "If I want to know what's going on, I have to make her think I trust her again."

"What about Alex? Do you apply the same crazy logic to him?"

"Alex is keeping a low profile. I will deal with him when the time's right."

"You don't think he could be behind what's going on?"

Karl shook his head and smiled. "No. Alex is weak. He takes after his mother. I'm sure he isn't involved."

Danny shrugged. "Well, what are you going to do? You

can't keep dodging the bullet all your life."

Karl inhaled deeply. "I've got the feelers out," he said, "but until the lads come up with something, there's not really much I can do."

"Except take precautions?"

"Exactly."

37

Joe hugged Charlotte tightly and kissed her gently on her cheek. "It's good to see you again," he said. "You're looking great."

"You too," Charlotte said. Removing her coat, she handed it to the waitress. "Is Sarah not coming?"

Joe tilted his head. "I'm afraid not, but she sends her love. Where's Marion? I thought she would be here with you."

"You're not going to believe this, but Marion got married."

Joe gasped. "Married? When did this happen?"

"When we visited Barbados," she said. "The first restaurant we went into, who should be sitting at the next table but Marion's friend from years ago. His name is Bernard."

Joe smiled. "When you say old friend, you mean an old client?"

Charlotte giggled. "That's right. Bernard was one of her regulars when Marion was working in Leeds."

"So, Bernard was holidaying in Barbados?"

"No, he lives there. He has a fantastic six-bedroomed villa and owns two restaurants."

"When did all this happen?"

"They got married two months ago. They really seem besotted with one another."

"Good for her. I hope he makes her happy."

Charlotte reached over and took Joe's hand in hers. "How are things with you? Have you had any more trouble from Karl?"

"I haven't heard a word from him since that night at the casino."

"He certainly has the luck of the devil, doesn't he? What's he doing with the casino? Has he sold it?"

"No, he's kept it operating. He changed the name, though. It's called *The Four Aces* now."

"Would you care to see the wine list, sir?" the waitress said, handing Joe a velvet-bound book. "We have a large selection of wines."

"Chardonnay, please," Charlotte said, not bothering to confront the wine menu. "What about you, Joe? Do you want wine, or would you prefer something else?"

Joe smiled as he closed the book and handed it to the waitress. "Chardonnay's fine," he said.

Left alone, Joe leant forward, frowning. "Charlotte, like I told you in my letter, there's an ex-policeman snooping around asking questions about Karl and David Glendenning. He's writing his memoirs and wants to include the incident in his book."

Charlotte took a deep breath. "Only four people know the truth behind what happened that night. Me, you, Karl and Marion. Karl won't say anything, and I know Marion won't."

"Even so, I just want you to be aware that he's looking for answers, and from what I saw of him, he means to get them."

38

Paul spent the following morning in the main library in Leeds, looking through national newspapers on the electronic viewer. It was almost an hour before he found what he was looking for. He read and then re-read the article before printing it off. Then, going into the street, he took out his mobile and rang a number.

"Bob? Bob, it's Paul," he said.

"Hello, Paul," Bob said. "This is a surprise. How are you, mate?"

"I'm fine," Paul said. "I need a favour. Can we meet?"

Bob huffed. "You never change, do you? Most people would ask how I am or how the wife and family are doing after not being in touch for all this time, but not you. Straight to the point as always." He chuckled. "What is it you're wanting, anyway?"

"I don't have time for pleasantries. I need your help."

"Are you in trouble?"

"No. It's nothing like that. Can we meet later?"

"I suppose so, but I'm working until two," Bob said. "I'll meet you at the Duck and Drake."

"Great. I'll see you there."

Bob Riley ordered two pints of lager and walked to one of the booths on the far wall. Deep in thought, he placed the drinks on the table and shuffled into the chair. Paul arrived a couple of minutes later. "Ah, great to see you," Bob said. "I've got you a lager. I hope that's okay?"

"Lager's fine," Paul said as he sat in the booth.

"It's good to see you," Bob said, "even though it has been nearly three years."

Paul shrugged. "Yeah, sorry about that. I've been busy. But what is it they say? *Tempus fugit?*"

Bob picked up his drink and swallowed greedily, putting the glass noisily onto the table. "So, what's up?" he said and wiped his mouth with the back of his hand. "It must be important for you to dig up an old hack like me."

"You're hardly an old hack," Paul said. "Back in the day, you were the best investigative journalist around."

Bob sniffed. "That was then. A lot of water has gone under the bridge since I made headlines." He picked up his glass and gulped its contents greedily. "Did you know those bastards on the paper have moved me to the sports section? They said I've lost my edge."

"You're a sports writer?" Paul said. "I don't believe it. You're far too good a reporter to be doing that."

"Tell them." Bob placed his glass to his lips and gulped the remaining lager. "Fancy another?"

"No, I'm fine," Paul said and handed Bob a ten-pound note. "I'll get this."

Bob gave a sharp nod as he strode to the bar, returning a few minutes later with another pint of lager. "So, what are you up to?" he said after he had taken a drink from the glass. "Still working for Karl Maddox?"

"That's right," he said. "I'm responsible for security in his clubs and his casino in Manchester."

"Good for you. Is it true Karl won the casino on the spin of the roulette wheel?"

Paul grinned. "Something like that."

"I also heard—"

"Bob, I'm not here to talk about Karl Maddox's exploits."

"Then why are you here?"

Paul removed the printed document he had taken from the library and handed it to Bob. "What do you know about this?"

Bob reached into his pocket and removed a pair of spectacles. "Let's have a look," he said, taking the document from Paul.

It was a photocopy of the front page of the *Western Morning News*, the most popular newspaper in Devon.

"Oh, the fire at the vicarage," Bob said, frowning. "I remember that. The vicar and his missus were both killed."

"Did you ever hear anything… anything suspicious about the fire?"

"What do you mean, suspicious? Are you saying this wasn't an accident?"

"I'm not saying anything yet," Paul said. "I just wondered."

"Bollocks. What's going on? Do you know something about this fire? Something the police don't know?"

Paul leant closer to his companion. "All I want you to do is take a closer look, that's all."

Bob picked up his glass and swigged his lager. "Why can't you? As I remember, you were always pretty good at sniffing out information."

"I don't have the time, mate, that's why. There's stuff going on at the clubs that need my attention."

"Are you going to tell me why you think there's something wrong?"

"Just instinct," Paul said. "They had an adoptive son, Ryan. I want you to see what you can find out about him."

Bob frowned. "It says here that he was away at the time. Do you think he had something to do with it?"

"What I think is irrelevant," Paul said. "I want you to look at it unprejudiced."

"I suppose I can call on colleagues at the Western. See what they've heard."

Paul shook his head. "No. I want this done on the QT."

"You want me to go to Devon?"

"That's right, as soon as you can." Paul patted Bob's arm. "Don't worry," he said. "I'll make it worth your while." He grinned as he removed a bulky envelope from his inside pocket and slid it across the table. "Besides, you're looking a bit peaky. A few days at the seaside will do you good."

39

"When exactly were you proposing to tell me you were moving?" Lydia demanded as Matthew entered the kitchen that morning. "Why do I have to find out from some furniture delivery firm?"

Matthew perched on the stool at the breakfast bar. "I was going to tell you, Mum," he said. "Chris and I are moving into the penthouse by the river."

Lydia sniffed. "I suppose this is her idea," she said, "dragging you away from your family home?"

"Mother, Christina and I are married. We want our own place to live. A place to have a family."

Lydia stomped across the kitchen towards Matthew. "With her? Are you mad?" she said, prodding him in the chest with her finger. "Have you forgotten—?"

"That's enough," Matthew said, grabbing Lydia's wrist and distancing himself from her. "Christina's my wife."

"Did I hear my name mentioned?" Christina said as she glided into the kitchen to stand beside her husband. "Is something wrong, darling?"

"Mother's a bit upset," Matthew said. "She's found out we're moving out."

Christina frowned. "I thought we weren't going to say anything until nearer the time?"

"The furniture people rang the house phone to speak to me," Matthew said. "She took the call."

"It's a good job I did, or I wouldn't have known until you crept away like two thieves in the night."

"That's unfair,' Matthew said. 'We were going to tell you we were moving, but we wanted to discuss it calmly and rationally. Not like this."

"I want you both out of my house now," Lydia said. "I don't want to hear from you again. From either of you."

Matthew held up his hands. "Don't be ridiculous. I'm sorry you heard about it that way. Let's all sit down and—"

"I want you out of my house by the end of the day," Lydia

said as she stomped towards the stairs. "And take that tramp with you."

40

When Geoffrey Lawrence arrived, Shirley was lounging on her friend Susie's couch. Susie showed him into the front room. "Would you like some tea?" she asked, "or there's coffee if you prefer. I've only got instant, I'm afraid."

"Tea will be fine," Lawrence said. "Milk and two sugars."

"Do you want anything, Shirley?"

Shirley shook her head. "No thanks, love," she said. "I'm fine." Susie disappeared into the kitchen.

Lawrence looked around the dingy room with its threadbare carpet and faded curtains before perching on the edge of a battered leatherette armchair. He smiled at Shirley. "You look like you've been in the wars," he said. "Are you all right?"

Shirley did not return his smile as she gazed at some spot on the floor. "I was in a fire," she said. "My arms are going to need skin grafts." She slightly raised her bandage-covered arms. "I've got burns to my legs too, but they're not as bad."

"I'm sorry about that," Lawrence said. "I'm sure you'll be on the mend soon. It's marvellous what they can do for burns these days."

Shirley wiped the tears from her face. "They can't do anything for my Colin, can they? He didn't manage to get out."

"That's terrible."

"Colin wasn't a bad man," she said, more to herself than her visitor. "We were really happy in Spain. He treated me like a princess."

"I'm sure he did," Lawrence said soothingly.

"They said the fire was started deliberately. Someone actually wanted to hurt us."

"You've no idea who that could be?"

Shirley scowled. "Of course, I know. It was that bastard, Karl Maddox."

"Why would Karl want to kill you both?"

"Because Colin took… he only took what was due to him, nothing more."

"You mean he stole money from Karl?"

She dabbed her eyes with a tissue. "It wasn't much," she said. "Just a few thousand, that's all. He deserved it after all the money he saved in taxes and stuff. Colin was Karl's accountant, you know."

"I suppose Karl had an alibi?"

She nodded. "They said he was in England, but Karl wouldn't have struck the match himself. He would have paid somebody else to do his dirty work. That's the sort of bloke he is."

Lawrence hunched his shoulders. "Well, I guess we'll never know what happened."

"Are you from the insurance people? Susie said they were coming today."

Lawrence smiled and shook his head. "No, I'm not from the insurance company. I'm here on quite a different matter. I was given your name by Magda. She said you might be able to help me."

"Help you with what?"

"I was hoping you could help me find a young woman you worked with years ago. Her name was Paula."

Shirley frowned. "I haven't heard from Paula in years. Nobody has. Paula and I weren't exactly close. She was Erica's friend, really."

"Did you know that Erica died?"

She nodded. "I heard. It was a bloody shame. She was a lovely person. The best thing she did was going off with Joe and leaving that bastard, Karl."

"Did you know Paula had a child? A daughter."

"I heard Marion looked after it while Paula went back to work. After Paula disappeared, Erica took the kid to her sister in Ireland to prevent her from going into care. Like I said, Erica was a lovely person. Surprising really with what the poor girl had had to go through."

"Oh? What do you mean by that?"

Shirley inhaled. "Well, I heard Paula telling somebody once that Erica's dad was a bit too fond of his daughters, if you know what I mean."

"Are you saying he was a paedophile?"

"I never say anything I can't spell," Shirley said. "All I'm saying is that Erica's sister got out of that house as soon as possible. From what Paula told me, Erica didn't shed any tears when he was found dead. She was put into care after he died. That's where she met Paula."

"What can you tell me about Paula's boyfriend? Did you ever meet him?"

Shirley grinned. "No, but Paula talked about him all the time. His name was David something. He was a policeman, would you believe?" She giggled. "Paula loved to tell stories that David had told her about things which had happened to him at work."

"What sort of stories?"

"Oh, all sorts of things. Fights he had broken up, people he had arrested, that sort of thing. She told me David had once found a dead body in Cooper's Alley. That's just off Cedar Road, where I had my beat while working for Karl. It fair gave me the creeps walking down there at night after that."

"Whose body was it?"

"A schoolteacher, I think. He'd been mugged and had his throat cut. The last time I saw Erica was in the café on Cedar Road. I pointed out Cooper's Alley, where it had happened. She nearly fainted. She was so upset."

"Did she say why?"

"She didn't get the chance. Joe arrived at the café, and off they went into the sunset."

41

Arriving home late that evening, Geoffrey went straight to his wife's room. The curtains had been drawn, and a small bedside lamp glowed through the darkness. Amanda was asleep, so he lightly kissed her forehead before leaving the room.

Once in his study, he began to type up the interview with Shirley. Tomorrow, he decided, he would ring his friend, Inspector Nigel Bennett, and establish the identity of the body in Cooper's Alley.

Joe had just turned off the bedroom light when his mobile rang. He recognised the caller at once. "Shirley," he said, "what on earth's the matter? I thought you and Colin were in Spain."

"We were," Shirley said, "until some bastard burnt down our villa. Colin's dead."

"I'm sorry to hear that. You're saying it wasn't an accident?"

"No, it was deliberate," Shirley said. "I know Karl was responsible, but—"

"Do you have proof?"

"No, but I know he was behind it."

Joe sighed. "Well, I'm sorry for your loss, Shirley, but I don't see what I can do."

"Oh, I wasn't ringing about that," she said. "I've moved in with Susie for the time being. You remember her, don't you? She used to work for Karl back in the day."

"Yes, I remember her."

"Well, today, a bloke called Geoffrey Lawrence called to see me. He was asking a lot of questions about that girl Paula who went missing and asking about Erica."

"What did you tell him?"

"Nothing much. I never had much to do with Paula. She was too wrapped up with that fella of hers to mix with the likes of me."

"You said he asked about Erica?"

"That's right. I told him the last time I saw her was in that café, the day you two were running away together."

"Why the fuck did you tell him that?" Joe said.

"I got reminiscing about those days, I suppose."

"What else did you tell him?"

"Nothing, only what Paula had said about David finding his first dead body down Cooper's Alley. I just said how it had upset Erica."

"You told Lawrence that?"

"I was making small talk, I suppose. Did I do something wrong?"

"Shirley, if this man tries to speak to you again, tell him to piss off. You mustn't speak with him, okay?"

"Sure, if you say so. By the way, I was sorry to hear about Erica."

"Thanks. I have to go."

"Okay, Joe. Goodnight."

But Joe had already hung up the phone.

42

Inspector Bennett took less than half an hour to return Lawrence's phone call the following morning. "That body in Coopers Alley," he said. "You'll never guess who it was?"

"Surprise me," Lawrence said.

"Go on, guess," Bennett teased.

"I have no idea," Lawrence said irritably. "Are you going to tell me or not?"

"This is going to cost you a couple of drinks."

"You can have as many drinks as you want. Now, what's the bloke's name?"

"Meadows," Bennett said triumphantly. "Thomas Edward Meadows."

Lawrence sighed. "Never heard of him. Who was he?"

"A teacher, but that's not the interesting bit."

"Then what is?"

"Meadows had a daughter, Erica. She was fourteen when her dad got murdered. A couple of years later, she became Karl Maddox's common-law wife."

"Mm, that is interesting. How exactly did Meadows die?"

"His throat was cut," Bennett said. "He had a laceration to his head, and his body bore signs of a good beating, but it was the loss of blood from his throat that killed him."

"Nobody was ever prosecuted? There were no suspects?"

"There had been a few muggings in the area at the time. None of them fatal, though. It was assumed it was the same bloke responsible," Bennett said.

"You don't suppose Maddox had anything to do with Meadows' death, do you?"

"He was never a suspect. What reason would he have for bumping off his girlfriend's father? It doesn't make sense."

"Probably not. Time will tell."

"Geoff, you will be careful, won't you? If Maddox finds out you're sniffing around."

"He'll what? Karl's a lot of things, but he's certainly not stupid."

"So, how are you going to handle this? You can't go up to him and accuse him of killing Meadows."

"Stop worrying. I know what I'm doing. I have a few more people to speak to before confronting Maddox."

"Is it worth it, Geoff? This bloody book, I mean? Glendenning's dead. Why don't you leave it at that?"

"Because I made a promise to Lydia, that's why. She's never got over what happened to her husband."

"I didn't realise you two were close."

"I was good friends with Lydia's father, George. He and I were at training school together back in the days when dinosaurs roamed the earth. Lydia asked me as a personal favour to find out why David did what he did, and I intend to find out."

"Despite the possible consequences?"

"David Glendenning wasn't the best copper in the force, but to do what he did… well, it was out of character. I know it was something to do with Maddox, something really bad. I have to find out what."

"Well, I think you're a bloody fool getting involved. So, take my advice and just leave it alone."

"Thanks for the advice," Lawrence said, draining the last of his coffee from its cup. "I'll be in touch."

43

Matthew picked up the telephone and dialled room service. He had it on good authority that The Park Plaza Hotel did a fantastic breakfast. "Fancy something to eat?" he said, turning to Christina. "I thought we could have breakfast in our room."

Christina shook her head. "Just coffee. I'm too angry with your mother to eat."

"She can be a cow when she wants to," Matthew said. "It's understandable why Dad turned out like he did."

Matthew placed his order with reception. "I have to pop into the office today," he said. "I should only be a couple of hours. What are your plans?"

Christina sat at the dressing table and began to apply her lipstick. "I suppose I could see if Charlotte wants to go shopping," she said.

Matthew frowned. "Do you think Charlotte's all right? She seemed a little… a little distracted at dinner last night."

"It's probably jetlag catching up with her. She'll be okay today."

"You don't think she's worrying about that ex-husband of hers, do you? I know he's on the run abroad somewhere, but—"

"Patrick? I don't think so. He wouldn't dare show his face in England again."

"Let's hope you're right," Matthew said. "After losing his inheritance to Charlotte, he must be pretty pissed off."

"Your sister did come out of it all rather well, didn't she? A lump sum from Erica, then all that money from Shamus's estate."

"She deserves it," Matthew said. "The poor kid has had a hard life."

There was a sharp rap on the door. "Ah, breakfast," Matthew said. "I'm starving."

After Matthew left the hotel, Christina telephoned Charlotte's room. There was no reply. She went down to the dining room, but there was no sign of Charlotte. Sighing, Christina went to the foyer and, stepping through the revolving door, went out into the busy street.

44

Lawrence had been parked outside Joe's house since dawn. He waited until he saw him leave and drive away in his blue Range Rover. Lawrence walked briskly up the drive and knocked on the door. Sarah answered it almost immediately.

"Oh, it's you," she said, attempting to close the door. "Joe's not here."

"I know. I saw him leave." He placed his hand firmly against the door. "It's you I want to speak to, Sarah."

"I've nothing to say to you. Please go away."

"It will only take a minute, and it is important."

Sarah's eyes narrowed into slits. "I said go away or I'll—"

"You'll what? Call the police? I am the police."

"No, you're not. You're retired. Joe told me."

"I'm still part of the police," Geoffrey said. "One word from me, and Joe will be taken away. Is that what you want?"

"You can't do that. Joe's done nothing wrong."

"Hasn't he? I think he's covering up for Karl Maddox."

"What do you mean covering up? He has nothing to do with Karl anymore."

"Maybe not now, but he used to work for him."

"That was years ago."

"Did he ever speak about David Glendenning?"

She scowled. "That cop who shot Karl?"

"I believe Joe knew why Karl got shot."

"If he did, he didn't tell me. Now, will you please leave? Joe will be back soon."

"Sarah, is there anything you can tell me about the shooting incident? It could help Joe if you co-operate."

"Joe wasn't even there when Karl got shot. He was on his way to meet Erica."

"He must have said something to you about what happened. Think, Sarah. Think."

"Joe only said he hadn't realised just how wicked Karl could be until that day."

"What did he mean by that?"

"He didn't elaborate, and I didn't ask."

"I know Glendenning was in Karl's office when Joe and Karl were arguing. I don't understand how he could have heard what was being said if he was upstairs?"

"I have no idea what the argument was about. Joe thinks David was probably listening to the whole thing from behind the false wall."

"What false wall?"

"It's at the back of the club. There's a staircase that leads from the office. Karl uses it all the time to spy on people."

Geoffrey arrived home mid-afternoon and, after speaking to Nurse Walters, went straight to his wife's room. Amanda was in her bed, propped up with pillows. "You're looking better today," he said. "How are you feeling?"

Amanda smiled weakly. "A little stronger, I think. I managed some soup for lunch."

"That's good," he said, dragging a chair close to the side of the bed. "Would you like a cup of tea? I'm having one."

"Tea would be lovely," she said as the nurse entered the room carrying a tea tray.

"Thanks," Geoffrey said. "Put it on the bedside cabinet. I'll pour."

"Very well," the nurse said, putting down the tray. "Please don't tire Mrs Lawrence. She needs her rest."

"I'll be ten minutes," Geoffrey said as he began to place milk into the china cups.

When the nurse left the room, Amanda giggled. "She really is a bit of an ogre, isn't she?"

Geoffrey grinned. "She's efficient. That's what matters," he said as he handed his wife a cup. He poured himself a drink and leant back into his chair. "I never told you this, but Nurse Walters was married to a real villain back in the day."

Amanda's eyes widened. "Really? Who was that?"

"His name was Harry. Harry Walters was quite a competent jewel thief until he fell out with the wrong people."

"What happened?"

Geoffrey sipped his tea. "I don't know all the details, but about ten years ago, Harry ended up dead in a ditch with his throat cut."

"That's terrible. Do you know who was responsible?"

Geoffrey pursed his lips. "Nobody was ever charged with the murder, although we did have our suspicions back at the nick. A bloke called Bernard Coates was prime suspect, but he was a slippery bastard, and nothing was ever proven."

"Is that how you met Nurse Walters? Through her husband's murder?"

Geoffrey nodded. "I interviewed Sandra a couple of times, but it was obvious she knew nothing about Harry's life of crime. She was working in a Nursing Home in Leeds at the time. To be honest, I felt sorry for her. She seemed a decent woman who made the mistake of marrying the wrong man." Geoffrey drained his cup and placed it back on the tray. "When you became ill, I contacted her and offered her the position here."

"She didn't mind taking care of a policeman's wife?"

Geoffrey patted his wife's hand comfortingly. "As I said, Sandra Walters is a good woman." He kissed her hand before walking towards the door. "I'd better write up my notes on Maddox whilst they're still fresh in my mind," he said. "You lay back and rest."

"Aren't you going to tell me how you got on? Have you found out any more information?"

Geoffrey grinned. "I've found out plenty," he said. "In fact, I have a pretty good idea of what happened."

"So, what are you going to do?"

"First, I'm going to type it all up, and then I'm going to visit Karl Maddox and confront him with what I know."

"But Geoffrey… you can't—"

"Stop worrying," Geoffrey said. "Everything will be fine. Now, you have a nap. I'll speak to you later."

45

Karl arrived at The Emerald at seven o'clock that morning. He was surprised to find Paul was not there. Leaving his office, he went down into the main club, where the humming of a vacuum cleaner could be heard in the distance.

"Let me know as soon as Paul arrives," he said to the cleaner, "and get me a coffee, will you? Black, no sugar."

"Yes, Mr Maddox," said the young woman in a pale-blue tabard. "Would you like something to eat? The café across the road is open and—"

"No, just coffee."

Karl returned to his office just as the phone on his desk gave out its shrill ring. "Yeah?" he said.

"Boss, it's me."

"Paul? Where are you? We have some accounts to go through this morning."

"I'm at the hospital."

"Why? What's the matter?"

"It's Peter. He's… he's dead."

"Dead?"

"It was a blood clot in his leg. It… it went to his heart, and… he died ten minutes ago."

Karl clenched his fist. "I'm sorry, mate. Is there anything I can do?"

"Yes, there is," Paul said. "You can help me find the bastard that killed my brother."

"Don't worry, I will." Sweat ran down the back of Karl's neck. "How's Victor doing?"

"How do you think? He's in bits."

"Do you want me to come to the hospital?"

"What for? There's nothing you can do here."

"Well, you know where I am," Karl said, running his hand through his hair. "Give me a bell if you need anything."

Karl put down the phone and took out the sheet of paper from his desk drawer, the paper containing the names of the suspects. He scanned it for several minutes before returning it to the drawer and slamming it shut in frustration.

"Anything else, Mr Maddox?" said the cleaner as she placed the mug of coffee on his desk.

Karl shook his head as he picked up the desk phone and began to dial a number. "No thanks. Close the door on your way out, will you?"

It was several seconds before the phone was answered. "Danny, it's me," Karl said. "I need your help, mate. I've just heard Peter has died."

46

Freddie arrived at The Topaz at eight o'clock that morning. He was halfway across the foyer before he noticed something was wrong. The glass display cabinet behind reception was smashed, and the computer screen was on the floor. He rushed through into the main club and gasped. Furniture had been ripped open, and all four silver podiums had been covered with black paint. The paint had also been thrown over the carpet. Behind the bar was carnage. Glasses were broken, and the bottled spirits had been emptied onto the floor.

Freddie raced up the stairs to the VIP Lounge. Broken furniture was strewn around the floor. Table lamps had been smashed and the walls smeared with black paint. Freddie felt his heart pounding as he reached into his pocket, took out his phone and dialled his boss.

Karl and two of his minders arrived at The Topaz in Bradford within the hour. "How the fuck did they get in?" Karl said as he strode around the main club. "Were the alarms on last night?"

"Yes, boss," Freddie said. "I set them myself."

"Who else knows the combination?"

Freddie shrugged. "Just a couple of the minders. They lock up sometimes when I'm not working."

"What about the cleaner? Does she have the combination?"

"No, there's no need. She starts at ten in the morning, so there's always somebody here."

"Have you checked the CCTV?"

"It's been smashed," Freddie said, placing his hands on top of his head. "Everything's been smashed. Do you want me to call the police?"

Karl shook his head. "No, we'll keep this quiet for now. Close up the club. Say there's a burst pipe or something."

"Okay. I'll ring round the staff and let them know."

"Before you do that, give me the details of everyone who

knows the alarm combination."

Freddie exhaled. "You can't suspect one of them is responsible. The lads have been working here for years."

"Until I'm proved wrong, I suspect everybody."

"What?" Freddie said. "Even me?"

"Especially you."

Karl telephoned Simon at The Sapphire. "Some bastard has done The Topaz over," he said. "Make sure you take extra precautions."

"Sure, boss," Simon said. "Was anybody hurt?"

"No. Just my pocket. I want you to ring Tommy at The Amethyst and tell him what happened. I have to get back to Leeds."

"Karl, what the hell's going on? First, somebody tries to kill you, and then they trash one of your clubs. Things are getting crazy."

"You can say that again. Peter died this morning. I've just heard from Paul."

"Oh fuck. I thought he was on the mend?"

"It was a blood clot." Karl clenched his teeth. "When I find out the bastard responsible, I'll kill him with my bare hands."

"Not before Victor and Paul have killed him first."

47

Lisa hurried along The Headrow. It was a nice surprise, Christina inviting her to go shopping. "Darling, there you are," she said as she approached her daughter. "You're looking well. How's Matthew?"

Christina huffed. "He's all right, I suppose. He's always working these days. I don't see much of him."

"And how are things with Lydia? Is she any sweeter towards you?"

"Actually, Mum, she threw us out of the house. Matthew and I are staying in a hotel at the moment."

Lisa grabbed her daughter's arm. "She did what? Why would she do that?"

Christina linked arms with her mother and began to walk down Briggate in the direction of the Victoria Quarter. "She found out Matthew and I were planning to move into our own place and went ballistic."

"But you and Matthew are married. Surely, she realises you want a home of your own?"

"She was upset because she found out from a third person before Matthew had the chance to tell her."

"Even so… The woman sounds quite unhinged."

Christina smiled. "She reacted exactly as I knew she would."

"What do you mean?"

"Let's just say that I arranged for her to find out. I had to get out of that house, Mum. It would be weeks before all the furniture got delivered, and I couldn't stand living there a minute longer."

"Does Matthew know what you did?"

"God no, and he mustn't find out. I know he loves me, but unfortunately, he loves that witch too."

"You must be careful, dear. Matthew's not a fool."

Christina shrugged. "We'll be in the apartment soon, then I'll have Matthew all to myself." They walked into the arcade and stood outside *Madam Flora's Boutique*. "Mum, what do you think of that blue dress over in the corner? I love it. I think I'll try it on."

Charlotte was coming out of the hotel dining room that evening when Matthew and Christina entered.

"Where were you this morning?" Christina said. "I was hoping you would come shopping with me."

Charlotte smiled. "Sorry," she said. "I had an appointment first thing in town."

Christina huffed. "Never mind. I went with Mother instead. She bought me this dress. What do you think?" Christina spun round, giving the full effect of the blue chiffon outfit. "It's gorgeous, isn't it?"

Charlotte nodded. "Very nice," she said.

Matthew leant forward and kissed Charlotte lightly on the cheek. "Did you meet up with Joe?" he said. "How is he?"

"He's fine. He looks really happy."

"We should try to get together, the four of us, and have a catch-up."

Christina inhaled deeply. "Catch up on what you all tried to do to Dad?"

"Of course not," Matthew said, attempting to put his arm around her shoulders. "I just thought we could—"

"Could what? Gloat? Don't forget, Dad got the better of you. Of all of you." She turned sharply and hurried in the direction of the foyer. "I'm not hungry after all," she said. "I'm going up to my room."

"I'll come with you," Matthew said.

"Don't bother. I think it might be best if you got another room this evening, or better still, you could always go back to your bloody mother."

"Chrissie, don't be like that," Matthew said, following her across the foyer to the staircase. "I—"

Christina began to quickly ascend the stairs. "Keep away from me, Matthew," she said, tears streaming down her cheeks. "I don't want to speak to you tonight."

Matthew stopped, turned around and walked slowly

towards Charlotte. "Sorry about that, Sis," he said. "Christina is upset. Her dad won't have anything to do with her since she got together with me. He thinks she knew what was going on with Alex at the casino."

Charlotte frowned. "Christina knew nothing. We all made sure of that."

Matthew hunched his shoulders. "She's still bitter about what happened. She doesn't accept what a bastard Karl is."

Charlotte linked her arm in Matthew's. "I heard from Marion earlier," she said. "She's coming over to Leeds for a few days. She's bringing Bernard with her."

"Ah, the new husband? I'm looking forward to meeting him. When are you expecting her?"

"Probably tomorrow, if not the day after. I'll be booking them a room here."

"Well, make sure you let me know. I'd love to see her again."

"I will," Charlotte said. "I think you'd better go and make peace with Christina, don't you?"

"Wish me luck," Matthew said as he slowly ascended the staircase. "See you soon."

48

The next afternoon Paul Borowicz was standing by the lounge window of his father's house, surrounded by his grieving family, when his mobile rang. His first instinct was to ignore it, but the persistent ringing made this impossible. He walked into the kitchen before removing the phone from his pocket. "Yeah?" he said quietly.

"Paul, mate," said a chirpy voice. "It's me, your favourite hack reporter."

"Bob, this isn't a good time," Paul said. "Can we speak later?"

"Why, what's up? You sound like you've just buried your cat."

"Peter has died," Paul said solemnly. "I don't want to—"

There was a sharp intake of breath. "Sorry to hear that, mate," Bob said. "I always liked Peter. He was a decent bloke."

"Yes, he was," Paul said.

"Well, if you don't want to meet now, can we arrange another time? Not too long, though. What I have to tell you is dynamite."

Paul's curiosity was piqued. "You found something out about Ryan?"

"You bet I did. This is going to put me back in vogue with my editor."

"I don't want you speaking to anyone until we've had a talk."

There was a pause. "Well, make it soon. I've got a job to do, don't forget."

Paul sighed. "What about this evening at the Duck and Drake? Say, seven o'clock?"

"Okay," Bob said. "Make sure you bring some cash with you. What I have to tell you is hot."

"See you then."

Paul returned to the lounge and sat on the couch next to

his father. "Leave the funeral arrangements to me," he said, placing his arm around Victor's shoulders. "I'll take care of everything."

Victor sighed, his head buried in his hands. "Have you let Katya know?" he said. "She was fond of Peter."

"Don't worry, Dad. All the family will be here."

"It was kind of Karl to offer to pay for the funeral, wasn't it?"

Paul nodded but remained silent.

"I want you to promise me something, son," Victor said quietly.

"Anything, Dad, you know that."

"When you find the bastard that caused my son's death, you let me know first. Will you do that?"

"Dad, I can take care of it. You don't have to get involved."

"Paul, promise me. I need to avenge my son."

"All right. I promise." Paul got up from the couch, walked to the dresser, and poured a large vodka. "Here, Dad," he said, handing the glass to Victor. "You'll feel better after this."

49

A few miles away, in an attic room of a terraced house in Chapeltown, Alex Maddox drank the remnants of the cheap bottle of whisky he had stolen from the corner shop earlier that day. He staggered towards the worn, purple couch, which had been his bed for the last two weeks. Throwing himself on top, he reached over to the small table, took a cigarette, held it to his lips, and lit it before picking up his phone. He dialled a number which was answered almost immediately. "Chris?" There was a pause. "Chris, I have to see you. Meet me at the same place as last time, okay?"

Christina pulled into the multi-storey car park. She could see Alex leaning against a concrete pillar. He looked dishevelled as he smoked a cigarette. She parked the car and walked towards her brother. "Alex," she said, "are you all right? You look like shit."

Alex snorted. "Thanks for that, Sis," he said, drawing heavily on his cigarette. "I... What the hell is she doing here?"

Lisa stepped out of the car and walked towards her son. "Alex," she said, rushing towards him. "Are you all right, son?" She attempted to put her arms around him, but Alex pulled away.

He turned sharply to face Christina. "Why did you bring her here? I told you to come alone."

"You need her," she said. "You know you do. You can't carry on like this."

Alex clenched his fists. "I don't need anybody," he said. "Leave me alone, both of you."

"But Alex, you—"

He turned abruptly to face his sister. "If you really want to help me, you can give me some money."

Christina shook her head. "No, that's not the answer," she said.

Lisa opened her bag and withdrew an envelope. "Here's two hundred pounds," she said, handing the envelope to Alex.

"I'll try to get you some more as soon as I can."

Scowling, Alex grabbed the envelope from his mother. "Thanks," he muttered, putting it in his pocket, "but I'll need more than this. A lot more."

"I'm going to speak to Karl," she said. "We can get this mess sorted out once and for all."

"Are you mad? Karl will kill me."

Lisa shook her head. "Of course he won't. He's angry with you, but I'm sure I can talk him round."

"Dad hates me. He never liked me since we first met at the club."

"That's not true, Alex. Your father helped you a lot. He paid off your debts with the casino. He wouldn't have done that if he didn't like you, would he?"

Alex huffed and lit a cigarette. "It wasn't my fault what happened," he said. "I was played by Joe and Matthew. You do know that?"

"It doesn't matter now, son, does it? What is done is done."

"But Matthew was to blame," Alex said, pointing his finger at Christina. "He's responsible for what happened, and my sister, my stupid dumb sister, goes and marries him."

"I'm not listening to this," Christina said, walking back towards the car. "You can sort your own mess out from now on." She climbed into the car and turned on the engine. "Are you coming, Mother?"

"You go," Lisa said. "I need to talk with Alex."

Christina huffed. "Suit yourself," she said as the car roared into life.

50

It was almost eight o'clock when Paul arrived at the Duck and Drake. Bob Riley stood by the bar, a half-empty glass of lager in front of him. "Another when you're ready," he said to the barman as he put the glass to his lips and gulped the contents.

"I'll get this," Paul said, handing over a ten-pound note to the barman, "and I'll have a whisky."

"You're late," Bob said, not bothering to look up. "I thought we said half-seven?"

"Sorry about that. I got held up. Anyway, I'm here now." Paul glanced around at the busy pub. "There's a table over there," he said, nodding in the direction of the far wall. "It's a bit more private."

"What, next to the ladies' bog? I don't think so. They'll think we're a pair of bloody perverts sitting outside the bog."

"Never mind about that," Paul said. He took the drinks from the bartender and pushed his way through the crowd to the vacant table.

Muttering to himself, Bob followed.

"For fuck's sake, stop whinging," Paul said. "Now tell me what you found out from Devon."

Bob gulped at the lager. "Show me the money first," he said.

"Don't worry, I've brought the cash. I'm not going to flash it here, though, am I?"

Bob leant back into his chair, assuming an air of importance as he inhaled deeply. "It would seem all was not honey and roses with the Reverend Nigel Grimes and his stepson. Far from it, in fact."

"What do you mean by that?"

"I had an interesting conversation with Hilda. She did the flowers in the church and a bit of cleaning for the vicar. According to her, Ryan and his father were barely on speaking terms in the few months leading up to the fire."

"Did she say why?"

Bob hunched his shoulders and gave a loud sniff.

"Apparently, it was Ryan's relationship with his real mother, Roxanne." He drained the last of the lager from his glass and looked up at Paul expectantly. "When Ryan was at university, he contacted Roxanne. He became quite obsessed. The vicar threatened to disinherit him if he continued seeing her."

"Why would he object to Ryan seeing his mother? I would have thought he was old enough to make up his own mind."

"Hilda said Ryan wanted Roxanne to move into the vicarage."

"What did the vicar say to that, I wonder?"

"Well, you can guess. Who wants a hardened junkie in their spare room? According to Hilda, there had been a mighty argument, and the vicar threatened to disinherit Ryan if he continued to see her."

"That sounds a bit harsh," Paul said.

"There's more," he said. "There was something fishy about the fire at the vicarage."

"What do you mean, fishy?"

"The cause of the fire was unclear. A discarded cigarette was thought the most likely, but the thing is, no door keys were found. Even if the vicar and his wife were alerted to the fire, they couldn't have got out."

"So, they were locked in? But who'd want to murder a vicar?"

Bob shrugged. "Ryan was the obvious suspect, but he had an alibi. He was at a party with his girlfriend that night."

"With dozens of witnesses to vouch for him, I suppose?"

"The party was an illegal rave in one of the warehouses by the river. A few people came forward to say they had seen Ryan and the girl throughout the night, but to be honest, not many wanted to admit they had been there."

"So, it's possible Ryan could have left, set the fire and returned to the party without being missed?"

"I suppose so, but suspecting something and proving it are two completely different things."

"If it was him, what was the motive?"

Bob grinned. "Money, of course," he said. "What else?

Not all vicars are poor as church mice, you know. Nigel had inherited quite a stash from his parents. He was worth over half a million by all accounts."

"And Ryan is the beneficiary?"

"Probate hasn't been completed yet, but yes. Young Ryan will soon be a wealthy young man."

"What about the girlfriend? Did you manage to locate her?"

Bob leant back in his chair, placing his hands palm down on the table. "Talking makes me thirsty," he said. "It would really help if I had another drink."

Paul indicated for the barman to bring over another pint. It was a couple of minutes before the glass of lager was placed on the table. "Stop pissing about," Paul said impatiently. "What do you know about Ryan's girlfriend?"

Bob put the glass to his lips and drank greedily. "A pretty little blonde, by all accounts," he said. "She worked as a stripper in a nightclub in York. Her name is Barbara, but she works under the name Phoenix."

51

After their meal, Marion and Bernard relaxed in the hotel restaurant, enjoying a glass of cognac.

"It's a pity Charlotte couldn't join us this evening," Bernard said. "Where did you say she was?"

"She's out with Christina and Matthew. I think they've gone to the cinema."

Bernard leant forward and gently took Marion's hand in his. "Do you remember our first proper date?" he said. "We went to the Odeon."

Marion giggled. "I remember you dropped a giant carton of popcorn all over the floor. The usherette was furious."

"The film was Indiana Jones, as I remember," Bernard said.

Marion sighed. "That was a long time ago, love. A lot of water has gone under the bridge since then."

"It certainly has," he said, gently stroking the side of Marion's acid-scarred face with his finger. "If I ever find out who did this to you …"

Marion pulled away. "It doesn't matter now, not after all this time."

"I might not be able to avenge you, my love, but I sure as hell can avenge Paula. That bastard Maddox deserves all that's coming to him."

"Darling, you must be careful. Karl Maddox can be ruthless."

He reached for his coat on the back of a chair. "Stop worrying," he said. "Killing scum like him is going to be a pleasure."

"But you're not a young man anymore. I'm worried you might get caught."

"Stop worrying. I've not been caught yet."

"Do you think we should tell Charlotte about… about everything?"

Bernard shrugged. "That's up to you, dear," he said. "Do what you think's best."

He began to put on his coat. Marion reached over and grabbed his arm. "Darling, you will be careful, won't you?"

He bent down and kissed her lightly on the cheek. "Stop worrying," he said. "I'll be back before you know it."

Fifteen minutes later, Charlotte bounded into the dining room. "Oh, there you are, Gran," she said. "Where's Bernard?"

"He had to go out, but he'll be back soon. How was the film?"

Charlotte screwed up her nose. "It was a romance," she said. "Not my sort of film at all."

"Oh? You don't believe in romance?"

"I did... until I met Patrick. He managed to kill any romantic notions I might have had."

"Darling, that's a terrible thing to say. You're still young, and you're beautiful. I would have thought men would be throwing themselves at your feet."

She shook her head. "No, not interested, I'm afraid. I don't think I'll ever trust a man again."

"Not all men are like Patrick," Marion said, taking Charlotte's hand in hers. "Look at me and Bernard, for instance."

Charlotte smiled. "You two are made for each other. He seems besotted with you."

"Do you think so?"

"Of course he is. Where did you meet?"

Marion slowly ran her tongue across her lips. "Bernard was one of my first clients when I worked in Chapeltown," she said. "He visited me at least once a week and always brought me flowers. Not many punters did that."

"So, how did you lose touch?"

Marion shrugged. "Back in the day, Bernard was a bit of a bad boy," she said. "He liked to rob banks. He was good at it too until Walters ratted to the police." Marion picked up her glass and sipped her brandy. "The police were waiting for him inside the bank. Poor Bernard got five years in Wakefield nick." She picked up her glass and drained the contents. "Wakefield is one of the worst prisons in the country. Did you know they call that place *Monster Mansion* because of the animals put away there?"

"No, I didn't know that."

"It was whilst Bernard was inside that I was expecting your mother."

Charlotte gasped. "Are you saying that… that Bernard was the father?"

"Of course he was. Paula was the image of him."

"So why didn't you and Bernard get together when he came out of prison?"

"Because of this," Marion said, placing her fingers on the purple mottling on her left cheek. "About a year after he was sent down, I got attacked with acid by some disgruntled punter and ended up like this. I was in hospital for months. That's when the authorities took Paula off me and placed her in care."

"But what about Bernard? Surely when he was released he—"

Marion shook her head. "He didn't know he had a daughter. By the time he got out of the nick, I was long gone. I didn't see him again until that night we walked into the bar in Barbados."

"It must have been a shock when he found out about your attack and his daughter being murdered."

"He was devastated, especially when I told him Karl Maddox was the one who had murdered Paula."

"We can't prove it, though, not without implicating Joe."

"Bernard's not bothered about proving anything. He's vowed to kill Maddox, which is exactly what he will do."

Charlotte gasped. "What? You have to talk to Bernard. He can't—"

"Stop worrying," Marion said, taking Charlotte's hand. "Bernard knows what he's doing."

"You can't go around killing people," Charlotte wailed. "You just can't."

"Don't be silly, dear. Of course, you can. In fact, that's exactly what Bernard is doing now."

"What do you mean?"

"He's gone to kill Karl Maddox, the man who murdered his daughter."

52

Geoffrey Lawrence entered The Emerald at nine o'clock. He purposefully strode over to the bartender. "I need to speak with Karl Maddox," he said. "Tell him it's important."

The man scowled suspiciously. "Mr Maddox is a busy man," he said. "May I suggest you make an appointment?"

"And may I suggest you tell Mr Maddox that Geoffrey Lawrence is downstairs and wishes to speak to him urgently."

A slim redhead wearing a skimpy black dress sidled over. "Is everything all right, Lenny?"

"This bloke wants to see Karl," Lenny said. "He doesn't have an appointment."

"I'm Chanel," the girl purred.

"Of course you are," Geoffrey scoffed.

"Can I help?"

Geoffrey pushed past her and headed towards the foyer. "My business is with the monkey," he said, "not the organ grinder."

Chanel followed in close pursuit. "You can't just go barging into Karl's office like this without an appointment," she said, reaching out and grabbing his arm. "Leave me your details, and I'll—"

Geoffrey turned and, taking hold of her shoulders, spun her round. "Piss off," he said gruffly. "Get out of my way." He ascended the stairs, two at a time. Chanel ran into the club and signalled two of the minders, Alan and Steve.

"There's a bloke on his way to Karl's office," she said. "You have to stop him."

The two men rushed past Chanel and bounded up the stairs just as Lawrence pushed open the office door. He stopped abruptly in the doorway of the dimly lit room. Karl was laid back in one of the armchairs, his trousers down by his ankles. Kneeling in front of him was a young, scantily dressed woman performing oral sex. She screamed at the intrusion and reached for her dress lying on the floor.

Karl growled as he attempted to pull up his trousers.

"What the fuck do you think you're doing barging in here?" he said.

"Sorry, boss," Alan said, grabbing Lawrence by the arm. "This bloke forced his way in."

Karl dressed quickly and rushed over to Lawrence. "How dare you burst into my office?" he said, the veins on his neck pulsating. "This is private and—"

"Calm down, Maddox," Lawrence said, raising his arms in mock surrender. "Your dirty little secret's safe with me if that's what you're worried about."

Alan and Steve attempted to frogmarch Lawrence to the door. "We'll throw him out, boss," Steve said, "after we've given him a bloody good kicking."

"I wouldn't do that," Lawrence said, "not unless you like prison food."

Karl frowned. "Who the fuck are you anyway? And what do you want with me?"

"If you get your gorillas off me, I'll tell you."

Karl indicated for the two minders to release him. "Well? What's so important that you have to barge into my office?"

"I need to speak to you about … a delicate matter," Lawrence said, "in private."

Karl's frown deepened. "What delicate matter would that be?"

"David Glendenning."

"David's dead. The stupid bastard shot himself."

"I know that, but I want to know why."

Karl huffed, then, walking over to the cabinet, poured himself a whisky before settling behind his desk and lighting a cigar. "Get out," Karl said. "All of you. Get out of my office." The two minders walked over to the door, followed closely by Chanel. "You too," he said to the young girl cowering in the corner of the room. "Close the door behind you."

Left alone with Lawrence, Karl leant back into his chair. "You must be the ex-cop Paul told me about," he said, pointing his finger. "He told me you had been snooping around. You're writing a book, aren't you?"

Lawrence nodded. "My memoirs. Cases I have worked on through the years."

"And you think your readers will be interested in a crazy cop who goes on the rampage with a gun?"

"My readers will be interested in the truth," Lawrence said. "They want to know why David would shoot you, a man he had been friends with for years, and then turn the gun on himself."

Beads of sweat formed on Karl's brow. "Because he was fucking nuts, that's why," he said, banging his fist on the desk. "Ask anybody. He'd got the push from his job. His wife was leaving him, and he was at his wit's end." He sipped at his drink. "Anyway, what business is it of yours?"

"I've been commissioned to write a chapter by his wife," Lawrence said. "She doesn't believe your explanation of what happened any more than I do."

Karl huffed. "From what I heard, David's wife was as mad as him. She's been in and out of looney bins for years."

"Lydia Glendenning was in a Nursing Home for a time after suffering a breakdown," Lawrence said. "Understandable, really, in view of what happened to her husband, I would have thought."

Karl took another sip of his whisky. "Well, I'm very sorry for her, of course, but I'm afraid I can't help you." He pointed towards the door. "Now, Mr Lawrence," he said, "get the fuck out of my office before I have you thrown out."

Lawrence stood firm. "Could David's breakdown have had anything to do with what happened to his girlfriend?"

Karl scowled. "What girlfriend? David was a married man."

"So are you, but it doesn't seem to stop you having extras on the side."

Karl laughed. "Oh, you mean the girl who was in here earlier. She's just a… perk of the job."

"I'm sure your wife won't see it like that."

Karl curled his fingers into fists. "I hope you're not

thinking of speaking with my wife," he said. "I promise you that you'll regret it."

"What you do in your private life is none of my business," Lawrence said. "I'm only interested in the truth about what happened between you and David Glendenning."

"David's dead, and as far as I'm concerned, that's the end of it."

"Tell me about Erica, your common-law wife."

Karl scowled. "What about her? She took off with another bloke. She died, and before you ask," he said, raising his right hand, "it was nothing to do with me. It was cancer."

"Her father was murdered, wasn't he?"

"Was he?"

"Thomas Edward Meadows was stabbed to death in Cooper's Alley. The police wrote it off as a mugging that had gone wrong, but I think we both know that's not true."

"I don't know what you're talking about," Karl said. "His death had nothing to do with me. I barely knew the man."

"I heard Meadows was a paedophile. How did you feel about your girlfriend living under his roof?"

"My, my, you have been a busy little bastard, haven't you?" Karl said, rising from his chair. "I think it's time you were leaving, don't you?"

"Why? Have I touched a nerve?" Lawrence walked over to the window. "Do you know what I think, Karl? I think you murdered Erica's father, and somehow David's girlfriend found out. I believe she was trying to blackmail you, and that's why you killed her."

"You're talking out of your backside," Karl said, sweat trickling down the back of his neck.

"Am I? I'll tell you what else I think. I believe David overheard you arguing with Joe Stevens on the night he died. He was probably in the secret passage at the end of the club, the passage where you spy on your punters. I think David overheard what you did to Paula, and that's why he shot you."

Karl lunged towards Lawrence with his fists raised. Suddenly, there was a loud crash as the windowpane smashed, spraying glass into the room. Karl flung himself onto the floor. Alan and Steve, who had been standing behind the door on the landing, burst into the room.

"Are you all right, boss?" Steve asked, rushing towards Karl. "We heard a shot."

Steve stopped abruptly, staring at the bloodstained body on the carpet. "Bloody hell," he gasped. "He's been shot."

Karl's hands shook uncontrollably as he struggled to his feet. "Is... is he dead?" he gasped.

Alan bent down to examine Lawrence. "No, he's still breathing. He's wounded in the shoulder."

Steve reached for the desk telephone. "I'll get an ambulance."

"No, leave it," Karl said. "We don't want the cops round here asking questions. Go and look around outside. The shot must have been fired from the car park."

"Okay, boss," Steve said as he rushed towards the door.

"Alan, you get the CCTV from the camera in the car park. Don't say a word to anyone downstairs about what's happened here, either of you."

"Of course not, but I doubt anyone heard anything with the music being so loud."

"Let's hope so," Karl said as he picked up the desk phone. He dialled a number. "Danny? There's been an accident. I need you at the club immediately and bring your medical bag with you."

53

It was almost eleven o'clock when the telephone in Lydia Glendenning's lounge gave out its shrill ring. "Hello?" she said, frowning at the wall clock.

"Lydia? Lydia, it's me, Amanda."

"Is everything all right, dear?"

"It's Geoffrey. He hasn't come home. He isn't there with you, is he?"

Lydia shook her head. "No, I haven't seen him in a couple of days."

"Oh dear, I… I don't know who else to ring. He isn't answering his phone. When he left, he promised he would be back by ten at the latest."

"Where was he going? Did he say?"

"Well, that's just it, Lydia. He told me he was going to confront Karl Maddox at The Emerald Club."

Danny Davies had been a medic in the British Army until his dishonourable discharge. He was known in criminal circles as *the doc* and had often been called upon when the patient preferred not to go to the usual medical treatment. A few years previously, Danny had tended to Karl when he had been involved in an altercation resulting in his face being slashed.

Danny rushed up to The Emerald Club's office. "What's happened?" he said, placing his bag on a chair and removing his coat. "Are you all right, Karl?"

Karl nodded. "It's not me this time," he said. "It's him." He pointed to the couch where Geoffrey Lawrence was slouched. "Some bastard took a pot shot through the window."

"I take it the bullet was meant for you?"

"Who else?" Karl said and swigged back a whisky. "See what you can do for him, will you, mate?"

Lawrence's bloodstained shirt had been removed, and Danny bent over to examine the wound. "The bullets grazed his shoulder," he said after a couple of minutes. "The heavy bleeding is due to him being cut with glass." He slowly began to pick out glass shards from the wound. "This should be a piece of piss to put right."

Lawrence groaned as Danny treated the wound. "It won't take long, mate," Danny said. "I've got all the glass out. I have to clean and stitch it, and then you'll be as good as new." He reached into his bag and removed a bottle of tablets. "Here, swallow a couple of these," he said. "It will help with the pain."

Half an hour later, Lawrence was sitting on the couch, a glass of whisky in his hand. "I need to get home," he said. "My wife… she's ill."

"I'll get one of my men to drive you," Karl said. "But first, we need a little talk."

"I thought we'd said all there was to be said."

"Not quite. I want to know where you got all this bullshit about Erica's father from."

"Does it matter?"

"Of course it fucking matters," Karl said, moving forward menacingly. "If you want to see your wife again, tell me everything."

Lawrence's breathing was shallow as he leant back into the couch and closed his eyes. "One of your old tarts told me about Meadows," he said. "She really hates your guts."

"Does this old tart have a name?"

"Her name's Shirley. She's convinced you had her villa burnt down in Spain and lost her old man in the fire."

"The silly cow doesn't know what she's talking about. Where is she now?"

"She was staying in Chapeltown with some mate she used to work with. I think her name was Suzie."

"How did Shirley know about Erica's dad?"

"She didn't. She just relayed a story to her of a bloke being found stabbed to death in Cooper's Alley. Erica must have realised it was her father." Lawrence sipped at the whisky. "I made enquiries and confirmed that it was her dad that had been killed."

Karl sniffed. "That paedophile bastard deserved to die, but it had nothing to do with me. If I knew who did for him, I'd buy him a drink. In fact, I'd buy him a whole bottle." He walked back to his desk and flung himself into the chair.

Lawrence licked his lips. "I don't feel well," he said. "I need to get home."

"Not yet. Who told you there was a secret passage in the club?"

"Does it matter?"

"Who told you?"

"If you must know. It was Joe's wife."

"Sarah? Are you sure about that?"

Lawrence nodded. "Joe confided in her that David had probably been hiding there listening when you two had your argument." He struggled to his feet, holding on to the chair's arm for support. "Now, I need to get back to my wife," he said. "She'll be worried."

Karl leant forward and steepled his fingers. "I don't want you saying a word about what went on here tonight," he said. "I'll deal with it."

"Somebody tried to kill you," Lawrence said. "They very nearly killed me instead. The police need to be told."

Karl fixed his gaze on Lawrence. "I said I'll deal with it," he said. "This place is surrounded by CCTV. I'll soon find out who was responsible."

"For Christ's sake, you can't just—"

"You're in my world now," Karl said, banging his fist on the desk. "This is what you get for sticking your nose into things which don't concern you." He got up and walked towards the cabinet. "Another?" Not waiting for a response, he poured two glasses of whisky, handing one to Lawrence.

"If you don't need me anymore, I'll be off," Danny said. "I'll leave some antiseptic and bandages for when you change the dressing."

"No, hang on, Danny. I need a word."

"I must see a doctor," Lawrence said. "A proper one."

Karl handed Lawrence a glass. "If Danny says you'll be okay, then you'll be okay. He knows what he's talking about."

"But—"

"There is no but. No doctor, understand?"

Lawrence gulped his whisky but remained silent.

"Do you want me to send one of my men over to change the dressing for you tomorrow?"

Lawrence shook his head. "No. I have a live-in nurse who attends to my wife. She can do it."

"Can she be trusted to keep schtum?"

"She works for me. She'll do as she's told."

"Well, let's hope so, for your sake."

Lawrence got to his feet. "I have to go. My wife will be worried sick."

Karl leant back in his chair. "Before you go," he said, "I want to know something."

"What?"

"How much?"

"What do you mean, how much?"

"How much will it cost to destroy your notes and forget everything you've learnt about Glendenning?"

54

Marion was alone in the hotel bar when Bernard arrived. He rushed over to his wife and flopped heavily on the chair next to her.

"Are you all right, darling?" Marion said. "You look a little… a little flushed."

Bernard lowered his head into his hands. "I shot the bastard," he said.

Marion leant forward and squeezed his arm. "Karl's dead?"

"I think so. The club was crawling with his lackeys when I got there. I had to go into the car park and take the shot from there. Karl was up in his office, but I saw his silhouette through the curtained window."

"And you're sure he's dead?"

"I didn't wait around. There wasn't much cover in the car park, so I had to get out quick."

"Are you sure nobody saw you?"

Bernard shook his head. "I don't think so. Anyway, what does it matter? We'll be back in Barbados in a couple of days."

"I think this deserves a celebration," Marion said as she indicated to the waiter. "Champagne?"

"Why not?" Bernard said, smiling. "By the way, where is Charlotte? I think she should be celebrating too."

"She's gone up," Marion said. "I think she was a little overwhelmed."

"What do you mean?"

"I explained to her that you were her grandfather."

"What did she think to that?"

"She was thrilled," Marion said. "Then I told her you were going to kill Karl."

Bernard scowled. "Oh, you shouldn't have done that. How did she react?"

Marion shrugged. "Shocked, I think. And, like I said, a little overwhelmed."

Bernard slouched back into the couch. "Have you got my pills?" he said, clutching his chest.

Marion reached into her bag and took out a small bottle. "Darling, I think you need to go back to the doctor when we get home. You don't look at all well."

Bernard took two pills and placed them on his tongue. "I'll be fine," he said. "It's just a twinge."

"You know what the doctor said. You must take things easy. You're not a young man anymore, remember?"

Bernard chuckled. "Maybe not," he said, "but I can still give the young 'uns a run for their money, eh, old girl?"

"Less of the old," Marion chastised. "We've both got a few miles left on the clock yet."

"Oh, here comes the champagne," Bernard said as the waiter put the ice bucket containing the champagne down on the table, along with two glasses. "Let's make a toast," he said, raising his glass. "To family."

"To family."

55

Nurse Walters was in the lounge when Geoffrey arrived home at almost midnight.

"There you are," she said, hurrying towards him. "I was about to call the police. Mrs Lawrence is sick with worry about you."

"Sorry, I got delayed," he said. "I should have telephoned. I'll pop in and see Amanda now."

"I've given her something to make her sleep," the nurse said. "It's best to leave it until morning now."

Geoffrey flopped onto the couch and closed his eyes. "Could you pour me a whisky?" he said. "A large one and get one for yourself."

"Thanks, I don't mind if I do. It's been a long day."

Geoffrey slowly sipped his drink and then leant forward. "Sandra," he said. "I need you to do something for me."

"Oh?"

"I… I had a slight accident tonight." He struggled out of his jacket.

Nurse Walters gasped. "Oh, your shirt, it's covered in blood."

"It looks worse than it is," he said. "I need you to clean the wound for me. Do you think you can do that?"

She removed Geoffrey's shirt. "What on earth happened?"

"A window got broken accidentally, and I got showered in glass."

She looked at him suspiciously. "This looks like a bullet wound," she said.

"It was an accident. I just need you to make sure the wound is cleaned properly."

"All right," she said, removing his shirt. "I'll get my bag."

Half an hour later, Geoffrey made his way into his study. He turned on his computer and retrieved his file entitled *Maddox/Glendenning*. Drumming his fingers on the desk, he read through his notes of the interviews he had conducted.

Deep in thought, he stroked his chin as he considered the evidence he had secured. Most of it was hearsay and guesswork. He knew Maddox's legal team could tear it to shreds in minutes. Then there was the threat from Karl. Destroy the file or… Geoffrey was well aware of Karl's ruthless reputation. He reached into his jacket pocket and removed the cheque Karl had given him. It was undoubtedly a great deal of money. It could provide first-class care for Amanda, possibly enabling her to try new treatments abroad. He studied the computer screen once more. "Fuck it," he muttered as his finger hovered over the delete button.

56

"Do you think he'll keep his mouth shut?" Danny said once Lawrence had left the club.

Karl scowled. "If he knows what's good for him, he will."

"Are you sure you don't know who's behind this? You've really pissed somebody off big time."

Karl turned to his computer. "I'll check the CCTV. There are two cameras in the car park, so let's hope we get lucky." He turned on the programme and leant over, examining the flickering images.

"There," Danny said. "Somebody is crouching behind the Audi."

Karl studied the figure. The man walked towards the building with his arm outstretched. There was a flash and the sound of breaking glass as the man turned and ran from the car park into the street.

"Fuck," Danny said. "You can't see the bastard's face."

"Let's check the other camera," Karl said. "That's just below the office window."

The second image was much clearer. Karl squinted at the picture as the man lifted his arm, and a gun could clearly be seen. He froze the screen and studied the man's face. "I don't know him," he said. "What about you? Do you recognise him?"

Danny turned the computer screen slightly to get a better look. "Yeah, I know him," he said. "He's a bit older, and his hair's a lot thinner than the last time I saw him, but I'd know that ugly mug anywhere."

"Who is he?"

"Bernard Coates," he said. "We shared a cell for a couple of years back in the day."

"What was he in for?"

"Bernard liked to rob banks. He was pretty good at it too. He got five years in Wakefield."

"Why would he come after me? I don't even know the man."

Danny shrugged. "There were rumours. Some people thought he was a mercenary for the underground."

"An assassin? That sounds ridiculous."

"Whatever he was up to, he did very well out of it by all accounts. The last I heard, he was living somewhere in the Caribbean."

Karl thumped his fist on the desk. "We have to find him. Somebody must have put him up to this."

"I'll put the feelers out," Danny said. "See if I can track him down. I still have a lot of contacts."

Karl poured himself a whisky. "Want one?"

"No thanks. I'd better get back to the casino."

"Yeah, you don't want that croupier giving all the profits away."

Danny grinned. "Oh, Zak's all right. We had a little talk, and… well, I suppose I'd better tell you. You'll find out anyway."

"Tell me what?"

"Zak is living with me in the flat."

Karl grinned. "Bloody hell, Danny, that didn't take you long."

"Needs must," he said. "I'll be back tomorrow for Peter's funeral. Two o'clock, isn't it?"

Karl nodded. "Yeah, I'll see you then."

"Good night, Karl, and stop worrying. We'll find the murdering little bastard, and when we do…"

Left alone, Karl studied the image on the screen. "I wonder…" he murmured. He picked up the telephone and rang Geoffrey Lawrence. "Do you know Bernard Coates?"

Lawrence frowned. "The bank robber? Why do you want to know about him?"

"I think he's the bastard who tried to kill me tonight. My people are out looking for him now. I don't suppose you know who he knocks around with?"

"Sorry. The last I heard, Bernard Coates was living in the Caribbean somewhere."

"Well, he's not in the fucking Caribbean now, is he?" Karl said and hung up.

"Will there be anything else, Mr Lawrence?" Nurse Walters said, hovering in the doorway. "I've got Amanda settled for the night."

"No, you get yourself to bed. I'll lock up."

"Goodnight then," she said.

"Goodnight," Lawrence said as he poured himself another drink.

57

Lydia had just finished breakfast the following day when the doorbell rang. She huffed as she put down the newspaper and went to the front door. "Geoffrey," she said, "what a lovely surprise. I wasn't expecting to see you today, and certainly not this early."

"Good morning," Geoffrey said rather stiffly, following her into the kitchen.

"Can I get you a coffee?" she asked. "It's Molly's Day off today, so… oh, what's wrong with your arm? It's in a sling."

"It's nothing," he said, "I had a slight accident." He leant against the kitchen island. "Lydia, I'm sorry, but I've decided not to carry on with my book."

She gasped. "What do you mean, not carry on? You can't stop now. You're getting close to finding out what happened."

He shook his head. "No, I'm not. It was all a blind alley. I'm afraid we must accept that David's mind was disturbed when he shot Karl and then himself."

"No, that can't be right," she said, tears welling in her eyes. "Karl caused David's death. I know he did."

"I'm sorry, Lydia, but there's no evidence to substantiate anything but the conclusions drawn at the time."

"Please, Geoffrey, I'm begging you. You must keep digging."

He pulled away from her grasp. "I have to think of Amanda," he said. "She needs specialist care. I'm taking her to America for treatment. It's amazing what they can do nowadays."

Lydia pursed her lips. "Has Maddox put you up to this?" she said. "Is that where you were last night when Amanda telephoned looking for you? Is he threatening you?"

"Don't be ridiculous," Geoffrey said, walking towards the hall door. "I've decided Amanda's welfare is more important. The book will have to wait."

"I don't believe you," she said, picking up her coffee cup and throwing it in his direction. "I think you're scared of

Maddox. I think—"

"That's enough," he said. "David is dead. Accept that and move on."

"Get out," she screamed. "Get the fuck out of my house."

Geoffrey hurried into the hall and through the front door to his car. "Sorry," he whispered as he turned on the engine. "But Amanda must come first."

58

Peter Borowicz's funeral was a small but dignified affair. His father, Victor, and his two brothers, along with Paul and his cousin Katya attended. Karl and Lisa arrived with Danny and Simon, the manager of The Sapphire, with half a dozen of the minders from the clubs. After the funeral service, the party went to Victor's house.

Victor sat in his usual armchair, a glass of whisky in his hand. "Thank you all for coming," he said. "Peter would be glad to know he had so many friends."

Paul perched on the chair arm and put his arm around his father's shoulders. "Everyone loved Peter," he said. "He hadn't an enemy in the world."

Victor's eyes were brimming with tears. "Maybe not," he said, "but somebody killed my son, and I won't rest until I find out who's responsible." He turned to Karl. "You still don't know?"

"We're getting close," Karl said. "We'll find him. You have my word."

Paul walked over to Karl. "I'll be back at the club tomorrow," he said. "I need to have a private word with you first thing."

"What about?"

"About your nephew."

"Ryan? What about him?"

"Not now," Paul said. "We'll talk tomorrow."

Early that evening, Karl was in the office when the telephone rang. It was Danny. "Yes, mate?" he said as he lit a cigar. "What can I do for you?"

"It's about Bernard Coates," Danny said.

"You've found him?"

"Yeah, he's staying at the Park Plaza Hotel."

"Good work. I'll get the lads together and—" Karl said.

"Before you go guns blazing, there's something you should know."

"Oh? What's that?"

"Coates didn't arrive in England until two days ago. I've had a mate check that with a contact at passport control."

"I don't understand. What are you saying?"

"We know Coates had a pop shot at you last night, but there's no way he could have messed with your car or tried to run you over at the hospital. He was still in the Caribbean."

"Then if he didn't, who the fuck did?"

"Just thought you should know," Danny said and hung up the receiver.

Karl drew on his cigar, drumming his fingers on the desk. His mobile rang, and he saw it was Lisa. "Yes, what is it? I'm busy," he said.

"Karl, I need to talk to you."

"Can't it wait until I get home?"

"No, I need to talk to you now. Can you come home?"

"I'm working."

"I'm sure the club can manage for an hour without you. It is important."

Karl huffed. "Give me an hour," he said. "I have a couple of things to sort out first."

"All right, but please don't be long."

Frowning, Karl put down the receiver and went downstairs into the club. Girls were already dancing on the poles, and several all-male groups were gathered around the podiums.

"Looks like it's going to be a good night, boss," Alan said, sidling up to him at the bar. "There's another four bachelor groups booked in for later."

"Great. Just keep an eye out. I don't want any trouble."

"Don't worry. That latest lot of minders Paul set on are pretty handy."

Karl placed his hand on Alan's shoulder. "I want a couple of your best lads for later," he said. "I have a job for you."

"No worries. What is it?"

"I'll tell you when I get back. I have some business to see to at home first, but I'll be back before midnight."

Alan smirked. "Sure, boss," he said. "Have fun."

59

Lisa was in the lounge when Karl arrived. "Well?" he said impatiently. "What is it that is so important?" He went to the cabinet and poured a whisky.

Lisa fidgeted uncomfortably on the couch. "It's… it's Alex," she faltered. "He's in a bad way, Karl. He needs our help."

Karl banged his glass down on the cabinet. "What the fuck have I told you about talking to that bastard?" he said. "He's no good. I don't want you to have anything to do with him. Understand?"

"He's my son," Lisa sobbed. "He's our son. He's in trouble, and he needs our help."

"Alex will always be in trouble. He's weak and feckless."

"Please, Karl, you have to help him."

"Help him do what? What is it this time? Another pretend job in Canada or paying off his gambling debts?"

"The poor boy is at his wit's end," Lisa said, dabbing her eyes. "He has no money, no job, no home, and no wife. We're all he's got. You can't see your own son on the streets. You couldn't be so heartless."

Karl picked up the glass and drained its contents in one gulp. "Where is he?"

"I've put him up in a bed and breakfast for a couple of nights."

"Where?"

"Does it matter?"

"What exactly do you want me to do?"

"I want you to give him another chance. I know what he did was bad, but gambling is an illness. He can't help it. You have a responsibility towards him, Karl. He's still your son, whatever he's done."

"That little bastard tried to bankrupt me, and you want me to trust him back in the business?"

"He's sorry for what he's done. I know he'll never do anything like that again. Please, Karl, I'm begging you. Give

166

our son another chance."

"And if I say no?"

"If you refuse to help him, then you and I are finished. Alex is my flesh and blood. I can't abandon him. I just can't."

Karl poured another whisky. "If I agree to bring him back in, it won't be as a manager. He does know that?"

Lisa flung her arms around his neck. "He'll do anything," she said. "He just wants his family back."

Karl grabbed her arms and forced them by her side. "And you'll be grateful too, won't you, darling?"

"Of course I will, Karl," she said. "You know I will."

Karl pressured Lisa to her knees. "Show me," he said, releasing his grip on her arms. "Show me how grateful."

60

It was just after midnight when the waiter entered the lounge of the Park Plaza Hotel. "Mr Coates," he said. "I'm afraid your car alarm is making a racket. Could you come and disable it, please?"

Bernard huffed. "Bloody hire cars," he said, retrieving the car keys from his pocket. "I won't be long, darling, if you want to go up."

Marion yawned. "Yes, I am rather tired tonight."

Bernard walked into the foyer and out into the car park.

Marion swallowed the remaining wine in her glass and went to her suite. Her clothes had already been packed into her suitcase for the early morning journey back to Barbados. She turned on the radio for the late evening news, but still there was no mention of a shooting at The Emerald Club. Exhausted, she got ready and climbed into bed.

The sound of a church clock striking two was the first thing Coates was aware of, that and the excruciating pain in his arms and back. He opened his eyes. Everything was blurry and out of focus. He ran his tongue along his parched, swollen lips. "Where… where am I?" he murmured. His voice sounded weak and tinny. "What do you want?"

Alan grabbed the pulley which was suspending Coates's half-naked body by the arms, and hoisted him up from the ground another few inches. "Please," Coates pleaded. "I'm an old man… I have a weak heart."

Steve was perched on a pile of used tyres across from him, smoking a cigarette. "Someone is coming to see you," he said. "He wants to ask you some questions."

Coates squinted through his swollen, bloodshot eyes. "What's going on?" he said. "I don't know you."

The sound of the lockup's iron door being opened caused everyone to turn. Karl Maddox strode briskly into the room and stood directly in front of Coates. "You tried to kill me," Karl said, punching Coates in the chest.

"No, you're wrong," Coates protested. "I—"

Karl pressed his face close to Coates. "You were seen," he said. "I have cameras everywhere, mate. What I want to know is why? Who put you up to it?"

Coates shook his head. "It wasn't me. You've made a mistake."

Karl brought back his fist and punched Coates hard on the jaw. "Stop lying to me," he said. "Who are you working for?"

Coates' breathing became irregular. "Please, I… I have a weak heart," he said.

Karl walked over to Steve. "Do you have the pliers?"

"Sure, boss," Steve said, handing him a pair of pliers. "Would you like me to do it?"

Karl grinned. "No," he said. "I'm going to take this bastard's fingers off one by one myself. Then I'm going to make him eat them."

Coates struggled violently against the chains. "Please, please stop this. I'm begging you," Coates said as Karl approached him, pliers in hand. "It… it was a mistake."

"The only mistake is that you're a lousy shot. You missed me and hit some other poor bastard."

"Just let me go. I won't bother you again. I should never have… I should never have tried taking revenge after all this time."

"What do you mean, revenge?"

Coates raised his head slightly. "You killed my daughter," he said weakly. "You killed my little girl."

Karl scowled. "What the fuck are you talking about?"

"Paula," he said. "You killed my Paula."

"Who told you that?" he said, prodding him in the chest with his finger. "Tell me, who the fuck said that?"

Coates' head lolled to the side, and he closed his eyes. Karl grabbed him by the shoulders and shook him. "I asked you a question. Who told you?"

"Marion," he whispered. "Marion told me."

"Marion? That ugly old tart that ran the brothels? What's it got to do with her?"

"Paula was her daughter."

"And who told Marion?"

Coates spat blood onto the floor. "Joe," he said. "Joe told her."

The creaking of the lockup's door caused Karl to spin round. A woman hurried forward, holding a gun in her hand. "You're the bastard that killed my Harry," she said, her voice heavy with emotion as she pointed the weapon at Coates' temple. "Now, I'm going to kill you. I'm going to blow your fucking head off."

Coates struggled against the chains binding him. "Get that mad bitch away from me," he yelled. "She's crazy."

Karl rushed forward, grabbing her by the arm, causing the gun to clatter to the ground. "What the fuck do you think you're doing?" he yelled. He pushed her to the floor and picked up the gun.

Sandra Walters flinched with pain as she struggled to get back to her feet. "Let go of me," she said. "That bastard deserves to die. He killed my husband."

"Who are you, and how did you know where to find him?"

"I… I heard Geoffrey Lawrence on the phone talking to you. I heard him mention Coates by name."

"That doesn't explain how—"

"I followed you," she said. "I waited outside The Emerald and saw you leave, so I… I followed you here."

"And the gun? Where did you get the gun?"

"It belonged to Harry. The police never found it when they searched the house, so I kept it. I knew it would come in useful one day."

Karl grabbed Sandra's upper arm and frogmarched her to the door. "Go home," he said. "We'll deal with Coates."

Sandra threw back her head defiantly. "He deserves to die. He's a killer. He—"

"I said we'll deal with him. Now go home and keep your mouth shut. You haven't seen anything here tonight. Understand?"

She was silent for a moment. "You promise he'll be

punished?"

"Leave it with me," Karl said. "Bernard Coates will get what's coming to him. You have my word."

61

Paul arrived early at The Emerald the following morning. He was sitting on the couch in the office sipping coffee when Karl arrived.

"You're an early bird," Karl said. "Pissed the bed or something?"

Paul huffed. "Very funny. What's happened to the window? It's boarded up."

"Oh, that? Some stupid bastard took a pot shot at me last night, but as you can see, he missed."

Paul jumped to his feet. "Why the hell didn't you tell me? It must have been the bastard who killed Peter."

Karl shook his head. "No," he said. "He didn't do for Peter. The bloke last night wasn't even in the country when Peter had his accident."

"Then who? You must have some idea."

Karl shrugged. "I've got all my people out there asking around, but so far, there's nothing."

Paul sighed heavily and flopped back onto the couch. "Are you saying there are two different people out to get you?"

Karl shrugged. "It certainly looks like it, and I haven't a clue who. Anyway, you said you had something to tell me about Ryan?"

"Yeah, so I did. It's a couple of things, really." Paul relayed the conversation he had had earlier with Bob Riley. "It seems young Ryan isn't as squeaky clean as he would have you believe."

Karl sat back in his swivel chair and slowly stroked his chin. "He's coming to the club later today," he said. "He wants to talk to me about something important. I'll have a word with him then."

"What are you going to do about the girl?"

"I'll decide what to do about her after I've spoken to Ryan. Did your mate know where to find this Roxanne woman?"

"She moves around quite a bit from one squat to another."

"Try and find out, will you? I'd like a word with her. By

172

the way, Paul, I want you to do me a favour later."

"Oh, what's that?"

"I want you to supervise the renovations to The Topaz. Freddie's a good lad, but I think he's out of his depth."

"Okay. Still no idea who's responsible?"

Karl shook his head. "Probably some punter with a grudge."

"You don't think it's the same joker who's trying to knock you off?"

"No idea. All I know is things have gone crazy these last few weeks since I got back from Spain."

"Have you heard any more from that Lawrence bloke? The one that was asking questions about Glendenning?"

"Stop worrying about him," Karl said. A wry smile spread across his face. "I don't think we'll be having any more trouble from him."

"Don't tell me you've—"

"I've what? Bumped him off?" Karl laughed. "I admit I was tempted at one point, but no, Geoffrey Lawrence is alive and well and is probably halfway across the Atlantic as we speak."

"You mean you've bought him off?"

Karl shrugged. "That's for me to know," he said, smiling. "Oh, there is one other thing."

Paul raised an eyebrow. "What's that?" he said.

"I'm seeing Alex later this morning. I want you to take him with you to The Topaz. I'm sure you can find him something to do there worthy of his talents."

"Eh? You've got to be joking. Alex is trouble, Karl. You know that."

"Of course, I know that, but as Lisa keeps pointing out, he is still my son."

"And you seriously want him back on the team?"

"I didn't say that. I'm sure he's more than capable of sweeping the floors or cleaning the bogs."

"Okay, if that's what you want," he said. "I'll see what I can find for him to do."

The desk telephone rang. "Yeah," Karl said. "Oh, it's you, Roger. Hold on a minute." He put his hand over the mouthpiece. "If you don't mind…?"

"Sure," Paul said, walking towards the door. "I'll get things sorted downstairs."

Left alone, Karl removed his hand from the receiver. "Sorry about that," he said. "Things have moved on. We're going to have to speed up what we discussed."

62

Marion paced the hotel lounge, wringing her hands nervously. "Something's happened to him," she said through her sobs. "He was lured outside last night and… and taken."

Charlotte put her arm around Marion's shoulders. "I'll check the hospitals," she said. "He could have been in an accident."

"I've rung all the hospitals. He's not there."

"His car is missing," Charlotte said. "He must have gone somewhere on business and didn't have time to tell you."

Marion shook her head. "No, he wouldn't do that. He tells me everything. Something's happened to him, I'm telling you. I bet it's something to do with Karl Maddox."

"I thought you said—?"

"There's been nothing on the news. I have to know if that bastard's dead," Marion said. "Go and speak with his daughter. See if she knows anything."

"Christina? Okay. I've arranged to help her later today anyway. She's having the furniture delivered to the flat this morning."

Marion huffed. "Good for her. That girl certainly has a charmed life."

Charlotte smiled. "Christina's not bad. She can't help what her dad gets up to, or her brother for that matter." She reached out and took Marion's hand in hers. "Are you sure you don't want me to call the police, Gran?"

Marion shook her head. "No, I don't want them getting involved."

"Then what are you going to do?"

"Bernard said if anything happened to him, I was to go straight back to Barbados, so that's what I'm going to do. I have to leave for the airport soon. Are you coming with me?"

Charlotte shook her head. "No, I think I'll stay a bit longer. I'm meeting Joe later. He might be able to help."

"You will let me know as soon as you find out anything, won't you?"

"Of course," Charlotte said. "Try not to worry. I'm sure Bernard will turn up."

"I do hope so," Marion said, dabbing at her eyes with a tissue. "I do hope so."

63

It was just before noon when Alex arrived at The Emerald. He went straight up to Karl's office.

"Hello, Dad," he said, timidly walking towards Karl. "You're looking well."

Karl was behind his desk, head down with pen in hand and a pile of documents in front of him. It was a couple of moments before he spoke. When he did, his voice was quiet and composed. "Your mother tells me you are having problems," he said, not bothering to lift his head.

Alex grimaced. "I… I know I've been a fool," he said, "but if you let me back in, I promise nothing like that will ever happen again."

Lifting his head, Karl raised his right hand. "Enough. I need you to get over to Bradford with Paul. He has some jobs for you at The Topaz."

Alex clasped his hands together and smiled. "Of course. Anything I can do to help. I really am sorry about what I did."

Karl's gaze returned to his paperwork. "Paul's waiting for you downstairs," he said. "And Alex…"

"Yes, Dad?"

"I don't normally give out second chances. But, because you're my son, I'm making an exception. If you let me down again…"

Alex inhaled deeply. "I won't, I promise. You can count on me."

"Well, let's hope so for your sake," Karl said, waving his hand dismissively.

Later that day, Karl was on the phone when Ryan entered the office.

"That's great news, Roger," Karl said. "It's a relief to know everything's going through without a hitch." He hung up the receiver before turning to Ryan. "Take a seat," he said, indicating the chair in front of his desk. "I think you and I have some things to discuss."

"What do you mean?" Ryan said, settling himself into the chair. "Is something wrong?"

"Tell me about your stepfather."

Ryan frowned. "What about him? He was a vicar, and now he's dead."

Karl banged his fist hard on the desk. "Don't be so fucking flippant with me, young man."

Ryan inhaled deeply. "I didn't mean… What I mean is Nigel was… how can I put this… he was very set in his ways."

"I've heard you two were not on good terms. In fact, you were barely speaking."

"Who told you that?"

"Never mind who told me. Is it true?"

"We'd had words, but there was nothing unusual in that. Nigel and I often had disagreements. It didn't mean—"

"Didn't mean what? It didn't mean you would set fire to the vicarage?"

Scraping back the chair, Ryan stood up. "That's enough," he said. "I don't have to listen to this garbage. I came here to get to know my family better, not to be accused of murder."

Karl glared at Ryan. "Sit down," he said through gritted teeth. "We're not done."

Ryan hesitated for a moment before perching on the edge of the chair.

"Did you have anything to do with the fire at the vicarage?"

"No, of course I didn't. Whoever told you that is a liar. The fire was an accident."

"I heard it was arson."

"Nigel was a heavy smoker. Ask anyone. He was always leaving lighted fags around. Lucy was always yelling at him about it."

"No door keys were found. It looked like they had been locked in."

"The house was burnt to the ground. It would have been almost impossible to find keys amongst the rubble."

Karl frowned. "Tell me about Roxanne."

"What about her?"

"Where is she?"

Ryan shrugged. "The last time I saw her, she was in a hostel."

"Where exactly?"

"Why do you want to know about my mother? You've never even met her."

Karl leant forward. "Ryan, I've asked you a question. I don't like to repeat myself. Now, *where* is she?"

"If you must know, she's in St Jude's Hostel. It's in Chapeltown."

"St Jude's? The saint of lost causes. I thought that place was just about derelict?"

"I'll have her out of there as soon as I'm able," Ryan said. "I'm just a bit strapped for cash at the moment."

"Until your inheritance comes through, you mean?"

"How did...? It's true my parents left me a little something in their wills."

"Oh, I think it's more than a little something, Ryan. I think you're hoping to inherit quite a fortune."

"That's none of your business," Ryan said.

"Why did you lie about Phoenix?"

"Phoenix? What do you mean? I haven't lied."

"She was your girlfriend when you were living in Devon. In fact, Phoenix was your alibi on the night of the fire. Why did you pretend not to know her in the club?"

Ryan's fingers curled into fists as sweat ran down his neck. "Leave her out of this. She's nothing to do with... with anything."

"Why did you come here, Ryan? Why did both of you come here?"

"I... I just wanted to get to know my family, that's all. I thought if you knew Phoenix was with me, you wouldn't have given her a job and to be honest, we really do need the money."

"I thought social workers earned a decent wage?"

"Oh, they do, but... but I quit."

"Why did you do that?"

Ryan shrugged. "I realised that social work wasn't really for me after all. It was Nigel's career choice, not mine." He leant forward. "Actually, I was wondering if your offer to work for you here in the club was still open."

Karl arched an eyebrow. "If you come to work here, you should know I don't tolerate liars."

"I've never lied to you," Ryan said.

"You haven't told the whole truth either."

Ryan ran his tongue over his lips. "What about Phoenix? Can she stay on?"

Karl exhaled deeply. "You can both work for me on a trial basis, but make sure you keep your private lives out of my club."

"Thanks, Karl. You won't regret it."

"I'd better not, for your sake. Be here tomorrow at six o'clock. I'll get one of the lads to show you the ropes."

64

"Wow, what a difference," Charlotte said as she glanced admiringly around the apartment. "I love the furnishings."

"Yes, I'm pleased with it myself," Christina said. "Have a look at the bedroom. It's pure luxury."

Matthew came in from the kitchen carrying three glasses of champagne. "Let's make a toast," he said and handed a glass to the girls.

Smiling, Christina raised her glass. "To freedom from your mother," she said and placed the glass to her lips.

Matthew frowned. "I was going to say *to us.*"

"Of course, darling, but you must admit getting away from your mother is worth celebrating."

"You mean you preferred staying in the hotel rather than at the house?"

"Didn't you? I couldn't have stayed under the same roof with that old bat a day longer. Moving into the hotel was the best thing we did."

Matthew's frown deepened as he put his glass down on the table. "Did you have anything to do with Mother finding out about the move the way she did?"

"Oh, Matthew, what does it matter? We got away from her a few weeks early, didn't we? Now we can start our life here in this beautiful apartment."

"That was a wicked thing to do," he said, "wicked and cruel."

"For goodness sake, what does it matter? We're free of her now. That's all that matters."

"I'm going out," he said, walking towards the door. "I need to apologise to Lydia."

Christina stomped her foot. "Don't you dare go running to her," she screamed, flinging back her head. "I need you here."

Matthew opened the door. "We'll talk later," he said. "I have to put things right with her." He stepped out into the corridor, slamming the door behind him.

Charlotte turned to Christina. "What on earth was that all about?" she said. "I've never seen Matthew so angry."

Christina shrugged. "Don't worry, he'll get over it," she said, flopping down on the couch. "The old bat was annoyed because we didn't tell her about this place. Matthew thought she might make a fuss if she knew we were planning to move out of the house. He wanted to wait until we had the apartment furnished before telling her."

"So, what went wrong?"

Christina giggled. "I arranged for one of the delivery firms to ring the house for further instructions, only I made sure Matthew and I weren't at home when they rang. Lydia was furious when she found out and ordered us to leave."

"So that's why you were staying at the hotel? I did wonder."

"It wasn't perfect, but it was better than staying with her."

"Still, you can see why Matthew is upset. Lydia is his mother, after all."

Christina huffed. "Don't you start taking his side too. You've no idea how difficult she made things for us when we lived with her."

Charlotte sipped her champagne. "How is Karl keeping these days?" she said, eager to change the subject. "He's not planning to open any more clubs, is he?"

Christina shrugged. "I've no idea. I spoke to him briefly this morning, but we're no longer close since I married Matthew."

"He'll come round. You just have to give it time."

"I suppose so, but I miss him. I miss Alex too."

"You're in touch with your brother?"

"I spoke to him last night. He seems to be back in Dad's good books again. He's hoping to manage The Topaz over in Bradford."

"Really? I didn't think Karl had such a forgiving nature."

"Actually, I'm thinking about asking Dad for the salon back. I'll be bored to tears here all day on my own. There are only so many times you can go shopping."

"But I thought you and Matthew were—"

"Were what?"

"Well, with you giving up work and then getting your own home, I assumed you'd be thinking about starting a family."

Christina threw back her head and gave a harsh laugh. "You've got to be joking," she said. "I've no intention of having kids." She picked up her glass and drained the contents. "I love Matthew, but I didn't marry your brother to spawn his brats."

"Then why did you marry him?"

"Money, of course," she said. "What else?" She poured another glass of champagne and, throwing back her head, drank it in one gulp. "Oh, that and to get one back at my dad, of course."

Charlotte gasped. "That's a terrible thing to say. Matthew adores you."

"Of course, he does, just like Guido adored me, and we all know what happened there."

"I really don't like you when you're in this mood," Charlotte said, walking towards the door. "I think you've had too much to drink."

"Oh, do you, Miss prim and proper? What the hell has it got to do with you how much I drink?"

"I'll speak with you when you're sober," Charlotte said, making her way out into the corridor.

"Don't bother," Christina said, flinging herself onto the couch. "I don't need you. I don't need anybody."

65

When Charlotte returned to the hotel, Marion was in the foyer, her suitcase by her side. "Darling, I'm glad I've seen you before I leave," she said, leaning over and hugging her granddaughter.

"Still no word from Bernard?" Charlotte said.

Marion shook her head. "No."

"Gran, I've been talking to Christina. She never mentioned a shooting. Karl is alive and well."

Marion frowned. "But that can't be right. Bernard said he shot him."

"If he did shoot someone, it certainly wasn't Karl Maddox."

"I think… oh damn, here's my taxi."

"Gran, you go back to Barbados, and I'll see what I can find out, and please, try not to worry."

Marion sighed as she followed the porter carrying her suitcase to the taxi. "Be careful, Charlotte," she said. "Get in touch with Joe. He'll know what to do."

Charlotte nodded as she waved Marion off before taking out her phone and ringing Joe.

Joe arrived at the Park Plaza Hotel at six o'clock. Charlotte was waiting in the lounge. She rushed over to him, flinging her arms around his neck.

"Charlotte, what on earth's the matter?"

Charlotte took Joe's hand and guided him to one of the foyer's couches. "It's Bernard," she said. "He's missing."

"What do you mean, missing?"

"A couple of nights ago, he shot Karl Maddox, or at least he thought he did. Then the night before last, he just… he just disappeared. Marion's out of her mind with worry."

"Where's Marion now?"

"She's flying back to Barbados. She didn't know what else to do. She couldn't go to the police and report him missing."

Joe leant back on the couch, gently stroking his chin. "Why

did Bernard try to kill Maddox?"

"Long story, but it turns out Bernard was my mother's dad, my grandfather."

Joe arched an eyebrow. "Bloody hell," he said. "I never knew that. Bernard had a bad reputation back in the day, but I had no idea he was Paula's dad. You say Maddox wasn't shot?"

"I spoke to Christina this morning. She said he's fine. Busy as ever."

"Then who did Bernard shoot?"

"I've no idea, but I'm certain Karl's behind Bernard's disappearance. It's the only thing that makes any sense."

Joe sighed heavily. "You realise Bernard's probably dead by now, don't you? If it was Maddox who took him, there's no way he'd let him go."

Tears welled in Charlotte's eyes. "Then what are we going to do? We can't let him get away with another murder. We just can't."

Joe reached over and took Charlotte's hands in his. "I've been thinking about contacting the police for some time," he said. "I think it's time we put the record straight about what happened to your mother, don't you?"

"No, Joe. You can't do that. You'll go to jail too."

"Perhaps, but it will be worth it to see Karl Maddox behind bars for murder."

"Can you prove he killed my mother? I thought you got rid of the evidence."

"The knife? Erica insisted I got rid of it. She didn't want me to end up in jail either. I had left it with my solicitor."

"Where is it now?"

Joe exhaled deeply. "I did what Erica asked," he said. "I removed it from my solicitor's office, and then… and then I buried it."

"Where?"

"Somewhere, it will never be found, but I can retrieve it if and when the time is right."

Charlotte sighed. "Are you serious about going to the

police? Once you go down that road, there'll be no turning back. You do realise that?"

Joe reached over and took Charlotte's hand in his. "I know that," he said, "but Matthew has a right to know why his dad shot himself. I owe him that."

"I suppose so," she said hesitantly, "but… but there are other considerations too."

"Such as?"

"Matthew is married to Karl's daughter, don't forget. What do you think will happen when Matthew finds out the truth?"

"Matthew should never have married that girl. I warned him she is too much like her father. There's too much bad blood."

"Don't do anything rash, Joe," Charlotte said. "Think everything through carefully before you act."

"I've thought of nothing else since that bloke Lawrence came to see me. In fact, I think I'll speak with him before I go to the police. If he's insisting on writing this damned book, at least I'll give him my side of the story." He took out Lawrence's business card from his coat pocket. "I'll ring now. The sooner I get this over with, the better."

Charlotte reached out and rested her hand on Joe's arm. "Let's have dinner first," she said. "You can ring Lawrence in the morning if you still feel the same way."

He smiled weakly. "All right. I suppose it can wait until tomorrow. I'll give Sarah a ring and let her know I'm staying in Leeds tonight."

"Good. I'll book a table and get you a room."

66

It was just after six o'clock. When Ryan arrived, Karl was talking to Lenny and Paul in the main club.

"Lenny, this is Ryan," he said. "He's going to be working here. Show him the ropes, will you?"

"Sure, boss," Lenny said. He turned to Ryan. "Have you worked behind a bar before?"

Ryan nodded. "When I was at university, I worked in the student bar for a few months."

Lenny grinned. "You'll find this a lot different to any student bar," he said. "Come with me. Let's see what you know."

Ryan followed Lenny behind the bar, and Karl turned to Paul. "Keep an eye on him," he said.

"Don't worry, I'll watch him like a hawk," he said. "Him and Phoenix."

"By the way, how did Alex do today at The Topaz? I hope you gave him plenty to do."

Paul grinned. "Oh yes, I kept him busy. I don't think there's much about cleaning bogs and sweeping floors he doesn't know."

"How did he take it?"

Paul began to chuckle. "He sulked at first when I told him what I wanted him to do. I got the impression he thought he would be managing the place."

Karl huffed. "Over my dead body. Is he still over there?"

"Yeah, Freddie's finding him plenty to do. Actually, I think Freddie's rather enjoying it."

"Let's hope Alex learns a valuable lesson," Karl said.

"What? On how to clean a bog?"

"No. That fucking with me has consequences."

Karl went to his office and, picking up the phone, dialled a number. "Sarah? Is that you?"

"Who's this?" Sarah answered.

"A little bird tells me you've been blabbing to a certain

retired policeman."

"I… I don't know what you mean."

"You told him about the staircase at the back of the club. That's right, isn't it?"

"Not exactly. I only said—"

Karl's growled. "I'll tell you this just once. You open your big mouth to anyone again about my business, and I promise you will regret it. Do I make myself clear?"

"Karl, that's not fair. I—"

"What do you think Joe would say if he knew it was you that told me about his plans at the casino?"

"No, you can't tell him. You promised."

"Don't tell me what I can and can't do. If you want to continue your comfortable life with Joe, keep your mouth shut. Understand?"

"I—"

"I said do you understand?"

"Yes, Karl. I understand."

67

It was almost midnight. Geoffrey Lawrence stood beside his wife's bedside, watching the doctor take her blood pressure.

"Is Amanda going to be all right, doctor? Her breathing seems very shallow."

"Mrs Lawrence is a very sick woman," the doctor said. "I think it might be best if I arrange for her to be admitted into hospital."

Geoffrey shook his head fervently. "No, no, you can't do that. Amanda doesn't want to go to hospital. She wants to stay at home with me."

"I understand you have a nurse taking care of Mrs Lawrence?"

"Yes, Nurse Walters. She's been feeling a bit under the weather for the last couple of days, but she will be back on duty first thing in the morning."

The doctor sighed deeply. "I'm afraid Mrs Lawrence may not last that long," he said. "Her pulse is very weak."

"No, Amanda can't die yet. She can't. I've arranged to take her to a clinic in Texas. They can do wonders for her complaint."

The doctor reached out and sympathetically patted Lawrence's arm. "Mr Lawrence, there's no way in the world your wife can travel anywhere in her condition," he said. "I suggest you prepare yourself."

Tears streamed down Geoffrey's face. "No, I can't lose her. Not yet," he said. "Amanda is my world. What will I do without her?"

The doctor perched gently on the corner of the bed. "I know it's hard losing your wife," he said. "I lost my wife last year, but somehow you know… somehow, you get through it."

Lawrence lowered his head as sobs racked through his body. Half an hour later, Amanda Lawrence was dead.

It was mid-morning. Joe and Charlotte were having

breakfast in the hotel.

"I hear Matthew's moved into his new apartment," Joe said before sipping his coffee. "I must call in and say hello."

"I was there yesterday. It really is lovely, but…"

"But what? Is something wrong?"

"I'm not sure Matthew's relationship with Christina is going well. They seem to argue a lot these days."

Joe frowned. "What do they argue about?"

Charlotte shrugged. "Christina is thinking of asking Karl for the salon back. She thinks being at home will be too boring."

"What does Matthew think about that? I wouldn't have thought he would be pleased with her getting involved with Karl again."

"She hasn't told him yet, but when she does, I'm sure it will cause a massive row."

"Well, that's their business, I suppose. It's best not to get involved. But what about you? What are your plans for the future?"

"I suppose I'll go back to Barbados. Gran will need the company."

"You can't hide yourself away, Charlotte. Life's too short for that. You should be out having fun."

"I'm not hiding away," she said, fidgeting nervously with her napkin, "but there is still the matter of Patrick Flynn, don't forget."

"You haven't heard anything from him?"

"Not a whisper, but he's out there somewhere, and until the police catch up with him, I'm never going to be safe."

Joe pushed his empty plate to one side. "Well, I can't put this off any longer," he said. "I'd better give Lawrence a ring and arrange a meeting."

"You're still determined to speak with him?"

Joe nodded. "Yes, it's the right thing to do. Karl's got away with things far too long." He dialled Lawrence's mobile but got no reply. "I think I'll go round there anyway," he said.

"Do you mind if I come with you for moral support?"

Joe smiled. "If you're sure," he said. "That would be great."

Charlotte sipped the last of her orange juice and headed for the foyer. "Give me five minutes," she said. "I just need to pop upstairs and get my coat."

Joe parked his car outside the address printed on Geoffrey Lawrence's business card. He was surprised to see all the curtains in the house were drawn. Standing in the porch, he rang the doorbell. It was several minutes before it was opened by a woman in a nurse's uniform.

"Is Mr Lawrence at home?" Joe asked, noting the nurse's eyes were red and puffy.

Nurse Walters shook her head. "I'm sorry," she said, "but Mr Lawrence can't see anyone at the moment."

"I need to speak with him as a matter of urgency," Joe insisted. "It's very important."

Nurse Walters stood her ground. "Mr Lawrence is not available today," she said. "I must insist that you leave him in peace."

"Is anything the matter?" Charlotte asked. "You look a little… a little upset."

Nurse Walters sniffed loudly and stepped into the porch, closing the door behind her. "I'm afraid there's been a bereavement," she said in a hushed tone. "Mrs Lawrence died this morning."

"Oh, I'm sorry to hear that," Charlotte said. "Please pass on my condolences."

The nurse nodded as she stepped back into the house. "Mr Lawrence is in no state to speak to anyone at the moment. I'm sure you understand."

"We're sorry to have bothered you," Joe said.

Nurse Walters tilted her head. "Who should I say called?"

"When he's up to it, tell him that Joe Stevens called about the book he's writing."

Nurse Walters sniffed. "Very well, Mr Stevens, I'll see he gets the message."

68

"Are you sure this is the place?" Karl said as he pulled up his car opposite a three-storey building. "It looks deserted."

"This is St Jude's Hostel," Lenny said.

"You wait here," Karl said as he got out of the car and entered the double doors with their peeling green paint. Inside the gloomy lobby was the distinctive smell of disinfectant, boiled cabbage and stale urine. Karl walked up to the makeshift reception desk consisting of a couple of trestle tables pushed together, covered in an off-white bedsheet. Behind the table sat a pale, thin man in his mid-twenties. As Karl approached, the man placed a protective hand over the documents in front of him.

"Can I help you?" he said.

"I'm looking for Mrs Maddox," Karl said. "Mrs Roxanne Maddox."

"Are you a relative?"

"Yeah, that's right. I'm a relative."

The man frowned as he looked through the appointment book. "Is Mrs Maddox expecting you? I don't have a record of a requested visit."

Karl leant over the desk. "Stop pissing about," he said, making eye contact with the man. "Where is she?"

"Room twenty-two," he said, pointing down the corridor. "Roxanne Maddox is in room twenty-two. It's the last room on the right."

Karl snorted. "There," he said, "that wasn't too difficult, was it?"

He strode down the corridor and rapped on the door before pushing it open. The room was small and gloomy, with only one small window. An electric flex hung from the ceiling with a solitary bulb. The room was sparsely furnished with a single bed, a chest of drawers, and a table with two wooden stools. A bookcase containing half a dozen paperbacks was on the far wall, with a small television perched precariously on top. Roxanne was seated on the only armchair in the room.

"Who the hell are you?" she said, struggling to her feet and pulling her shabby dressing gown around her thin body. "What do you want?"

Roxanne looked older than Karl had expected. Her long hair was greasy and lank, tied back with a rubber band. Her skin was sallow, with dark shadows beneath her eyes. "What do you want?" she repeated, suspicion flashing in her watery-blue eyes.

"I'm Karl," he said. "I'm Jason's brother."

Roxanne grabbed the chair arm for support. "So, you're the famous Karl Maddox?" she said. "Ryan said he'd met you."

He walked into the room and pulled out one of the rickety stools from underneath the table. "Do you mind?" he said, balancing unsteadily.

She shrugged. "Help yourself," she said, plonking herself back into the armchair. She reached into her dressing gown pocket and removed a half-bottle of vodka. Holding the bottle to her lips, she gulped greedily before replacing it in her pocket.

"Ryan is working for me now at The Emerald. Did you know that?"

"I thought he was with social services. Why would he want to work for you?"

"He fancied a change, I suppose," Karl said. "Besides, I pay more."

Roxanne grinned. "I don't suppose you can get me a job?" she said. "I always fancied working in one of them posh clubs." She chuckled. "You probably wouldn't get many punters wanting to look at my skinny arse, though, eh, Karl?"

"I want you to tell me more about Ryan," Karl said. "How did he find you after he was put in care?"

"I don't know. He just turned up over a year ago. I thought I'd never see my son again when he was taken from me."

"It must have been a shock seeing him after all those years."

"It was, but I recognised him at once. He's the image of

Jason, don't you think?"

Karl nodded.

She frowned. "He's got his dad's temper too."

"Oh? I hadn't noticed."

"There's anger inside him, like a pressure cooker. It builds and builds until, eventually, it explodes. Jason was just the same."

"So he's aggressive?"

Roxanne pursed her lips. "He's a good boy, really. He knows the difference between right and wrong."

"Has Ryan ever lost his temper with you?"

"A couple of times, but… well, like I said, he's his father's son."

"Does he visit you regularly?"

"What is it you want, Karl? You're asking a lot of questions about my boy."

"Just curious. I like to know about the people I employ."

"I can't understand why Ryan would choose to give up a good job with prospects to work in a pole dancing club."

"I've told you, I pay more," Karl said.

"He doesn't need the money, or at least he won't when he gets his inheritance from the vicar."

"You know about that?"

"Of course I do. Ryan talks about nothing else. He will get me out of this shithole when he gets the money and buy me a proper house."

"So, he's going to take care of you?"

"Yes, he is. I'm his mother. I'm glad he got away from those people when he did."

"Which people?"

"That vicar and his wife. They were supposed to take good care of my boy, but Ryan said the vicar was nothing but a filthy kiddie fiddler. She knew what he was up to but did nothing about it."

Karl stared at her. "That's a serious accusation to make. Are you sure it's true?"

"I'm sure. Ryan said it had been going on for years."

"Why didn't Ryan come to me for help?"

Roxanne squinted. "Why, what would you have done? You're his rich and famous uncle, the main honcho of the sex industry. Everybody knows that."

"I could have stopped the abuse. I could have—"

"Could have what? Nobody would have believed Ryan. Everyone in Devon knew he had come from a dysfunctional background. Adding you to the mix would only have made things worse."

Karl huffed. "You should still have told me," he said. "Have you met Ryan's girlfriend yet?"

She shook her head. "Ryan doesn't bring her here. You can't blame him, really, can you?" She reached back into her pocket and removed the vodka once again. "Want some?" she asked, holding out the bottle.

"No thanks," Karl said as he stood up and pushed the stool back under the table. "I'm a whisky man myself." He reached into his jacket pocket and pulled out a bundle of notes. "Here," he said, leaning forward and handing the money to Roxanne. "Treat yourself to something nice." He turned and headed towards the door, leaving Roxanne counting the money.

69

When Karl returned to the Emerald, he was surprised to find Christina waiting in the office.

"What are you doing here?" he said. "I thought I told you to keep away?"

She smiled weakly. "Dad, I… I've made a terrible mistake. I know that. I need to make things right between us."

"Things will never be right between us," he said, flopping on the chair behind his desk. "Marrying Glendenning was unforgivable."

"I'm so sorry," she said. "Please, believe me, I knew nothing about the casino scam. I was so besotted with Matthew that I didn't see what was happening with him and Joe."

"You expect me to believe that?"

She sniffed and took a tissue from her bag. "It's the truth. I only found out about it afterwards. I was furious with Matthew."

"You still went ahead and married him, though, didn't you?"

"That… that was a mistake. I should never have done that, but you were so angry with me and… and Matthew was kind. I thought I was in love with him, but I realise now that maybe I made a mistake."

Scowling, Karl reached into the desk drawer and took out a cigar. "Pour me a whisky," he said.

Christina strode to the cabinet and poured the drink, handing the glass to her father. "Aren't you having one?" he said.

She shook her head. "No thanks. I… I need to keep a clear head."

He arched an eyebrow. "For fuck's sake. You're not pregnant, are you?"

"I'm not a total idiot."

"I hear you've been seeing your mother quite a bit."

"Mum and I go shopping sometimes," she said. "I think

she's lonely."

"What do you mean lonely? She has me, doesn't she?"

"You're not at home very much, though, are you?"

"Lisa has just spent two months in Spain with me. What more does she want?"

"Dad, I… I was wondering."

"Wondering what?"

"If I leave Matthew, could I move back home with you and Mum?"

Karl snorted. "After everything you've done, you expect me to forgive and forget?"

"Please, Dad," Christina said. "I'll make it up to you, I promise. I don't want to be with Matthew anymore and—"

"That didn't last long, did it?"

"You were right. I should never have married him. It was a mistake."

"What is it you really want, Christina?" he said, leaning back in his chair, his arms folded across his chest.

She tilted her head. "I don't know what you mean. I just want to come home, that's all."

"I don't believe you," he said. "You have ten seconds to tell me the truth. Otherwise, I'll throw you out of the office myself."

Christina inhaled deeply. "I… I want the salon back. I miss working in the salon and want to start over again."

"Ah, so that's what this is all about? I thought as much."

"Please, Dad, the salon is just standing empty."

"Does Matthew know you're here? Why you're here?"

She shook her head. "No. We're barely speaking these days."

Karl sipped his whisky. "Is Matthew still in contact with Joe?"

"Yes. Charlotte's back in Leeds at the moment, and Joe's been over to see her a couple of times. The three of them usually meet up."

"Does he indeed? Where is Charlotte now?"

She shrugged. "She was staying at the Park Plaza Hotel,

but she's going back to join Marion out in Barbados."

Karl's eyes narrowed, and he drummed his fingers on the desk. "I'll tell you what I'll do," he said. "Arrange for Joe to meet you at some place quiet. That little pub at the end of Millennium Square should do it."

"You mean The Four Feathers?"

"Yes, that's the one. Get him there tomorrow night at eight o'clock."

Christina frowned. "Why? You're not going to—"

"Going to what? Kill the cheating, deceitful little bastard? No, of course I'm not. I need to talk to him in private, that's all. If I ring him, he won't come."

She looked expectantly at her father. "Does this mean… does this mean I can come home?"

"It means I'll think about it. You still have a lot of bridges to mend first."

Smiling, Christina walked over to the cabinet. "If you don't mind, I will have that drink after all. Can I get you another one?"

70

Joe had just finished his lunch when his mobile rang. It was a number he did not recognise.

"Yeah?" he said.

"Is that Joe Stevens?"

"Who's this?"

"Mr Stevens, my name is Geoffrey Lawrence. I understand you called to see me the other night?"

Joe inhaled deeply. "Yes," he said. "I was sorry to hear the sad news about your wife. Please accept my condolences."

"Thank you," Lawrence said. "I was hoping that we might meet?"

"I think that would be a good idea if you're sure you're up to it."

"Would this evening be convenient?"

Joe frowned. "No, I'm sorry. It's my wife's birthday, and I've booked a restaurant. Any time tomorrow would be good, though."

"Okay, shall we say two o'clock? Perhaps you could come to my house?"

"That's fine," Joe said. "I think it's time we cleared the air, don't you?"

Joe put the mobile in his pocket as Sarah entered the room.

"Who was that?" she asked.

"Nobody important," Joe said. "It's just some business I must take care of tomorrow."

"What sort of business?"

"Sarah, please don't pry. It's nothing for you to worry about, I promise."

"Is it to do with that policeman that called round the other day asking about the shooting?"

Joe sighed. "I have to put the record straight, Sarah. The guilt of what happened is eating away at me. I must do something to stop Karl, or he will kill again. I know he will."

Sarah grabbed Joe's arm. "You promised me you'd stay away from Karl Maddox. That business with Glendenning will bring that bastard back into our lives."

Joe placed his arms affectionately around Sarah's waist. "No, it won't," he said. "I won't let it."

"Don't do this. Please, I'm begging you."

He released his hold on Sarah. "That's enough," he said. "Don't you have an appointment at the hairdresser in half an hour? You want to look your best this evening, don't you?"

She huffed as she pulled away from him. "Who else is coming?"

"Just the two of us," he said. "I invited Matthew, but he said Christina was under the weather. Marion's returned to Barbados, and Charlotte said she didn't want to play gooseberry."

Sarah sighed as she put on her coat. "That's a shame. It would be nice to see Charlotte again."

"We'll meet again soon, I promise," Joe said. "Now hurry up. You don't want to be late for your appointment."

71

It was six o'clock when Matthew returned to his apartment from work. Christina was in the kitchen cooking a Bolognese.

"Mm, something smells good," he said, sauntering over to her and encircling her waist. He leant forward and attempted to kiss the nape of her neck, but she pulled away.

"Stop it," she said, anger flashing in her eyes. "Don't touch me."

Matthew frowned. "What's the matter, Chris?" he said. "Are you still angry with me?"

"Yes, I am. How dare you humiliate me like that in front of Charlotte?"

"The last thing I wanted to do was humiliate you but… but what you did to Mother was wrong. She was very upset."

"Your mother is an interfering old witch," Christina said. "I hate her."

Matthew exhaled, and the colour rose in his cheeks. "I'd rather have a witch for a mother than a murdering bastard like your father." He strolled over to the cabinet and, taking a bottle of whisky, poured a large quantity into a glass.

Christina picked up a plate from the table and flung it at the wall. "How dare you say that? What about your father? He's the one who shot at Karl."

"That's not fair. My dad was sick, you know that. He didn't know what he was doing."

"Your father was a lying philanderer and a cheat," she screamed, prodding Matthew in the chest with her finger. "Don't you dare try to defend him to me."

Matthew took a step back and slowly shook his head. "Chris, where is all this going? I… I don't want to fall out over our parents. I thought we were past all that."

Christina rushed over to the coat rack and picked up her jacket. "I'm going out. I need some air."

"What about dinner? You can't just—"

"You eat it," she yelled as she went out into the corridor. "And I hope it chokes you."

Christina's eyes welled with tears as she walked along the canal path. She removed her phone from her pocket and rang a familiar number. "Joe? Joe, it's me," she said.

"Hi, Chris. You've only just caught me. Sarah and I are going out for dinner tonight. It's her birthday."

"I need to see you. It's really urgent."

"Is everything all right, Chris? Matthew said you weren't feeling too well."

She snorted. "I'm perfectly well. He fusses too much."

"Okay, if you're sure. Where do you want to meet?"

"Can you come over to Leeds? I thought we could meet at The Four Feathers near Millennium Square at eight o'clock."

"Sure, if that's what you want. I'm in Harrogate tomorrow afternoon on business, so I can pop over to Leeds afterwards. Are you going to tell me what this is about?"

"Not over the phone. I'll see you tomorrow. Oh, wish Sarah a happy birthday from me."

"Sure, I—" But Christina had already cancelled the call.

She quickly dialled another number. "Dad, just to let you know, Joe will be at The Four Feathers tomorrow night. Do you want me to be there too?"

"No," Karl said. "I need to speak to him alone."

"All right, if you're sure. I don't suppose you've reconsidered—?"

"Goodnight, Christina," he said.

"Goodnight, Dad."

72

Joe pulled onto the drive of Geoffrey Lawrence's impressive, detached house just before two o'clock that afternoon.

Geoffrey opened the front door. "Come in. Glad you decided to speak with me," he said. "Just down the corridor, the first door on the right."

Joe entered the large room, which was being used as an office. An oak desk was in front of the window, and one wall was lined from floor to ceiling with books. Two comfortable brown-leather armchairs were in front of the open fireplace on either side of a small glass table. The table contained several buff-coloured files.

"Please, take a seat," Geoffrey said, indicating the chair on the left. "Can I get you something to drink? Tea or coffee perhaps, unless, of course, you would prefer something stronger?"

Joe shook his head as he perched on the edge of the chair. "No thanks. I'm fine."

"Okay, Joe. You don't mind if I call you Joe, do you?"

"Of course not, but are you sure you really want to do this so soon after your wife's passing?"

Geoffrey smiled weakly as he walked to the drinks cabinet and poured himself a whisky. "It was Amanda's idea, writing my memoirs," he said. "She has always shown a keen interest in my work." He put the glass to his lips and sipped the whisky. "Are you sure you won't join me?"

"No, I've got some driving to do, but thanks."

Geoffrey shrugged as he plonked into the armchair. "You don't mind if I record this interview, do you?" he said. "It's so much more convenient than writing everything down."

"However you want to do this," Joe said.

Geoffrey smiled weakly again as he turned on the recording device on the table next to the files. "As I mentioned when we first met, David's widow, Lydia Glendenning, commissioned me to dedicate one chapter in my book to the circumstances leading to her husband's demise."

"David Glendenning shot himself," Joe said. "I hope you're not trying to suggest anything else?"

"No, of course not, but it's the circumstances leading up to the shooting that I'm interested in."

Joe frowned. "You realise I wasn't in the club when the shooting happened?"

"So I understand, but from what I've discovered from my enquiries into the affair, you and Karl were very close. You must have known everything that went on there."

"It's true we'd been friends for a long time, but—"

"Joe, let's start at the very beginning, shall we? What do you know about Erica's father?"

Joe's frown deepened. "I never met him. Why do you want to know about him?"

"Thomas Edward Meadows was murdered in Coopers Alley, but I'm sure Erica told you that."

"Yes, of course, but I don't see what this has to do with me, or Karl, for that matter."

"You never suspected Karl had any involvement in Meadows' death?"

Joe shook his head. "No, how could I? I hadn't even met Karl when Meadows was killed. I always understood it was a mugging that went wrong."

After taking a sip of his whisky, Geoffrey picked up one of the files from the table and opened it. "When you worked for Karl, did you ever meet a young sex worker called Paula? She worked in Cedar Road."

"There were lots of girls working for Karl back then."

"Paula disappeared. Nobody seems to know where she is."

"Girls were always moving on," Joe said, lacing his fingers on his lap. "It happened all the time."

"But Paula left her baby behind. Didn't anyone find that bizarre?"

Joe tensed but remained silent.

"Nobody reported Paula missing at the time. Why was that?"

Joe shrugged. "Like I said, girls were always coming and going. It was the nature of the job."

"I understand Erica took the little girl to Ireland, and she was adopted by Erica's sister."

"That's right."

"Don't you think it strange for Erica to have taken Paula's child to Ireland like that?"

Joe pursed his lips. "Not really. Erica and Paula had spent time in care together, so I suppose they had a kind of bond."

"Even so… What about the child's father? Did you know who he was?"

"David Glendening was Charlotte's father," Joe said.

"David never got to meet his daughter, did he?"

"I don't know. I don't think so."

Geoffrey swirled the contents of his glass. "Do you know what I think, Joe? I think Karl killed Meadows, and somehow Paula found out about it. She tried her hand at blackmailing Karl, and… well, we can guess what happened next."

"And you can prove that?"

Geoffrey shrugged. "It's all circumstantial, but I'm working on it."

"So, where do you think I come in?"

"I believe you know exactly what Karl did, and either through fear, or misguided loyalty to him, you have kept quiet all these years."

Joe lowered his head into his hands but made no reply.

"I don't know if you're aware of this," Geoffrey said, "but somebody is trying very hard to kill Karl Maddox. On the last attempt, whoever it was almost killed me."

Joe sat upright. "I… I don't know anything about that. Karl and I don't mix in the same circle these days, as I'm sure you are aware."

"Would you be surprised to learn that Karl offered me a substantial amount of cash to keep quiet about the shooting and not to continue with my book?"

"Did you accept the bribe?"

"I still have the cheque," Geoffrey said, patting his trouser pocket. "I had intended to use the money to provide for the expensive treatment Amanda needed, but unfortunately, it was too late. She died, so now there's no reason not to go ahead with the book."

"If Karl finds out you're still going ahead, he'll—"

"He'll what? I'm not frightened of Karl Maddox." He lifted his glass to his lips and drained the contents. "Have you come across a bloke called Bernard Coates?"

Joe nodded. "Bernard is married to a friend of mine."

"Do you know why he would want to kill Maddox?"

Joe exhaled and stoked his chin slowly. "Are you suggesting it was Bernard who took a pot shot at Karl?"

Geoffrey nodded. "He was seen on the club's CCTV, apparently. Clear as day."

Joe ran his tongue over his lips. "I think I will have that drink after all."

Geoffrey poured two large whiskies. "Don't you think it's time all this business came out into the open once and for all?" he said, handing Joe a glass and resuming his seat. "Do you know where Coates is?"

"All I know is he went missing a couple of days ago. His wife is frantic with worry."

"What I can't figure out is what reason would Coates have to kill Karl?"

Joe sighed. "Bernard Coates is Paula's father."

Geoffrey's eyes widened, and he inhaled deeply. "I see. It's all starting to make sense now," he said and took a sip of his whisky. He leant forward. "I'm going to ask you straight out. Do you know what happened to Paula?"

Joe drained his glass and leant back into the chair with his eyes half-closed. "I'll tell you everything that happened that night," he said, "under one condition."

"Oh, what's that?"

"You help me find Bernard Coates."

"You think he was abducted by Karl?"

"Who else could it be?"

"If you're right, I wouldn't put money on Coates being

found alive," Geoffrey said.

"Maybe not, but if you want all the facts for your book, you'll use every resource you have to help me find him."

"I'm not a policeman anymore, you do know that?"

"Maybe not, but you still have contacts who are. Now, do we have a deal?"

Geoffrey reached over to the recording device and turned it off. "Okay. We have a deal."

73

It was six o'clock when Joe left Harrogate and headed along the A61. He hadn't eaten all day, so he decided to pull into The Silver Fox pub for a quick snack. He had just ordered a pint and a round of ham sandwiches when his mobile rang. He could see it was Charlotte.

"Hi," he said, striding over to a booth carrying his drink. "Is everything all right?"

"Joe, I… I've just been talking to Marion."

"What's the matter? Has she heard from Bernard?"

"He's telephoned. He says he'll be in Barbados in the next couple of days. He has some business to attend to first."

"But, I thought Karl—"

"Bernard wouldn't say what happened. I'm flying over to Barbados tomorrow to be with Marion."

"Okay. Let me know what happened as soon as you find out."

"Yes, I'll call you later."

The waitress brought the plate of sandwiches to the table. "Anything else?" she said.

"No thanks. This is fine."

She shrugged as she hurried back to the bar, her stiletto heels clattering on the tiled floor.

Twenty minutes later, Joe was back on the road heading towards The Four Feathers. He pulled his car into the half-empty car park just before eight o'clock. He was about to get out when the passenger door flung open, and Karl Maddox deposited himself on the seat.

"What the—?"

"Calm down," Karl said, "I just want a quick word, that's all."

"You couldn't speak to me yourself? You had to hide behind your daughter?"

"Yeah, sorry about that," Karl scoffed, "but I had to make sure you came."

"What is it you want? I thought our business was finished a long time ago."

"Joe, I'm being stalked by some twat who's writing his memoirs. He's asking about David."

"You mean Geoffrey Lawrence?"

"Ah, I take it he's been in touch?"

Joe nodded but said nothing.

"What have you told him?" Karl said.

"I haven't told him anything. Not yet."

"What's that supposed to mean?"

Joe gripped the steering wheel. "Where's Bernard Coates? What have you done to him?"

"How… how did you know about him?"

"Never mind how I know. Where is he?"

"That bastard tried to kill me the other night. Did you know that? He tried to shoot me."

"You can't blame him, can you? After all, you killed his daughter."

"That was an accident. You saw what the silly cow did to me." Karl ran his finger over the scar down his left cheek. "She would have killed me if I hadn't—"

"If you hadn't killed her first?" Joe said. "Paula was just a kid. She didn't deserve to die like that."

"For fuck's sake, don't try and come the innocent with me," Karl said. "You helped me get rid of the silly cow, so your hands are tainted too, don't forget."

"The difference between us is I have regretted what I did every single day of my life. I doubt you even give the girl a second thought."

"The slag tried to blackmail me. She deserved all she got."

"You haven't answered my question. Where's Coates?"

The muscles in Karl's neck tensed, and he clenched his fists tight. "Don't worry," he said, "that lowlife is still breathing."

Joe's eyes narrowed. "Where is he?"

Karl shrugged. "My boys gave him a going over, and then… well, let's just say we came to an arrangement."

"What sort of arrangement?"

Karl gave a shrill laugh. "It's surprising how much people are prepared to pay to keep breathing God's clean air," he said. "Coates is loaded. Did you know that?"

Joe snorted. "So now you're in the protection racket? That's pretty low, Karl, even for you."

Karl reached over and grabbed Joe's lapel. "Don't look down your nose at me. The only reason I didn't put a bullet through that bastard's head was the finger could have pointed straight back in my direction."

"So, where is he? What have you done with him?"

"Don't worry. He'll be joining that ugly bitch of a wife of his once he liquidates certain… certain assets."

"You really are an evil bastard, aren't you?" Joe said. "Why are you so desperate to get his money anyway? Aren't the girls bringing in enough cash these days?"

Karl leant back into the car seat and half-closed his eyes. "The girls are doing just fine, but you can never have enough cash, can you? Especially when you're planning to disappear."

"What do you mean *disappear?*"

"I'm getting out," he said. "I've had enough of all the shit going on in my life. Someone is trying to kill me, and then there's this Lawrence bloke poking his nose into the past. I've had enough."

"You can run, Karl, but you can't hide."

"Yes, you can if you know where to go."

"What about Lisa and the kids?"

"What about them?"

"You can't just up and leave them."

"Watch me," Karl said. "The only problem left is you, Joe. You're always going to be a loose end. The only witness who knows I did for that slag."

"And you're afraid I'll blab to Lawrence or the police? Is that it?"

"Well, won't you? You've always been too soft for your own good."

"Don't talk bollocks," Joe said. His breathing was erratic

as sweat ran down the back of his neck. "I wouldn't—"

Karl half-turned towards Joe, a steely look in his dark eyes. "I'm sorry, mate," he said, plunging the knife deep into Joe's chest, "but I can't take that chance."

Polly Reaves steered her Ford Fiesta into the car park and, after checking her appearance in the car's mirror, took off her sandals and slipped into her stiletto heels. She climbed out of the car and hurried towards the pub. Walking along the rough ground, she caught her heel and lunged sideways, banging into the side of a blue Range Rover. Glancing inside, Polly could see a man's blood-stained body slumped across the front seat. Screaming, she ran into The Four Feathers for help.

74

Alex arrived at the Buttered Scone café in Leeds at ten o'clock the following morning and, walking up to the counter, ordered a black coffee and a round of toast.

"You're late," said a voice behind him. "We agreed half-past nine."

Not bothering to turn round, Alex paid for the coffee and toast. "Keep your hair on, cuz," he said. "I'm here now, aren't I?"

Alex walked to the small table and sat on the bench across from Ryan. "Your mates really fucked up with The Topaz," Alex said.

"What do you mean? I thought you wanted the place trashed?"

"No, mate. I wanted it destroyed. Karl's having it re-furbished, and he's making me help clear up the mess."

"You're joking. His own son?"

Alex bit into his toast. "I told you the man's a bastard. He's put me back on the payroll but as a fucking cleaner. Can you believe that?"

"What about The Sapphire? Do you still want me to arrange to have that done over too?"

"Of course I do, but this time make sure it can't be repaired so easily." Alex reached into his pocket and removed a set of keys. "This one is the main door," he said, "and this is for the office. I've written down the security codes." He handed Ryan a slip of paper. "Memorise it," he said, "then get rid of it."

Ryan studied the paper containing the alarm code before tearing it into small pieces. "When do we do the big one?" he said, grinning. "I can't wait to destroy the Emerald."

"All in good time," Alex said and sipped his coffee. "We may have to put that one on hold for the time being."

Ryan frowned. "Why? I thought you wanted to get rid of all of your dad's clubs?"

"I do, but The Emerald is crawling with his goons at the moment. Apparently, someone's trying to bump him off."

Ryan stared open-mouthed. "Kill Karl? Are you sure?"

"It's what I've heard through the grapevine," Alex said. "There have been a couple of attempts so far."

"Does he know who's responsible?"

Alex shook his head. "It could be anyone. Dad has made a lot of enemies over the years." He drained the remnants of his coffee before pushing his cup to one side and leaning back in his chair. "By the way, Ryan, these mates of yours, they will keep their mouths shut, won't they? If Karl gets to find out I'm behind the break-ins…"

Ryan grinned. "Don't worry. They're professionals. They won't blab."

Alex ran his hand through his hair. "It was a lucky break, bumping into my long-lost cousin in the casino. I didn't even know you existed."

Ryan patted Alex's arm. "It was fate," he said. "We're family. We should stick together. I think Karl was unfair, cutting you off the way he did." He sighed deeply. "I know only too well what it's like to be rejected."

Alex glanced at his watch and pushed back his chair. "I have to go," he said, heading towards the door. "I have to be at The Topaz by twelve."

Ryan joined him as they went out onto the street. "Tell me something," he said. "Did you plan to do your dad's clubs over when you had copies made of all the keys?"

Alex grinned. "No, not really. I had the keys copied so I could pop in occasionally on the QT and help myself to cash. Gambling can be an expensive hobby."

75

It had been a busy night at The Sapphire. Finally, Simon locked up the club and climbed into his car. He yawned as he turned on his car stereo and began humming to Ed Sheeran's new release. Being back at the club felt good, although he would never admit that to Karl. He was halfway home when he reached into his pocket for his phone and realised he had left it at the club. Cursing, he retraced his journey back to the club.

Three figures made their way across the empty car park in the direction of The Sapphire Club. Two were carrying large holdalls, and the third had a can of petrol. They skulked round to the back of the club and, placing the key into the lock, opened the heavy wooden door. The security alarm on the wall began to bleep. The first man tapped in the numbers he had been given into the pad. The alarm continued to bleep. He cancelled his attempt and repeated the numbers. Still, the alarm beeped. The red dial showed only ten seconds left to turn off the alarm.

"Are you sure you've got the right code," the second man asked.

"Of course, I'm sure. 7832, that's the number I was given." He tried once more. The alarm continued to beep. Then, a shrill, deafening noise suddenly filled the air, and bright lights flashed throughout the club.

"Let's get the fuck out of here," the third man said. "The bastards have changed the security code."

Just as Simon pulled into the car park, all three men raced out of the building and scattered in different directions. Simon drove after the man carrying the petrol can and trapped him against the wall. Jumping out of the car, he grabbed him, punched him hard in the face and roughly pushed him against the vehicle.

"Who the fuck are you?" he said, twisting the man's arm up his back, "and what are you doing here?"

The man struggled violently, but Simon held firm. He looked around, but there was no sign of the other two men. He quickly opened the boot of his car and forced the man to get in, closing the boot down firmly.

"Deja fucking Vu," he muttered as he drove the car to the club. He quickly dealt with the alarm before phoning Karl.

"It's happened again," he said when Karl answered his phone.

"What has?" Karl said.

"Some bastards have come after The Sapphire. I've locked one of the little turds in the boot."

"Have they done any damage?"

"I don't think so. They scarpered just as I came into the car park. It's a good job I changed the alarm code yesterday."

"Take the little bastard to the lockup. I'll meet you there."

"Okay, but hurry up. I'm knackered."

76

Simon was already there when Karl arrived at the lockup with Paul and Lenny.

"So, this is the little bastard that wants to destroy my business, is it?" Karl said, standing in front of a man suspended by chains from a girder. "Who are you, and who put you up to this?"

The man was no more than twenty. His face was bruised and swollen, blood trickling from his nose and the corner of his mouth. He spat at Karl. "Fuck off," he said.

Karl took a handkerchief from his pocket and wiped the spittle from his jacket. "That's not polite," he said, bringing back his fist and punching the man in the face. "Now, let's start again, shall we?"

"Fuck off," he repeated, thrashing against the chains.

"Look, mate, I can stay here all night if I have to," Karl said. "Now, stop playing silly beggars and tell me your name and who put you up to this."

Lenny walked over to Karl. "Do you need these, boss?" he said, holding a pair of pliers. "We can take the bastard's fingers off one by one." He laughed coarsely.

Smiling, Karl took the pliers and held them in front of the man's face. "Thanks, Lenny," he said, "but I think I'll start with the toes this time. Take his trainers off, will you?"

"Sure thing," Lenny said as he pulled off the man's Nike trainers and socks.

Karl crouched down in front of him, pliers in hand. "Tell me, do you prefer to lose the toes of your right foot or your left? You decide."

The man struggled violently. "You're mad," he screeched. "Everybody says you're a mad bastard."

"Mad? You think I'm mad?" Karl stood up. "If you don't tell me what I want to know, I'll show you how mad I am." He took a step back. "Now, for the final time, who are you?"

The man made a low, guttural sound as, leaning his head forward, he began to vomit.

Karl picked up a bottle of water from the table and opened it, putting the bottle to the man's lips. "Here," he said. "Drink this."

The man greedily drank some of the water.

"That better?" Karl asked, replacing the water back onto the table. "Now, where were we?" He crouched down once more in front of him, pliers in hand.

"Benny," the man said weakly. "My name is Benny."

Karl stood and patted Benny on the shoulder. "There, that wasn't so hard, was it? Now, Benny, I want you to tell me why you broke into my club carrying a can of petrol?"

"I… I can't," Benny spluttered. "He'll kill me if I do."

"Well, either way, you're fucked," Karl said. "At least with me, you'll have a fighting chance. Now, who sent you and why?"

Benny stared at Karl for a second, then slowly nodded. "All right, I'll tell you," he said. "I'll tell you everything, but promise you'll help me get away."

"I'll have you on the next train to wherever you want to go," Karl said. He turned to Lenny. "Untie the lad. We need to talk."

77

It was after three that morning when Karl arrived home. He was surprised to see the house lights were on. As he entered the hallway, Lisa came rushing towards him, followed closely by Christina.

"What's going on?" he said. "And what is she doing in my house?" pointing to his daughter. "I thought I told you to keep away."

Tears streamed down Lisa's face as she grabbed Karl's arms. "Is it true what Christina told me?" she said. "Did you stab Joe?"

Snarling, Karl pushed Lisa to one side. "I don't know what the fuck you're talking about," he said, striding past the two women and entering the lounge.

Christina followed Karl. "You promised me you only wanted to talk to Joe," she said. "Why did you stab him, Dad?"

Karl poured himself a large whisky, drinking it in one gulp. "How do you know Joe's been stabbed?"

"It was on the news that someone had been stabbed in The Four Feathers car park. It didn't mention Joe's name, but I know it was him."

Karl picked up the bottle, poured another drink, then walked to the couch and flung himself down. "Who else have you told?" he asked. "You didn't tell Matthew, did you?"

"No, of course I didn't. I only told Mum because she could see I was in a state."

"Well, keep your mouth shut," he said. "Both of you. What's done is done."

"But why? I don't understand why you stabbed him."

"The bastard knew too much. I had to kill him."

"Dad, Joe's not dead. He's in hospital. A paramedic was in the pub and was able to give first aid."

"Are you sure he's still alive?"

"Yes, Dad. Joe is still alive."

Lisa sat on the couch next to Karl, her arms folded across her chest as she gently swayed backwards and forwards.

"What are you going to do?" she said. "If Joe comes around and tells the police…"

Karl lowered his head into his hands. "That's never going to happen," he said.

"You don't know that," Lisa said as she got off the couch and walked towards the door. "It's late. I'm going to bed." She turned to Christina. "You'd better stay here tonight. The bed in your old room is made up."

Lisa began to slowly ascend the stairs when there was the sound of breaking glass in the direction of the kitchen. She ran along the corridor and opened the kitchen door. "Fire," she screamed. "Someone's setting fire to the house."

Karl raced to the kitchen just as a second petrol bomb was hurled through the window, engulfing the breakfast island. "Get out," he yelled. "Both of you get out of the house now."

Karl reached for the extinguisher from the wall and attempted to put out the fires.

Lisa was crying hysterically as she picked up the phone. "I'll ring for help," she said as she dialled the emergency services.

Karl ran into the hallway and herded the women towards the front door. "For fuck's sake, get out," he screamed. "The fire's out of control."

Smoke from the kitchen filtered through the house as Karl and the two women watched helplessly from the garden. The Fire Brigade took only minutes to reach the house and bring the fire under control.

"You were lucky," said the Fire Chief half an hour later. "If you'd have had a cheaper kitchen in there, the whole place would have gone up."

Karl arched an eyebrow. "Lucky?" he said. "I've lost half my fucking house. How is that lucky?"

The officer shrugged. "Do you know how the fire started, Mr Maddox?"

"No idea," Karl said.

"It looks to me like an accelerant of some kind was used.

Petrol, most likely."

Karl shrugged but said nothing.

"I've informed the police," the officer said. "They'll need to talk to you."

"What did you do that for? I don't want to talk to the police. I'll deal with this."

"Sorry, mate, but it's procedure. If somebody's going round lobbing petrol bombs into houses, the police need to know."

Karl walked over to Lisa, sitting on the grass, clinging to her daughter. "I want you to go and stay with Christina tonight," he said. "I'll sort this out."

Lisa sobbed. "Who would do this, Karl? Who wants to kill us?"

Karl inhaled deeply with his hands curled into fists. "Try not to worry. I've an idea who's responsible."

"Come on, Mum," Christina said. "I've telephoned Matthew. He's on his way to pick us up."

Lisa put her hand on Karl's arm. "What about you, Karl? You can't stay here. Come with us."

"I have things to do," he said. "There's… oh, isn't that Matthew's car?"

"Yes. Hurry up, Mum. Let's get out of here."

Lisa kissed Karl lightly on the cheek. "Be careful, darling," she whispered. "I'll see you tomorrow."

78

Inspector Wilson arrived at Karl's house just as Lisa and Christina were being driven away by Matthew. Karl was standing on the drive, his hands thrust deep into his pockets, watching as the fire crew prepared to leave.

"Mr Maddox," Wilson said as he approached Karl. "Are you all right?"

Karl shrugged but remained silent.

"I hear this was an arson attack," Wilson said. "Do you have any idea who is responsible?"

"Probably the same bastard who tampered with my car," Karl said. "I don't suppose you worked out who did that either?"

"I have a computer on my desk, Mr Maddox, not a crystal ball."

Karl snorted and walked away as Wilson followed.

"Have you received any threats recently? Any demands for money?"

"Are you serious? Don't you think if I had, there'd be a body in the morgue by now?"

"So, what you're saying is that someone is targeting you, but you don't know why, and you don't know who?"

"That's right, Inspector. I don't have a clue."

"I heard through the grapevine you'd been having a bit of trouble with Charlie Dexter trying to muscle in on the Emerald. You don't think he could be involved?"

"Do you?"

"Word is Charlie's gone up north."

"Well then," Karl said.

"What about that Irish bloke, Patrick Flynn? You had a run-in with him. He hates your guts, so I hear."

Karl turned abruptly to face Wilson. "If Flynn was anywhere in the country, I'm sure the boys in blue would know about it. As far as I'm aware, Flynn's keeping his head down somewhere. You can't blame him. Half of the European police are looking for him."

Wilson shrugged. "Yeah, you're probably right."

The fire engine hooted as it drove out of the drive and onto the road.

"I take it I can go into my house now?" Karl said.

"Not until forensics has done their bit. You'll have to find somewhere else to kip tonight."

"I'll stay at the club," Karl said, walking towards his car.

"Okay, but I'll need a statement from you tomorrow. Oh, by the way, I hear an old friend of yours got stabbed tonight."

"Which old friend would that be?"

"That black guy who used to run your errands. Joe Stevens."

"Joe was never my errand boy," Karl said.

"I understand Joe lives in Liverpool. Do you know what he was doing up in Leeds?"

"I have no idea. Joe and I don't mix."

"No, of course you don't. He ran off with your first missus, didn't he?"

Karl climbed into his car and turned on the engine. "If there's nothing else…" The engine sprang into life, and he sped through the open gates and into the night.

79

It was seven o'clock the following morning when Jeramiah Beauchamp arrived at the Emerald Club. Karl was waiting for him at the door.

"Thanks for coming," Karl said, ushering him through the foyer and up to his office. "Please take a seat."

Beauchamp perched on the edge of the couch, placing his briefcase across his knee. "What's so urgent that couldn't wait until a more savoury hour?"

"Two things," Karl said. "I want you to draw up a Sale Agreement for me."

Beauchamp frowned. "What are you selling?"

"Everything," Karl said. "All four of the clubs, as well as the casino." He handed Beauchamp a folder. "All the details are in there."

Beauchamp stared open-mouthed. "I see," he said, taking off his spectacles and rubbing them frantically with his handkerchief. "I must say, Mr Maddox, I'm a little more than surprised at your request. I always thought—"

"I also need you to transfer some money."

"Oh?" Beauchamp said, his curiosity piqued.

"I want you to open an offshore account for me at this bank," he said, handing him a slip of paper. "When you've done that, I need you to transfer two million pounds into that account from this one." He handed Beauchamp a second piece of paper. "Do you think you can do that?"

Beauchamp studied the papers for a few seconds. "This is… this is most irregular, Mr Maddox. You can't just transfer so much money without—"

"Yes, you can," Karl said. "Drug dealers do it all the time."

Beauchamp took off his spectacles and began frantically polishing them once more with his handkerchief. "You're not… you're not in that line of business, are you?" he said, the colour draining from his face. "I won't be a party to—"

"I'm not a fucking drug dealer," Karl said. "I want to get some of my assets out of the country, that's all. Now, can you do it or not?"

"Well, I… I suppose I can, but it is most unorthodox. I take it Mr… Mr Coates is not into drugs either, with all this money in his account?"

"No, Mr Coates is not a drug dealer. He is perfectly agreeable to transferring the money from his account into mine."

"Will Mr Coates be joining us? I will need his signature on a letter of authorisation."

"Mr Coates will not be joining us," Karl said, "but he did ask me to give you this." He reached into his jacket pocket and handed a signed letter of authorisation. Beauchamp studied the letter for a few minutes. "Mm, this seems to be in order," he said. "Now you say you want an account opening … in Caracas?"

"Yes, that's right. It's in Venezuela."

"I'm perfectly aware of where Caracas is, Mr Maddox," Beauchamp said. "I see you want to open your account at The Central Bank of Venezuela."

"That's right," Karl said. "I'd like it dealt with today."

Beauchamp pursed his lips and slowly shook his head. "Today is impossible, I'm afraid. I don't think you quite realise how much paperwork is involved in transactions of this type."

"And I don't think you realise the urgency of the situation," Karl said, the veins on his neck pulsating. "I need everything in place by tonight."

Beauchamp snorted. "I… I'll see what I can do," he said, standing up and collecting his briefcase. "I'll return to the office straightaway and put the wheels in motion."

"Okay. I want you to be at the Sphynx Hotel near Mirfield this evening at eight-thirty. Do you know where that is?"

"Oh yes. I've been to the Sphynx many times," Beauchamp said. "The wife and I enjoyed a very nice meal there last month for our anniversary, as a matter of fact. We're hoping—"

"Good, that's settled then." Karl held out his hand and shook Beauchamp's. "Thanks for coming. I'll see you tonight at the hotel. The vendor will be there to sign the Sale Agreement. I'll need you to transfer his money for the sale of my properties into the Venezuelan bank, so make sure to bring your laptop with you."

"I never go anywhere without it," Beauchamp said. "I take it you'll be paying my fee tonight?"

"Don't worry. You'll get well paid. There'll be a bonus too for keeping your mouth shut."

Beauchamp smiled weakly as he made his way to the office door. "I'll see myself out. See you at eight-thirty."

80

Half an hour later, Paul arrived at The Emerald. "You look rough," he greeted as he entered the office to see a dishevelled Karl behind his desk. "Been here all night?"

"I had no choice," Karl said. "Some bastard tried to burn my house down last night."

Paul dropped heavily onto the chair. "Fuck, Karl. Are you all right? Was anyone hurt? Lisa…?"

Karl raised his hand. "She's fine, thank god. I packed her off to Christina's last night. By the way, did you sort Benny out?"

Paul nodded. "He was on the first bus to Manchester," he said. "Karl, we can't ignore what he told us. Alex is your son, but the little bastard's out of control. You know he is."

Karl leant forward, stroking his chin. "Do you believe what Benny said last night about Alex being behind all this?"

"The lad was scared shitless. I don't think he would dare lie."

Karl frowned. "I'm not so sure. Benny was terrified of someone, but I'm not sure it was Alex. My son is weak and greedy and can be vengeful too, but I don't think he's capable of violence." He drew on his cigar. "Besides, where would Alex get the money to pay? Christina says he's broke."

Paul shrugged. "We both know Alex is a competent liar. Maybe he does have money stashed away somewhere."

"I don't think so. I've seen the B&B he's staying at. You wouldn't stay in that fleapit if you had cash."

"If Alex did try and burn down The Sapphire, he was probably responsible for the fire last night and the other attempts on your life."

Karl shook his head. "Alex would never hurt his mother. He adores her."

"So, what are you going to do?"

"He should be on his way to The Topaz this morning. I've asked Freddie to give me a call when he gets there."

"Do you really think he'll turn up?" Paul said.

"We'll have to wait and see."

"Fancy a coffee? I'm going to the café."

"Yeah, why not?" Karl said. "A couple of bacon rolls would go down well too."

At eleven o'clock, Karl arrived at The Topaz. Alex was scrubbing down the back wall, which was covered in black paint.

"Alex, a word," Karl said, striding into the club. "Upstairs."

"What… what is it, Dad?" Alex said, following Karl up the stairs to the office. "Is anything the matter?"

"Where were you last night?"

Alex scowled. "Why do you want to know that?"

Karl moved forward. "I asked you a question. Where were you?"

The colour in Alex's cheeks rose. "I went out for a drink," he said.

"Where?"

"Does it matter?"

Karl prodded Alex in the chest with his finger. "Yes, it matters. I want to know exactly where you were all night."

Alex shrugged. "Well, if you really must know, I was at The Black Bull in town," he said. "I was there until closing time."

"And after that, where did you go?"

"Home, of course, if you can call that fleapit I'm staying at home. What's going on, Dad?"

"Some arseholes tried to burn down The Sapphire last night. Did you know anything about it?"

Alex pursed his lips. "No, of course I don't. Why would I?"

Karl roughly grabbed Alex by the shoulders. "Because Simon caught one of the bastards in the act, and he mentioned your name."

"He's lying," Alex spat. "I was nowhere near The Sapphire."

"And you can prove that?"

"I… I was with a girl," he said. "I picked her up in the pub, and we went to her place."

"Does this girl have a name?"

Alex shrugged. "I'm sure she does, but I don't know what it is."

Karl brought back his hand and slapped Alex hard across the face. "Don't get smart with me, you little bastard. Unless you prove to me you were nowhere near The Sapphire, your card's marked."

Karl released his grip, and Alex rubbed his cheek. "Her name was Jane or Jean, I think. Something like that."

"And where do I find her?"

"She has a flat in Beeston. Pinewood Court, I think it was. Flat fourteen."

Karl grabbed Alex's arm and steered him towards the door. "You're coming with me. If you're lying about last night, you'll eat through a fucking straw for the rest of your life."

Jenny Greenwood had just finished washing up when the doorbell gave out its familiar tune. She frowned as she made her way to the door. "Who is it?" she said, opening the door a couple of inches. Then, at the sight of Alex, she smiled and opened the door wide. "Oh, it's you," she said. "Come back for round two, have you?"

Karl, standing to the side, pushed past his son and entered the flat.

"Who the hell are you?" Jenny said. "What do you want?" She turned to look at Alex. "Who is he, Alex?" she asked. "What's he doing here?"

Alex stepped into the room and closed the door behind him. "It's all right, Jane," he said. "This is my dad. He just wants to—"

"I don't care who he is. He's no right barging into my flat, and by the way, my name's Jenny, not Jane."

Karl scrutinised the woman. He guessed she was on the wrong side of thirty with short auburn hair cut into a bob. On her left arm was a tattoo vowing her everlasting love for *Eddie*.

228

Jenny picked up her mobile. "If you don't get out of my flat right now, I'm calling the police."

Karl leant against the door jamb. "Nobody's going to hurt you. I just need to ask you some questions about last night."

She scowled. "What about last night?"

"Where were you, and who were you with?"

Jenny flung back her head. "That's none of your bloody business."

Alex walked over to her and placed his hand on her arm. "Tell him, Jenny. Tell him, and then we're gone."

Jenny walked over to the dresser and, opening the drawer, removed a packet of cigarettes. "Got a light?" she said, addressing Alex.

Alex took out a lighter and lit her cigarette.

"I'm waiting," Karl said.

"Didn't your son tell you?" she said. "I was with him."

"How long?"

"All night. We met in The Black Bull, had a couple of drinks, and came back here."

"How long was he here?"

Grinning, Jenny ran her tongue over her lips. "All night," she said. "Your son certainly has staying power."

"What time did he leave?"

She shrugged. "Not sure. I got up for a pee about six, and he was asleep. When I woke up at eight, he'd gone."

"See, Dad. Now, do you believe me?"

Karl opened the door. "Come on, let's go. Sorry to have disturbed you, Jenny."

"You can stay if you want, Alex," Jenny said.

"Sorry, I can't," Alex said as he rushed out of the door after Karl.

81

Karl started up the engine, and the car roared into life. It was fifteen minutes before they came to a halt down a side lane.

Frowning, Alex turned to his father. "Why have we come here?"

"Alex, I'm giving you one chance and one chance only. If you don't tell me the truth, I swear I'll bury you right here."

Alex tensed, and his breathing became erratic. "What... what do you mean? I don't understand. One chance to do what?"

"I know you're somehow mixed up in the attacks on the clubs."

"That's not true. You heard what Jenny said."

"The Topaz and The Sapphire showed no sign of forced entry. Whoever got inside had a key."

"I don't have a key. You took them off me when... when I left."

"You could have had copies made. I think you memorised the alarm codes for the clubs. They've all been changed now, by the way."

Alex inhaled deeply. His hands shook. "Dad, that's... that's not true. I would never—"

"It is true, Alex. I want to know why?"

Alex banged his fist on the dashboard. "Why?" he said, anger flashing in his dark eyes. "I'll tell you why. Because I'm sick of being treated like a piece of shit by you, that's why." He reached over and tried to open the car door. "Unlock the fucking door," he said. "I want to get out."

"You'll get out when I say you can. Who put you up to this? Was it Christina?"

Alex gave a harsh laugh. "Christina? Don't make me laugh."

"Then who?"

"Everything is your fault. None of this would have happened if you cared half as much for your family as you do for your damned clubs."

"What do you mean by that?"

"Your life revolves so much around making more and more money you don't have any time for your family."

"That's rubbish. I had time for them last night when some bastard firebombed the house."

Alex's posture stiffened. "What… what happened?"

"They threw a couple of firebombs through the window. It's a miracle your mother and sister weren't killed."

Alex put his hands to his mouth. "Are they all right? Were they hurt?"

"Luckily, they both managed to get out. We all did."

"Dad, that… that was nothing to do with me. I swear it wasn't."

"What about the other attempts on my life? The car accident that killed Peter, for instance? I suppose that was nothing to do with you either?"

"You don't seriously think I… That I'm capable of doing that?"

"No, but I think you know who is, and before you get out of this car, you're going to tell me who they are."

82

After dropping Alex off at The Topaz, Karl drove to Christina's apartment.

"Mm, very nice," he said as he stepped into the entrance. "Is your mother here?"

"She's in the kitchen," Christina said. "She's terrified and didn't sleep a wink last night."

Karl walked through to the kitchen, where Lisa sat at the island, sipping a cup of coffee. At the sight of Karl, she ran towards him, flinging her arms around his neck. "Darling, are you all right?" she said. "Everything happened so quickly last night I—"

"I'm fine," Karl said, taking Lisa's hands in his. "The damage to the house isn't as bad as I thought. The insurance is dealing with it today, so you should be back in a couple of days." He walked over to the couch. "Sit down," he said, patting the cushions beside him. "I need to talk to you both." He glanced around the room. "Where's Matthew?"

"He had a meeting he couldn't get out of," Christina said. "He'll be back later."

"Before he returns, I have something to tell you both."

Both women sat down on the couch.

"What is it, Karl?" Lisa said. "Not more bad news?"

"I've decided to sell the clubs," he said, "and the casino too."

Christina gasped. "Dad, you can't. Why would you sell the clubs?"

Karl huffed. "I've had enough. It's all becoming too much hassle."

"But, Dad, what will you do if you sell up?"

"I don't suppose there's a whisky going?"

"Of course, I'll get you one."

"Me too," Lisa said, "I think I'm going to need it."

Christina got the drinks, and both women looked expectantly at him.

Karl inhaled deeply. "I've decided the time is right to

leave," he said.

"Darling, what do you mean, leave? Leave Leeds?"

"No. I mean, leave England," he said.

Christina reached out and grabbed Karl's arm. "Is this because of what happened with Joe? He'll probably die. Nobody will know it was you who stabbed him."

"I rang the hospital this morning," he said. "Joe is off the critical list."

Lisa clasped her hands tightly. "Karl, this is crazy," she said. "Moving to another country takes a lot of planning. You can't just—"

"I have been planning," Karl said. "Everything's in place."

"This is madness," Lisa said, jumping to her feet. "If Joe does talk, the police will drag you back."

"They'd have to find me first," Karl said. "And if the country has no Extradition Treaty... well, what can they do?"

"You're really serious about this, aren't you?" Lisa said.

"Of course, I'm serious. I don't think I have many choices, do you? I was hoping you'd want to come with me."

Lisa shook her head. "I... I can't do that, Karl. You know I can't. My children are here. I can't leave them."

Karl scowled and grabbed Lisa by the shoulders. "I'm your husband," he said. "Your place is with me."

"You can't make me go," Lisa said. "I won't go. My children need me."

"What about me? I need you."

"I'm sorry, Karl," Lisa said, "but I'm staying here." Karl released his grip, and Lisa stepped back. "Where... where are you going anyway?"

"Never mind about that. What you don't know, you can't tell," Karl said. "But don't worry. I'll make sure you're both well provided for." He turned to his daughter. "I'll arrange for the salon to be put back in your name, Chris, if that's what you want."

"Thanks, Dad, but I won't need it after all."

"Oh? I thought you were all set for regaining your independence from Matthew?"

"I was, or at least I thought I was, but I've changed my mind and decided to stay with him to work at my marriage."

"Our daughter is pregnant," Lisa said, putting her arm protectively around Christina's shoulders. "She and Matthew are going to have a baby."

83

It was almost six o'clock that evening when Karl returned to The Emerald. Paul quickly ascended the stairs and joined Karl in the office.

"How did it go?" he said, closing the door. "Did Alex admit to the break-ins?"

"Pour me a drink, will you, and one for yourself?"

Paul poured the drinks and, handing one to Karl, perched on the corner of the desk. "Well?" he said. "What did he say?"

Karl sighed heavily and leant back into his chair, closing his eyes. "Alex wasn't there last night," he said at last. "He admitted to having the clubs' keys cut and memorising the alarms, but he wasn't actually there himself."

"And you believe him?"

"Yes, I believe him."

Paul scoffed. "What about the fire at your house? I suppose he wasn't involved with that either?"

"Alex had an alibi for last night. I checked it out this morning. The fire wasn't down to him either."

Paul banged the glass down on the table. "Somebody killed my brother," he said. "I think it was your son, and I'm going to—"

"Paul, it wasn't Alex. I give you my word."

"Then if it wasn't him, who the fuck was it?"

"It was Ryan."

"Ryan? But Alex doesn't know Ryan. They've never met."

Karl shrugged. "Apparently, they met in the casino a few months back. Alex was telling him how badly done to he felt. So, Ryan offered to help him get even and got some of his mates to break into the clubs."

"Was Ryan responsible for your house being fire-bombed or the car accident that killed Peter?"

Karl shook his head. "No, I wouldn't think so. Why would he? He was helping his cousin get one over on me."

"Where's Ryan now? I need to speak to him. Is he working tonight?"

"It's his night off," Karl said. "I've tried ringing him, but his phone's switched off. Phoenix isn't working tonight either, so they've probably gone out for the evening."

"What are you going to do about him? You can't just let him get away with it."

"He won't, don't worry. But right now, I have more important things to deal with."

"Like what?"

Karl drank the last of his whisky and handed the glass to Paul. "Do you mind?" he said.

Paul walked over to the cabinet and refilled Karl's glass.

"Is everything all right, boss? You look a little distant."

"Sit down, Paul," Karl said. "We have stuff to discuss."

Paul plonked on the leather chair across from Karl's desk. "You sound very serious. What's up?"

Karl took a sip from his glass. "I've decided to sell up. The clubs, the casino, everything."

Paul stared open-mouthed. "What? Have you lost your mind? You can't sell up."

"I've been thinking about it for a while," Karl said. "I've had enough. What with Dexter and his crew, then the attack on The Topaz. I've had enough. He sipped his drink. "Not to mention the mad bastard out there who's trying to kill me."

"We'll find him, boss."

"Maybe you will," Karl said, "or maybe he'll find me first." He drained his glass. "Then there's this bloke Lawrence poking around."

"He'll soon get fed up and move on to something else."

Karl inhaled deeply. "I don't think so. I… I did something stupid the other night," he said. "I stabbed Joe."

"Fucking hell, Karl. What did you do that for?"

"Joe was going to spill his guts out to Lawrence. It was the only way I could stop him."

"Is he dead?"

"No, unfortunately. When he comes round, he'll send me to jail for a long time."

Paul frowned. "What is it Joe knows?"

"It's best you don't know, mate."

Paul jumped to his feet. "Karl, my brother's dead. If this secret you're keeping has anything to do with that…"

"It doesn't. You have my word."

"Is Lawrence the real reason you're running away?"

"I'm not running away. I'm just packing up and moving on."

"What will you do when you move on? I can't see you sitting on a beach for the rest of your life."

Karl shrugged. "Right now, that seems very appealing."

Paul walked over to the window and stared down into the car park. "Do you have a buyer for your businesses?"

"Yes."

"Who?"

"Nobody you know, but he has agreed to keep you on here, so don't worry. There'll be a big loyalty bonus for you too."

"Fuck your bonus," Paul said. "And fuck you."

He strode over to the door, turned and then pointed at Karl. "I want to speak to Alex myself," he said, "and Ryan. Especially Ryan."

84

Karl drove to the exclusive Sphynx Hotel on the outskirts of Mirfield and headed for the lounge bar. He was halfway down his first drink when his guest arrived.

Standing up, he held out his hand in welcome. "Roger," he greeted. "Thanks for coming at such short notice."

Roger Laverick shook Karl's hand before flopping into a tan-leather armchair. "What's so urgent, Karl? I thought we were going to meet up next week."

"Things change," Karl said. "I have to get our business done today."

Roger shook his head. "Can't be done, mate. These things take time."

"Roger, stop fucking about. Do you still want to buy my businesses or not?"

"Of course I do, but why the urgency?"

"Never mind why. Just arrange for the money to be in place. Jeremiah Beauchamp will be here in half an hour with the documentation. All it takes is your signature."

Roger's eyes narrowed, and he slowly stroked his chin. "Has something happened? Something I should know about?"

"Roger, don't ask questions I can't answer. Now, can you have the money in place or not?"

"I suppose so," Roger said, taking out his phone. "As soon as the papers are all signed, I'll transfer the money."

The waiter came over to the table. "May I get you, gentlemen, anything?" he asked.

"Whisky," Roger said. "A large one."

"Same here," Karl said.

The waiter walked away, and Karl turned to face Roger. "There's something else I need you to do," he said.

"What's that?"

"I need you to get me out of the country."

Roger grinned. "I think you'll find British Airways have cornered that market."

"I need to get out, leaving no trace."

"What have you done?"

"Nothing which concerns you. Now, can you help me or not?"

"Where exactly do you want to go?"

"Venezuela."

Roger pursed his lips and gave a low whistle. "Venezuela? I've heard the weather is very nice there."

Karl shrugged. "I couldn't care less. I just need to get away."

"I don't suppose you'll tell me what's going on?"

"What do you mean?"

"Nobody goes incognito to the other side of the world unless they've got the cops up their arse. Venezuela doesn't have an extradition treaty with the UK, does it?"

"Never mind about that. Are you going to help me or not?"

"I suppose it could be arranged," he said, "but it's going to cost."

Karl snorted. "Of course, it is. How much?"

"It depends. Will Lisa be going with you?"

"No, she wants to stay with the kids. I'll be on my own."

"Fucking hell, Karl, are you sure you've thought this through?"

"I have to get out of the country in the next day or so. Can you sort that?"

"Sure. I've established a regular route with South America. Can you be ready to move the day after tomorrow?"

"No problem," Karl said. "Let's get the clubs and casino transferred tonight, and then we can sort out the travel."

"If that's what you want," Roger said. "I... oh, is this your man?" he said, pointing. "That funny-looking bloke hovering in the doorway?"

"Yes, that's Beauchamp," Karl said. "Right on time."

85

Karl got back to The Emerald just after eleven. He went into the main club and strode up to the bar.

"What'll it be, boss?" Lenny asked, reaching for the whisky.

"Make it a double," Karl said as he looked around the club. Scantily clad young women gyrated seductively around the six poles to the beat of the music. Men were ogling the girls, some sitting at the tables drinking, whilst others were standing around in groups. "It looks busy tonight," Karl said.

"Yeah, and there's a couple more bachelor parties coming in later," Lenny said. "We could have done with Ryan working tonight."

"He'll be in tomorrow," Karl said as he turned and walked towards the foyer. "Where's Paul?"

"I haven't seen him all night."

"When he comes in, tell him I want a word."

"Okay," Lenny said as half a dozen men came to the bar demanding drinks. "I could really do with more help."

Karl pointed to one of the minders. "Give Lenny a hand behind the bar."

"Sure, boss," the man said. "But I've never pulled a pint before."

"Well, now's the time to learn," Karl said before he walked into the foyer and up the stairs to his office.

The office was in darkness as he entered. He reached into the room and turned on the switch, bathing the room in light. He walked wearily to his desk and was about to sit down when Ryan appeared from behind the door.

"What the… I want to talk to you," Karl said, rushing towards him. "Did you—" He stopped abruptly at the sight of the gun in Ryan's hand. "What the fuck are you playing at, Ryan?" he said as a cold shudder ran down his spine. "Put the gun down."

Steely-eyed, Ryan pointed the gun towards Karl's head.

"Sit down, Uncle Karl," he said mockingly. "Over there behind the desk, and keep your hands where I can see them."

"What the fuck's going on?" Karl said as he perched on the edge of his chair. "What's this all about?"

"You don't know? You really don't know?"

"I've heard you're behind the damage to The Topaz," Karl said. "And I know you arranged for The Sapphire to be vandalised, but what I don't know is why? Why would you do that to your own family?"

Ryan snorted. "Family? You talk to me about family?" He paced the room, his eyes fixed firmly on Karl. "You do know it was Alex who got me the keys?"

Karl shook his head. "I've spoken to him. I think we've straightened things out."

"He really is an idiot, your son. Do you know that? He's so naïve it's not true."

"What do you mean, naïve?"

"He thought I'd bumped into him by chance at the casino, but I'd been following him for weeks. The stupid bastard didn't have a clue."

"Why would you follow Alex?"

"I thought it was the best way to meet you."

Grabbing the arms of his chair, Karl stood. "So, you've got to meet me. What now?"

Tears trickled down Ryan's face. He wiped them away with the back of his hand, still pointing the gun at Karl's head. "Sit down," he said. "If you move again, I'll blow your head off."

Karl leant back in his chair and sighed, slowly steepling his fingers. "Is this something to do with Roxanne?"

"It's everything to do with my mother," Ryan said. "She's completely broken because of you."

Karl scowled. "That's nonsense. I didn't even know she existed until a few weeks ago." He leant forward. "Roxanne is a hopeless addict," he said. "She chose to put that filthy stuff in her body. I didn't make her. Nobody did."

"She's a junkie because of you," Ryan said. "You're responsible."

"For Christ's sake, Ryan, don't talk bollocks. Put the gun down, and let's—"

"Let's talk? All right, Karl, let's do that." He sat down heavily on the chair opposite Karl's desk. "Let's talk about my time working as a social worker in the prisons. I talked a lot to the inmates. That was my job. Talking and listening, of course."

Karl frowned. "I don't understand. What's that got to do with anything?"

"Sometimes inmates confided in me, almost as if I were their priest. You'd be surprised what I got told."

"You're not making sense, Ryan. I—"

Ryan raised his hand. "Keep your mouth shut and listen," he said. "Now, where was I? Oh yes, my role as a priest." He tilted his head and closed his eyes for a second. "I remember it was a warm, sunny day last August. I decided to counsel some of the inmates outside in the prison gardens instead of in my office. It was probably the feeling of normality, being more relaxed, that made some of them speak freely."

Karl frowned. "I still don't see what this has to do with anything."

"It's everything to do with it," Ryan said. Leaning back into the chair, he crossed his legs, the gun still pointing at Karl. "I got friendly with quite a few of the tearaways. As a matter of fact, that's where I met Benny and his two mates. They were only too happy to get paid for doing you over."

"Were they the ones who tampered with my car's brakes?"

"No, Karl. That was me. I couldn't leave something as important as that to anyone else, could I?"

"And the hospital car park? I take it that was you."

Ryan sipped at his whisky and nodded. "I must say, Karl, you're like a cat with nine lives. Last night I felt sure the firebomb would have seen you off, but… well, here you are."

"If you're going to kill me, Ryan, at least tell me why. You owe me that much."

Ryan drank the remnants of the whisky before banging the glass down on the desk. "All right. I suppose you deserve to know why you're going to die." He stood up and again began pacing the room. "Like I was saying, it was a perfect summer's day. One of my clients was a bloke called Raymond. An old lag that'd spent most of his miserable life behind bars."

"I don't know anyone called Raymond."

"No, maybe not, but you know the bloke Raymond took his orders from, Barney O'Dwyer." He wagged his finger at Karl. "Now, don't tell me you don't know Barney because we both know that's not true."

"Ryan, you're not making sense."

Ryan strode back over to the desk. "It was Raymond who killed my dad," he said. "He punched him in the showers, and Dad fell back and banged his head on the wall."

"Jason got into a fight in prison," Karl said. "He was always getting into fights, but I don't see how you can hold me responsible."

"Raymond was remorseful for what he'd done. He'd been ordered by Barney to start the fight as a favour to you. Dad was due for parole, but you didn't want him spoiling the opening of your poxy new club, did you?"

"Ryan, that's nonsense."

"It's not nonsense. Raymond didn't know it was my dad he'd killed." Ryan's breathing became erratic as sweat ran down his neck. "The next time I visited him, I slipped him some pills. The stupid bastard thought they were uppers."

"And weren't they?"

Ryan grinned. "It took just thirty seconds for him to die," he said. "About the same time it took my dad."

"Why don't you go and speak to Barney O'Dwyer? He'll tell you what Raymond said was a pack of lies."

"I tried," Ryan said, "but he's dead. He died five years ago of sclerosis of the liver."

"Tell me, what do you plan to do after you shoot me? Run away and hide?"

Ryan snorted. "My inheritance came through yesterday. After I get rid of you, I'm taking my mother out of that stinking rat hole, and we're going far away. We'll start again, just me, Mum and Phoenix."

"Does Phoenix know what you're planning to do?"

Ryan shrugged. "She knows about the clubs. In fact, trashing them was her idea."

"Does she know you were responsible for Peter's death?"

"No, but that was an accident. It should have been you. I—"

Paul, standing by the open door, leapt forward and knocked the gun from Ryan's hand, elbowing him in the face as he did so. Ryan yelped as he plummeted to the ground, Paul sitting astride his shoulders.

Karl rushed around the desk. "You took your time," he said. "This little bastard was about to blow my head off."

"You killed my brother," Paul said, reaching over and picking up the gun. "Now I'm going to kill you."

"For fuck's sake, put the gun down, Paul," Karl said. Paul held the gun next to Ryan's temple and slowly and deliberately pulled the trigger.

86

Karl opened the office door, looked out onto the stairwell and sighed in relief. The loud music downstairs had drowned the sound of the gunshot.

"You've done it now, Paul," he said, standing over the lifeless body of Ryan. "What the hell are we going to do with him?"

Paul was leaning against the desk for support, his eyes bulging. He swallowed hard. "I don't care," he said. "That bastard killed my brother. He deserved to die."

Karl walked over to the cupboard and opened the concealed door leading to the passageway. "Let's put him in here for now," he said. "We'll move him later."

Paul stood motionless, staring at the corpse.

"For fuck's sake, pull yourself together," Karl said. "Help me get him in here."

Paul grabbed Ryan's feet while Karl took his shoulders. Slowly they carried the body down the stairs to the passage below.

"I'll bring Dad's van round," Paul said when they were back in the office. "We can put the useless piece of shit in that and bury him on the moors."

Karl frowned. "We'll have to be careful." Then nodded in the direction of the car park. "Ever since Joe was stabbed, there's been a car parked down there with two blokes in it. I think they're cops."

"Are you sure?"

"More or less," Karl said as he strode to the cabinet and poured two glasses of whisky, handing one to Paul. "I'm getting out tomorrow," he said. "I've got everything in place."

"So, you were serious then about leaving?"

"I don't have much choice. Once Joe's able to speak to the police…"

"Where are you going?"

Karl shook his head. "Like I told you before, it's best you don't know."

"I don't suppose you can arrange for me to go too?"

"Are you serious? You'd leave everything behind?"

"Leave what behind? I don't think I have much of a future here, do I?"

"What about Victor?"

"Dad's going back to Romania. He's been talking about it ever since Peter died."

"And you're sure you want to leave? There'll be no coming back. You do know that?"

Paul shrugged. "What have I got to lose?" he said and sipped his whisky. "Besides, who's going to look out for you if I'm not there?"

Karl reached out and patted Paul on the shoulder. "I'll give Roger a ring," he said. "See what he can arrange."

87

The following morning, Inspector Wilson waited in the hospital corridor outside the room where Joe Stevens was being treated. A doctor and a couple of nurses stood by his bed. After a few minutes, the doctor turned and walked towards the door.

"The patient is beginning to make a recovery," he said to the policeman. "You may speak with him for a few minutes, but remember, he is still very weak."

"I just have a couple of questions," Wilson said. "It shouldn't take long."

Wilson entered the room and the two nurses left. He turned to Joe. "I hear you're lucky to be alive," he said. "Do you know who did this?"

Joe sank back into his pillows, closing his eyes.

"Joe, we both know it was Karl Maddox," Wilson said. "You're not going to let that bastard get away with it, are you?"

Joe opened his eyes and ran his tongue over his dry lips. "Get me some water, will you? I'm parched."

Wilson walked to the bedside cabinet and poured water from the jug into a feeder cup. He carefully placed the cup to Joe's lips, and Joe began to drink greedily. "Hey, steady on," Wilson said. "I think you're only supposed to sip the water." He replaced the cup back onto the cabinet, and pulling a leather chair close to the bed, he perched on the edge and took out his notebook.

"Can you confirm that Maddox attacked you?" he said.

Joe nodded weakly.

"Joe, you have to tell me. Was it Maddox?"

"Yes," Joe whispered. "Karl Maddox stabbed me."

"Why did he stab you?"

Joe exhaled but remained silent.

"Does it have anything to do with you running off with Erica?"

Joe closed his eyes and slowly shook his head. "You really have no idea, do you?"

"Why don't you tell me? I'm listening."

"It… it was Paula," he said. "It was all about Paula."

Wilson frowned. "Who's Paula?"

"Perhaps I can help," Geoffrey Lawrence said as he walked into the room. "I've been working on this case."

Wilson's frown deepened. "And who might you be?"

"I'm ex-Chief Superintendent Lawrence," he said. He turned to Joe. "How are you feeling? I hear you're on the mend."

Joe smiled weakly. "I'll live. Where's Sarah?"

"She went home to get some sleep," Wilson said. "The poor girl has been by your bedside for two days. She's exhausted."

Lawrence drew up a chair close to the bed. "I was right before, wasn't I, about you covering for Maddox?"

Joe nodded. "I… I—"

"Would somebody mind telling me what the hell's going on?" Wilson said.

Lawrence put his hand on Joe's arm. "I'll tell the inspector what I know," he said. "You tell me if I get anything wrong." Lawrence turned to face Wilson. "It all began a few years ago," he said, "with the death of a bloke called Thomas Edward Meadows…"

Wilson listened intently as Lawrence told him all he had uncovered since his investigations began. He took out his pocketbook and made notes. Occasionally Joe would correct certain details. Finally, when Lawrence had finished, Wilson turned to Joe.

"Where did you bury the girl's body?"

"She's in the cemetery near Church Lane," Joe said. "I put her alongside an old lady."

"Does this old lady have a name?"

"Winterbottom, I think," he said. "Gladys Winterbottom."

Wilson put down his notebook and sat bolt upright. "Joe, at this point, I must caution you. You do not have to say anything, but it may harm your defence if you do not mention, when questioned, something you later rely on in court. Anything you do say may be given in evidence. Now, for the avoidance of doubt, are you saying Paula's body is in the same grave as this woman?"

"She's underneath the coffin," Joe said. "I put the knife used by Karl in the same grave."

Wilson rose from his chair and hurried into the corridor. He radioed PC Black, who had been charged with keeping The Emerald Club under observation. "Is Maddox still in the club?" he asked.

"No, sir," the constable replied. "He's in his car heading towards town. I'm following."

"Get assistance and stop him," Wilson said. "I want him arrested for murder."

Karl's Mercedes was heading towards Beeston when two police cars, their sirens blaring and their blue lights flashing, brought it to a halt. PC Black jumped out of the patrol car and ran to the passenger door. The window was wound down.

"Are you Mr Maddox?" the officer asked. "Mr Karl Maddox?"

The driver shook his head. "No, mate," he said. "My name's Lenny Roberts. I've borrowed Karl's car to do an errand."

PC Black radioed to Inspector Wilson.

"Get everyone back to The Emerald," Wilson ordered. "I'll meet you there."

Grinning, Lenny drove to the lockup where Bernard Coates was being held. Steve was engrossed with his mobile phone when he entered.

"Everything all right?" Lenny said, walking over to the mattress where Bernard Coates lay. "He's not given you any trouble?"

Steve shook his head. "No, he's just moaning. He wants to get out of here."

Lenny smiled. "Can't blame him, I suppose. Anyway, Karl

says we can let him go tonight." He strode over to Coates and crouched down. "Karl said to remind you what will happen to your wife and daughter if you open your mouth about what's being going on here. Understand?"

Coates nodded.

Lenny walked back to the door. "There's a bonus waiting for you at the club," he said to Steve. "Then it's best if you piss off for a while. Take a holiday or something."

Steve smiled. "Sounds good. I'll see if Sharon wants to join me."

"I'm going back to The Emerald," Lenny said. "Let Coates loose at ten o'clock."

88

When the police arrived at The Emerald, it was locked down. Wilson banged on the door for several minutes before the elderly caretaker eventually appeared in the foyer.

"We're closed, mate," he said. "The club isn't opening today."

"Open up," Wilson shouted. "Open up now."

The old man fumbled with the locks until the doors were eventually opened. "There's nobody here. As I said, the club's closed today."

Wilson and half a dozen officers pushed past him and entered the main club. It was deserted. He dashed into the foyer and up the stairs to Karl's office. Again, it was empty.

He turned to the caretaker, grabbing him roughly by the shoulders. "Where's Maddox?" he said. "Where is he?"

The caretaker struggled from his grasp and gained his composure. "Mr Maddox left a couple of hours ago with Paul Borowicz," he said.

"Do you know where they were going?"

The caretaker shook his head. "No. It's not my place to ask, is it?"

Wilson bounded back down the stairs into the foyer just as a light-grey Lexus pulled into the car park, and two men got out. They walked briskly up to the front door, where a policeman blocked their path.

"What's going on?" said the first man. "What the hell are the police doing here?"

Wilson rushed outside to confront the men. "Who are you? And what are you doing here?"

"My name is Roger Laverick," said the first man. "I'm the new owner of The Emerald." He turned to his companion. "And this is Mr Rigby-Jones. Mr Rigby-Jones is my solicitor. Now, would you please tell me what the police are doing in my club?"

The dawn exhumation was a solemn affair. Permission to

exhume Gladys Winterbottom had been given by the family after the facts had been explained to them. Within an hour, the coffin of Gladys Winterbottom had been removed, and the remains of Paula were carefully placed in the waiting private ambulance.

"There's a knife here, sir," said the young woman from CSI as she carefully lifted a plastic bag containing the knife.

Inspector Wilson examined the weapon. It had a mother-of-pearl handle and a six-inch blade, a blade which appeared to be stained with blood. "Yes, that's it," he said, a wry smile spreading across his face. "We've got the bastard now. All we have to do is find him."

The CSI officer carefully placed the knife and plastic bag into her evidence bag and walked to her vehicle. "I'll get this to the lab. We should be able to get DNA easily enough."

Wilson strode towards his police vehicle, his hands thrust deep into his trouser pockets. "Where the hell are you, Maddox?" he murmured.

89

Karl sipped the beer and grimaced. "It's not exactly John Smith's," he said. "It tastes like cold piss."

Paul grinned. "I'll take your word for that," he said. "Personally, I've never tasted piss, cold or otherwise."

Karl scowled. "Very funny," he said, pushing the glass to one side. "I think it's about time we started planning for the future."

"What sort of plans? I'm enjoying doing absolutely nothing. I've enjoyed doing nothing for the last three weeks." Paul lowered his sun hat over his face and leant back into the lounger. "Why are you getting so edgy?"

Karl huffed. "I'm not edgy. I don't like being idle, that's all."

"Karl, we're on one of the most beautiful beaches on the planet. We're safe from the cops and have more cash than we could ever hope to spend. So why would you want to do anything to spoil that?"

Karl sat upright in his lounger. "I heard from Lisa yesterday," he said. "The police were round to the house again asking questions."

"What did she tell them?"

"What can she tell them? She has no idea where I am."

"It's a pity you couldn't get her to join you. She'd love it here."

"No. She'd miss the kids too much."

Paul propped himself up on his elbows. "Suppose we did look for a venture," he said, "what do you have in mind?"

Karl shrugged. "I don't know. Maybe we could buy a bar or a restaurant?"

Paul grinned. "I didn't know you could cook. What's your speciality?"

"I'm serious," Karl said. "We have to find something to keep us occupied until the heat dies down."

"You think it will? Let's face it, Karl, we're fugitives. We can never go back to the UK unless we want to spend the rest of our lives locked up."

"I've been thinking about that," Karl said. "We could have plastic surgery. I've heard they can work wonders in Brazil."

"Are you serious?"

Karl shrugged. "Just an idea." The waiter came towards them, carrying more beer on a tray. Karl raised his hand and shook his head. "No thanks," he said. He turned to Paul. "Let's go up to the bar and get a proper drink. I could murder a malt whisky."

Clad in blue shorts, Paul pulled his tee shirt over his bare torso and followed Karl up the beach towards the Caribbean Dream, purported to be the best cocktail bar in Playa El Yaque.

"Whisky," Karl said as the pretty young woman behind the bar came over to him. "Make it a large one." He turned to Paul. "What about you?"

"I'll have a beer," Paul said. "Actually, I find it quite refreshing."

Both men got their drinks and headed to a table by the door. "I'm serious, Paul," Karl said when they had sat down. "I think we ought to be—"

"British?" said a local man. "You're both from Britain?"

Karl scowled. "Yeah," he said. "We're British."

"Ah, you are the second British man I have met today." The man grinned broadly, showing a mouthful of discoloured teeth. "Never before did I meet a British man, and then I meet four in one day."

Paul grinned. "Oh? Where are the other two?"

"They were in my taxi this morning. I took them to the Melia Hotel."

Paul tilted his head. "The Melia? I've heard that's one of the best hotels in Caracas."

The man nodded enthusiastically. "Indeed, it is. They are staying for two months. Very generous they were. They give me a big tip." He turned to face Paul. "Britain is a small place," he said. "Perhaps you know them?"

Paul chuckled. "Britain might be small, but over sixty-six

million people live there."

The man shrugged and looked deflated. "Okay," he said. "I just thought you might know them."

"What were the men's names? Did they tell you?"

Karl huffed. "For fuck's sake, Paul, don't encourage the stupid bastard. Let's finish our drinks and go back to the villa. I have some calls to make."

The man turned to leave. "Patrick," he said. "One of the men is called Patrick, and the other, his name is Luke."

About the Author

Eva Carmichael followed her dream when she retired to live by the sea in Redcar in 2016. Shortly afterwards, Eva started work on her first novel, **'BAD BLOOD RISING'**, where she first introduced Karl Maddox, the main protagonist. This is a gritty murder/mystery set against the sleazy background of the Leeds sex industry. The book was released towards the end of 2019. It proved an immediate success with local residents when, after the lockdown, Eva began promoting the book regularly on Redcar Market.

The following year, Eva released her second novel **'MORE BAD BLOOD'**. Again, another gritty story, delving into the murky world of sex trafficking with Karl Maddox steering the way. This was released towards the end of 2020 and again proved exceptionally popular.

Eva's third book, **'A TWISTED MIND',** is set in her home town of Redcar. A police procedural, Eva takes the reader into the sinister world of the serial killer. This book was released in December 2021 to exceptional acclaim.

Eva's latest book, **'LET THERE BE BLOOD',** is the final part of the 'Bad Blood' trilogy. It brings closure to some of the unanswered questions in her previous two books. The reader will discover if the law catches up with Karl Maddox or does he manage once again to evade justice?

Eva will continue to promote her books on Redcar Market and welcomes you to come along and have a chat.

Other Books by This Author

Bad Blood Rising – When a young prostitute is murdered by her pimp, Karl Maddox, he thinks the terrible secret she had threatened to expose is buried with her.

But when the murdered prostitute's daughter arrives in Leeds eighteen years later, she is seeking answers.

Slowly but surely, Karl's life as the wealthy, powerful kingpin of his clubland empire begins to unravel as loyalty is replaced by treachery, and friendship is replaced by hatred.

Is Karl about to find out that no secret can remain buried forever?

AN EXCITING ROMP THROUGH THE CRIMINAL UNDERWORLD...

More Bad Blood – Karl Maddox is content with his lot as kingpin of the sex industry. However, his beautiful estranged wife is now back in his life, along with his son and daughter.

But, when one of his escorts dies after stealing a briefcase from a client, Karl finds himself caught up in the sinister and dangerous world of sex trafficking.

When danger knocks directly on his door, Karl needs every ounce of his ingenuity to keep those close to him safe.

The real threat is much closer than he realises. A danger which threatens everything he holds dear.

A THRILLING, GRITTY NOVEL WHICH DELVES INTO THE SEEDY UNDERBELLY OF THE SEX TRADE IN THE NORTH OF ENGLAND

A Twisted Mind – When a young girl goes missing from a crowded beach, Detective Inspector Andy Bainbridge of Cleveland Police is put in charge of the case.

Despite endless enquiries, no trace of the child is found, and it is assumed she had been swept out to sea.

Sixteen years later, when a number of young women go missing from the same resort, Bainbridge is horrified to realise that their disappearance, and that of the young girl years earlier, are connected.

BAINBRIDGE COMES UP AGAINST THE WORST TYPE OF EVIL – THE PURE EVIL OF A TWISTED MIND.

Printed in Great Britain
by Amazon

10578817R00148